Works by Andrew Barger

Fiction

The Divine Dantes: Paella in Purgatory (Book II)

The Divine Dantes: Cruising in Paradise (Book III)

Mailboxes–Mansions–Memphistopheles

Coffee with Poe: A Novel of Edgar Allan Poe's Life

Edited Anthologies

Edgar Allan Poe: Annotated Entire Stories and Poems

Leo Tolstoy's 20 Greatest Short Stories Annotated

Phantasmal: The Best Ghost Stories 1800-1849

6a66le: The Best Horror Short Stories 1800-1849

Mesmaerion: The Best Science Fiction Stories 1800-1849

Bloodeath: The Best Vampire Stories 1800-1849

Shifters: The Best Werewolf Short Stories 1800-1849

Orion: An Epic English Poem

For Ky,
who refused to let me give up on this trilogy no
matter how hard I tried.

The Divine Dantes
Squirt Guns in Hades

BOOK I OF THE INFERNAL TRILOGY

Andrew Barger

The Divine Dantes™
Squirt Guns in Hades

ISBN: 978-1-933747-41-5

Fonts: Arial, Bookman Old Style, Harrington

Bottletree®
BottletreeBooks.com

Prologue

BEA BROKE UP the band.

Serious. She did. It's easy to do when there are only two people in it and one leaves. No big deal, right? But it was one of America's greatest *rock* bands!

Anyone got a tissue?

It all got started around the clubs and back alleys of Upstate New York. If you go there today you'll hear rumors of the band. There's bound to be confusion over the actual name of the band and how big the lead singer's boots were and why the band drove around in a meter maid car. But hey.

Where there is no confusion, like I already mentioned, is that Bea broke up the band. Keep that in mind. No matter how many wild and outlandish stories (rock-n-roll stories to the nth degree, maybe even to the zth degree they're so good) you're going to read. It was Bea. It really was.

I'm here to confirm that all the stories are true. Even those that are false are true in their own way. The band rocked. Straight up. I was at every single one of their concerts. Granted, there weren't very many of them. About as many as Bea has strings on her Stratocaster. But I attended everyone nonetheless.

My miserable name is Edward T. Nad.

I was one of the two members of said band that rocked. It's brief—but glorious—history started to end when I pulled up to Bea's apartment with palpitations in my chest because our biggest gig was at hand. I felt sick. I wondered if I could even get out of the car. I honked. Well, I tried to honk but my horn wasn't working in the meter maid car. So I waited for my stomach to calm down and got out. Somehow I made it to the front door and figured out how to knock on it.

"Eddie!" She threw her arms around me as soon as she

opened it. "I'm so nervous."

"I'm not."

"Yeah, right. Then why is your cheek quivering?"

"That's me winking at you."

She smiled and we headed along the sidewalk. Bea's guitar was strapped to her back. She had her trademark pigtails tied off on the sides. They were a work of chaotic art the way she shook them while standing at the mike shredding on her guitar. It was enough to drive a guy crazy, especially from behind where I was pummeling the drums. That was pretty much it for our band. Electric guitar. Drums. Shrieking. Whorls of pigtails. What else do you need? Did I mention big boots?

My meter maid car was parked a few spaces down from the apartment door. From the side it resembled a guitar pick on wheels (if you ask Bea). First thing I did was trick it out with subwoofers and chrome wheels (had to buy four, even though it has three wheels, because the guy told me they were only sold in sets of four and that's the kinda screwed up world we live in). It's a two-seater. I mounted a skull (that matches my belt buckle) on the front bumper. It was the scariest meter maid car on the planet and still is.

"The Deathmobile," Bea said.

"A vehicle the size of a frozen fish triangle that goes twenty miles an hour—tops—is unlikely to kill anyone even if they are run over by it. It's actually the Lifemobile."

Bea slid in the passenger seat, leather squeaking against pleather. The front seat was still torn along the front despite Bea asking me to fix it a hundred times. Reddish foam poked out when she sat down.

"It's sticking its tongue out at you," I said.

"Or trying to lick me."

We both said, "Ewwww!"

We drove twenty minutes (that's five minutes in real vehicle time) to our gig. Bea was nervous, not me. Finally, we pulled up to the curb in front of Hard's Speakeasy. Bea read aloud from the wipeboard in the street window. "Playing Tonite - Hallelujah & the Southern Gothic!! 2 fur 1 drafts and wells."

"That's awesome," I said.

"Thought our name was Wroth? Did you change our band name without telling me?"

"Must be a typo."

"Suuuure. Hallelujah & the Southern Gothic is only ten or twenty letters away from Wroth."

"If you put thirty monkeys in a room with typewriters they'll eventually crank out the works of Shakespeare. I bet it'd only take them a week to change Wroth into Hallelujah & the Southern Gothic."

"How long did it take you, Monkey Boy?" Bea asked.

I hopped out of the car and immediately heard, "Uh, I was just leaving. I'm going right now. Right this very second, sir. Let me just get inside and start it up."

There was a dude standing there in jeans and cowboy boots, waving his hands. Stitched patterns ran across his chest. His huge belt buckle may've been a wagon wheel in another life.

I decided to play along. I walked over to the parking meter between our cars and peered down. "Time has expired," I announced in a gruff voice. "There will be civil fines and repercussions to last generations."

"I said I was just leaving. *Please* don't give me a ticket."

I rubbed my chin for a moment. Bea was standing behind the cowboy, grinning. The little, triangular, three-wheeled meter maid car brought abject fear on city streets and I was just the kinda guy who would take full advantage of it. It's worth driving just for the shock value alone. I got my two grand back out of it months ago from sheer devilish pleasure.

I heard the cowboy's boots click together as he stood up straight. He was still explaining. "It just expired. Just seconds before you pulled up. I don't know what happened."

"I have ways of knowing, right down to the very second of expiration. The municipality knows all. It's a wireless thing."

"No. Please sir."

Bea pointed at her wrist and I knew it was time to go inside and get set up. "Alright. I'll let it slide this time, but do not let the meter expire again."

"I won't. I won't. Believe you me."

"Thanks, Tex."

Bea was already unloading our instruments from the trunk. I helped her with the last snare drum. The back bumper that had stickers plastered across it: Arcade Fire, NIN, M83, Skinny Puppy, Ministry, Dead Milkmen. Bea commented on my latest (Wolfmother) as I shut the groaning hatch that protested on its thirty-year-old hinges.

We muscled our equipment up to the swinging front door.

In that moment, us standing there under the flashing neon lights of Hard's Speakeasy, we both locked on each other's eyes and exhaled. Bea's were a calming sea of green. For a split second I got lost in them and right after that I felt her hands clamp onto my shoulders.

"You ready for this?"

"Sure am, Hallelujah. But is the world ready for Hallelujah and the Southern Gothic?"

"I thought *you* were Hallelujah," she laughed.

I confessed that I would be feeling better if we had played for any audience larger than the Garden Nursing Home of Greater Florence or any audience with an average age less than seventy before this gig.

Bea gave me a kiss on the cheek and went inside. I struggled moving the drum set through the door, piece by piece. A rockstar doing manual labor. Not one person on the sidewalk asked for my autograph or offered to help. The indignity of it all.

I was jostling the kick drum from the sidewalk when I noticed a knitting store next to our venue. There was a banner tacked to the front door: I reed—laagh—niit.

"Well I sneeze—eat—drum," I mumbled on my way by.

My last trip to the car was to get the cymbals that were perched on a stand I had made from PVC. When I clanged inside with them I noticed Bea off to the right. She was talking to an impish Italian with long sideburns who she introduced as Gustavo Hardente. He wore a pinstriped suit and obviously owned the joint by the bling-bling on his wrist and fingers. I was pretty sure he had ties to the mafia so I was nice to him.

"Where's the rest of your band?"

"Just us," Bea said with a shoulder shrug. "We're twice as nice."

"I play drums and Bea here plays guitar and sings."

"I don't care if you spin on your heads. Just keep the customers happy and thirsty."

"Not to worry," Bea said. "The moshpit will form on our very first song."

"Slam dancing will make 'em parched in a hurry," I added.

"Who says 'parched' these days, Eddie? I mean really."

Gustavo flung back a dark velvet curtain and showed us the stage. "The amps, mikes, everything is up there for you. Good luck and try not to break anything."

With that I drug the kick drum up two steps and onto the wood platform that served as the stage. "Come on," I called back to Bea.

Her head shook back and forth.

"Don't tell me you're backing out."

"Not a chance. Just test the mikes and get set up. You can introduce me."

I wasn't sure if I saw anxiousness in those big eyes of hers or anticipation. Regardless, I rolled the kick drum across the stage and secured it in place. I did the same for the other drums and cymbals. When my percussion cave was complete, I flicked the mike near the drums and walked over and did the same for the one in front of the stage. They actually worked.

When I looked up I was surprised to see a rather large group (for us at least) of concertgoers mulling around the open floor below. In the back were expensive neon signs advertising cheap beer. There were no chairs to be found, which is good because at our last concert I had a folding chair thrown at me by one of the ladies at the Garden Nursing Home of Greater Florence. I really did.

I glanced over at Bea and was glad to see she was still in the wings. She gave me the peace sign and quickly turned it upside down to form an anarchy symbol. I smiled. She *always* makes me smile.

I took the mike in one hand and cleared my throat. "Hey all you thrashers, squelchers, mashers and moshers, I'm Edward T. Nad. Straight up. I play drums in this band and that makes me a thresher."

Yells rose up from the audience.

"This here is—" I glanced over to the side to check on Bea. "This here is my girl, Beatrice. She rips vocals and plays mad guitar. That makes her a shredder."

A smattering of applause arose as Bea made her way across the stage under the fresh-bruise lighting. I took my place behind the drums. Bea pulled her guitar over her shoulder so that it was in front of her. From behind I noticed that the strap fell just under her sunflower tattoo. It sat between her ripped shoulder blades. When she strummed her muscles would cause the sunflower to wave in an imaginary breeze that reminded me of a summer's day.

Bea reached down and plugged the guitar into a chord lying on the floor. She gave the guitar a hard strum. "We're Wroth!"

"Negative," I said from behind.

Bea glared back at me, then slowly addressed the audience. "I mean, we're Hallelujah and the Southern Gothic. We're still hammering out the name of our bandd, actualllyy."

Bea's voice slurred and I could tell—even from behind— she was looking at someone or something right beside her. But there was no one there.

"I, uh . . . uh," and for a moment it all went blank for Bea.

After the gig I learned that her father was standing right next to her, twisting a tuning peg on her guitar. He just couldn't help himself. No one could see him, though, except Bea. Folco Portinari never missed one of her concerts. Truth be told, he attended more of them now that he was dead than alive. Folco had been a struggling musician for his entire adult life. He was always searching for that *one hit* that could propel him to stardom in Hitsville, USA. By the time he got his life together in the late seventies, he suddenly found himself playing roles as both father and mother when his flowerchild bride died while giving birth to Beatrice. Not in Maui General Hospital, mind you, but in the back of Folco's rusted-out van with the bubble windows and floor covered in sleeping bags where Folco and Ryder used to spend many nights sleeping on the beach. "Ole Fisheye" they called the van.

And on that fateful day, that hippie-killing, responsibility-shaking day, he also inherited the job of naming Beatrice. A hundred times over Folco wished they had decided on a name for her prepartum instead of trying to be cool and wait to see how she looked in the first days and how the Inner Spirit led. So he picked the name Beatrice after having recently seen it in a tattered copy of *The Divine Comedy* he had been reading off-and-on while Ryder was in labor. He figured it was just as good as any other name used in the post-hippie, Hawaiian commune (Muddy Ponds, Rosebud Lane, and Justin Case) in which they lived on Maui.

You've got this, Bea.

I don't know, Daddy. What if I suck?

Heck, you've got my 1970s Stratocaster around your neck with my Welcome to Hotel California sticker on the back. What could go wrong?

You know your little girl is always trying to please you. I learned Stairway to Heaven *at the age of eight just to play it for you on your birthday. Remember?*

And Folco Portinari *was* proud of her musical talents during those few moments when he was not buried under his notepads, sitting on the floor of the hut and barking chords to Bea who was strumming the Strat from a corner of the room. "Give me a C with a quick transition to D flat then crank on the whammy bar, Bea. No. No. I said C then D. There's too much feedback on the amp. Try it now without the pick." As Bea played Folco would feverishly write down chords for his latest rock anthem—chords that would never get heard apart from the commune bonfire on Saturday nights as palm trees swayed overhead.

Play, Bea. Now's the time. It's your time. You've got the chance I never had.

I can do this for you if no one else, not even Eddie.

Do it for yourself, Bea.

No. I'll do it for you.

I saw Bea reached out into nothingness with an open hand that caressed an invisible cheek. Then she brought her hand back to the guitar. At that moment her posture straightened and she stared out into the audience. "Who cares what the name of our band is. Hades, we came here to rock and that's what we're going to do!"

The crowd roared.

"And remember, you're not dancin' unless you're slammin'."

With that the first chord reverberated into her wrist. Bea launched into a dark and brooding rock set.

"From Dust"
"Riven By Chance"
"Beautiful Rocker Boy"
"Asphodel Lowlands"
"Let's (The La, La, Lee Song)"
"Collecting Angel Eyelashes"
"Among Graves"

Have to admit, Bea rocked something fierce. I love a woman in leather and boots and pigtails. She was amazing to watch from behind and I can only imagine how she looked from the front snarling at the audience. It was the fastest tempo she had ever called out for our songs and it took all I had to keep pace on the skins. She broke off into a guitar solo during "Among Graves" that lasted nearly fifteen minutes. I can best describe it as psychedelic-infused shredding with a tinge of auditory domination. The slam dancers were chaotic ocean waves pushing out into the middle of night before being sucked back to the edges of the crowd.

When we finished with the hour-plus set, the crowd was going nuts. During the clapping I joined Bea at the front of the stage and we bowed.

Bea flicked her guitar pick into the front row. I took her around the shoulders and we walked off stage. "We got a standing O, Bea!"

"You do realize there were no chairs in the audience, right? They had no choice."

"Never thought of that. Thanks for ruining the moment."

"Tell me you didn't have a blast out there?"

"Alright. It was pretty much the coolest gig ever."

We now stood on the other side of the velvet curtain that served as a doorway to the stage. One question was nagging me. "You saw your dad again, didn't you."

"Yeah," Bea answered. Her eyes brightened in an uncommon way for a person who had just admitted to seeing a ghost. "Daddy's still there for me and I realize now that he always will be."

Gustavo came running up from the wings of Hard's Speakeasy. He was giving us the thumbs up. "Sweet! You got 'em real thirsty. Had to change out three taps." In one hand was a long strip of paper that must've been his drink sales for the evening. From his pocket he fished a money clip and paid us $100 cash. Bea saw the opportunity and booked us for a gig the following month. Gustavo was happy to oblige, though he didn't care much for our "raucous music" but he realized "that's what the young pups listen to these days."

The gig, though, never happened.

It was all Bea's fault, of course. It ended badly when we were standing in the alley behind Hard's Speakeasy that night. I was surrounded by my drum set and Bea had her guitar strapped across her back. We had just played our last gig, although we didn't know it at the time. Bea, hands on her hips. Me, cross-armed.

The fight was over the name of our band as usual. She thought we should be called Wroth, which is short for Wrath of Goth. "We can't start building our artistic integrity until we agree on a name," she said.

I shrugged and said we could do better. "Our artistic integrity, whatever is left of it, is all gunked up with crud like the end of a tube of toothpaste."

"Exactly, but I wouldn't compare it to a tube of toothpaste."

"I'm serious, Bea. It's gotten sticky anywhere you touch. The sink is full of grey spots that used to be our artistic integrity. Globs of them. They are clogging up the drain. Globs, globs, globs!"

"Why do you have to put things the way you do?" Bea took off down the alley in a huff that I heard over the *clunk-clunk* of her boots. It was totally unfair. She was more mobile. I had to carry drums and stuff.

"Hallelujah and the Southern Gothic is a great name for a band," I yelled to Bea as she tried to flag a cab at the other end of the alley. "It's Church Grunge. It's Chunge. A whole new genre. Think about it."

"Uh, we're a Northern band!" Bea screamed back. "It makes no sense whatsoever! You are so sophomoric!"

"Yeah, right. If I'm anything, I'm new and original. I'm way before that. I'm *freshmoric*. So there.

"More like *freshmoronic!*" Bea screamed. She's got a set of lungs on her.

A bedroom light flicked on in a studio apartment overhead and a guy yelled out the window, "It's three in the flippin' morning! People are trying to sleep!"

"Sorry your bedroom window has an alley view, buddy. You should have paid more rent. Can't you hear? I'm trying to salvage what's left of a great American band. Now listen, Bea, I'm a creative genius. Come to grips with it."

"I need more say in the band. Period."

"I let you pick the song order, didn't I?"

"Hey genius, quit being so stupid and let the woman have her input," the guy yelled from above.

"You don't talk to rockstars like that," I called up to him. Back to Bea, "Globs I tell you. Big gray globs in the artistic integrity sink! That's what this has come to."

"Quiet down!"

"I'm through speaking with you, buddy. Now shut the window to your smelly apartment before I pass out from the garlic smell."

Splat!

Right then I felt a greasy substance running off my head and into my ears. As best I could I wiped it off with my hands and flicked the gray substance onto the pavement. I glanced up. "What is this?"

"Bacon fat, buddy."

"Look what you did, Bea. I got swine lard tossed on my head."

She chuckled. "And you deserve it."

"Yeah you do," came the voice from above.

So Bea flung open the door of a cab, took off her guitar and set it inside. She climbed in the back and barked orders to the driver. There was no use trying to convince her. It's easy to bust up a band when only one person has to leave. She knew that, too. That's the kinda person she is.

Twenty minutes later, when I had cleaned my head off in Gustavo's bathroom and loaded my drums, I slunk back into the meter maid car as some guy said, "You were good tonight, kid. Real good. When is your next gig?"

I sighed as I shut the door on him.

The next week I learned Bea moved to Venice. That's in Italy.

Section I

A Dark Wood

BEA THINKS SHE dumped me, but I secretly dumped her without her knowing it. That's when she took off for Venice where she's probably being serenaded by some gondolier singing bad Italian love songs to her. I'm going to fly there from New York and plead with her on bended knee to take me back so our two-person rock band can rule the world again and we can rock on for all eternity.

Naw!

That's the plot of a novel or maybe three. Who knows? But I'm not a novelist. I'm a rockstar. I've certainly never written a novel. Geez, I've hardly read any. Most rockstars don't even read sheet music let alone big thick books.

And since there's no way I'm ever going to Venice to get my girl back, I suppose you'll want answers to a bunch of squirrelly questions like the name of our band and why Bea broke up the band and how come my parents gave me the sorry name of Edward T. Nad instead of something rock-n-roll like Sting or Bono or Slash. Next you'll want to know what model combat boots I wear on stage and the type of wood I use for my drumsticks and why I drive around in a meter maid car. The obvious questions.

There's no end to it, really.

Since I have time on my hands—being between girls and bands and all—I'll tell you my rotten story. It begins like any good rock-n-roll yarn: I was in a bunny costume being chased through a dark wood by my new band members on the day before Good Friday (let's call it Bad Thursday).

A lion. A wolf. A leopard. Satan's becostumed dark brood was after me. They were gaining. I'll give them that. Those buncha reverbmongers. There was no chance they would ever be rockgods or anything, like me, and that's probably at the heart of why they were so mad.

"The Beelzebubbas is a fantastic name for a rock band," I yelled from within the furry bunny head. "It's Devil Grunge. It's Dunge. A whole new genre!"

"Sounds like dung and smells like it, too," blurted Phil the spotted leopard.

"Takes dung to know dung."

"We've had it with your stupid names, Nad." Phil is a big fraud. Once, I caught him trying to swap out my amp for some piece of junk he got online. It was made in China and I told him, "A billion and a half people and not one rockstar worth mentioning. Think about it. Why should we use their equipment? What does China know about rock-n-roll? But we do need to tour there someday." Phil's jaws started popping. That's when I know he's mad. That's when he kicked in the amp. His foot got stuck in it and I laughed while he tried to extract it. To this day he carries a lot of angst around with him from the incident. What I should've done is *kick Phil* out of the band. Then he wouldn't be chasing me.

"My name's better than Guilloteens, Phil!" I said as I continued running and running, ducking under branches and hurdling bushes with all my bunny ability. "We're not even teenagers! For the last time, if you don't like *my* name for *my* band then get out of *my* band."

"We've already left," disclosed Tasha from her wolf costume. Guess you could say Tasha is a she-wolf. She's all big-lipped and lusty with a flowing mane of hair. She wants more than a fourth of the revenues from our gigs because she attracts both boy and girl fans. The greedy canine.

But forget Tasha, the heart of all my problems always reverts to Bea. She's the one who took off to Venice and broke up our original two person band. When she did she made me feel middle aged. I'm only twenty-one. And now that I've brought up Bea I suppose you want to know—in your list of squirrelly questions—what she's like and all that, what tat she's sporting on her shoulder that the Venetian guy is staring at right now from the back of the gondola. Bea played guitar and shrieked on lead vocals. I played drums and sang when Bea had blown out her chords. That happened often. It was so sexy. But enough of Bea. I could write my next rock anthem, Anarchy for Me, if I wasn't always telling you about Bea so stop asking already. I'll get to all that stuff eventually, but first let me summarize the situation for you: young rocker—being chased through the woods—bunny costume—not going to Venice. So there.

"We're getting closer, Nad," one of them yelled through cheap synthetic Asian fabric.

"Fat chance catching me. I'm a pink blur. You run like a bunch of dingleberries!"

"When we catch you, you're dead." That was the lion. Geri's the most angst-ridden of the bunch and the only one with a Mohawk. I know that's not the politically correct thing to say but it's the only way I know how to describe it. Really. Anyway, he's the most ambitious, too. If he got his way we'd have been playing gigs on the road for eighteen months straight.

"Go back where I found you, playing videogame guitar in your mommy's basement. What the—"

I turned around and a branch snagged one of my floppy ears. It spun my furry head to the side, which caused the lights to go out. Ever tried running blind through the forest in a bunny costume? It's not everything it's cracked up to be.

I began rolling (all poof and cottontail) down an embankment, over a tin can and what may have been a squealing forest creature. A few 360s later came the log. It sent me airborne, ears helicoptering. The two hundred pound pink snowball that I had become splashed hard into a creek bed. As I lay there in a semi-conscious state, I felt the slow creep of dank water into my costume. It was freezing.

There were blurry visions of budding trees and wild sunflowers. There was Bea singing on stage. And the flames of Hades!

After a few hazy moments I wrenched my head back to the front. I wriggled my pink body under a deadfall of branches in the hopes they wouldn't find me. I felt bruises marching up my side and issuing a purple salute. Let me tell you something, there's no padding in Easter bunny costumes no matter what your boss tells you at the miserable Zany Zoo Travel Agency.

Virg—who runs the place and is our sometimes manager for the band—started feeling sorry for us. So he offered us a job of sorts promoting the travel agency. It wasn't until he dragged out the costumes that we knew what we were getting ourselves into. My new band got mad at me for making them dress up in costumes to make a little extra money for a smog machine at our gigs. I said it was better than flipping burgers or frying chicken nuggets. "Musicians have to make money any way they can," I pointed out. "Besides, no one will know us in the costumes."

I got stuck with the bunny getup on account of me creating the whole the situation. As you might imagine that was the most embarrassing getup.

It's hard work waving at traffic for eight hours. My arms killed at the end of the day. I couldn't play any beats when I got back to the apartment. Plus, the lining in the costume really chaffed in all the wrong places. Can you believe somebody would throw a chocolate milkshake at the Easter Bunny? Last Sunday a trucker mooned me.

The same afternoon a woman approached me with her little brat kids and wanted me to conduct an Easter egg hunt right on the front lawn of the Zany Zoo Travel Agency of greater Florence (that would be Florence, New York for all you home readers). We don't even have a good Italian restaurant. Anyway, I told the lady to get lost and then Virg got all mad because he received an irate call from her husband who promised he would never use the travel agency again. Probably the same guy who mooned me.

That day it all came to a (furry) head when we got in a fight over our name. Not the first time. The Beelzebubbas rocks and it's the best name I've come up with. Why can't they understand my genius? The ruckus started right on the front lawn when Geri started beating me over the head with the Zany Zoo sign. Then they all got in on the action. Cars were honking. Kids stopping their bikes on the sidewalk.

Somehow I was able to duck out of the mêlée of pumping white signs. I heard some guy call out his window, "The Easter Bunny's crawling away. Hang him by his ears!" When the signs stopped flailing, I was already off and running.

I ran so far without looking back that I got crazy lost in the dense forest. When I stopped, the trees had closed in on me. It was turning dusk. Thanks to all the pink, my *former* band members could see me despite my head start.

From down in the culvert I heard their voices as they searched for me. My heavy breathing was thunderous in the bewhiskered head. I'd been focusing on my music career. I wasn't in the best of shape, okay? For a while I tried not to breathe. Breathing is so overrated except when you are out of breath.

At least ten minutes passed in my little soggy burrow. The taunts from the lion, wolf and leopard had stopped. The sound of tinkling water beside me grew comforting. A piece of driftwood spun by on its way down the rivulet. There was no sound from above. I felt safe under the deadfall. A frog issued a protest to the pink invader. A copse of leaves left over from last fall waved at me beneath the cold water.

Bea says fall colors suck the tones out of other colors in the world. If oak leaves change in Berlin, yellow drains from an Iowa sweater or a bowl of curry powder in Bangladesh. When Japanese maples turn colors in Fukuoka, the hues of a thousand burgundy New York knapsacks darken. Bea told me that's why all my black T-shirts fade. I said it was bleach. Bea lets me know color is like energy—it's neither created nor destroyed. Color fades somewhere and brightens in another place. She calls it the yin and yang of hue. I told her there was no way to prove her theory scientifically. That's the problem with her quirky theories, they make tons of sense when you think about them, but there is no proof. She was quick to point out that there is nothing that disproves her ideas, either.

Last fall we made a compost bin out behind the apartment. First, we had a huge leaf fight. I won, of course. When it was over and we had stuffed a bunch of leaves inside the bin, I reminded Bea that not only were we saving the environment, but a few baseball caps in Memphis had turned light green.

She just laughed and told me that's not how the color law

works. "It's only when colors are *created* that others are destroyed."

Can you believe her? Again, no proof. Like I was supposed to know that. Like they teach Bea's theories in colleges across the land. Not that I've ever been to college or anything. So you won't catch me using big stiff words like Virg. You'll see.

And what did I say about not wanting to talk about Bea?

In the bunny costume I began smelling a strange odor. The smell was coming from behind me. Hades, it was coming from *my behind,* from the back hatch where I do my bunny business!

My tail was on fire!

I scrambled out from under the branches. Let me tell you, it's hard to scramble and swat at your nether regions all at the same time. You'd better believe I got good at it in a hurry. When I jumped to my feet there was Geri. One of his lion paws was off and he was standing with a lighter in his hand. He's the only member of the band that smokes. The rest of the band was laughing their furry heads off.

"Enjoy your seat warmer," Geri chuckled.

One of them said, "Let's string his ears from the trees."

I turned to run and Geri moved in front of me. I stepped to the side and there he was again. When I darted the other way, Phil stopped me. That left no other choice than to push the she-wolf into the stream. She was the only one I could manhandle of the bunch since she's a girl.

As Tasha crash-landed into the water I darted up the embankment with fire dancing up my backside. I was giving off enough smoke signals to make any Boy Scout proud. Easter Bunny costumes aren't fireproof if you get them from the disgusting Zany Zoo Travel Agency. Keep that in mind.

At the top of the embankment I ran at least a hundred yards swatting and flapping with alternating hands. I hurdled a log, then another. My pink feet skidded on a patch of black mud. Then I went knee-deep into a puddle. I was in for a heck of a dry-cleaning bill from Virg.

S'ppose you need to know why I didn't just ditch the bunny costume so I could run faster. Well for starters, I don't run fast in stocking feet and it was way too cold to be running in boxer shorts. Easter season is chilly in Florence, New York. Plus the zipper was rusty and impossible to unzip. So yeah, that was another squirrelly question.

I scrambled past huge maples that densely populated the forest and a cypress or two. The voices of my pursuers were getting closer. I was working up a lather in the costume.

Finally the air began lightening and I realized I was reaching the outskirts of the woods. Off in the distance I glimpsed the blinking red sign of the travel agency EVERYBODY LIMBO. You can only imagine how cheap and gaudy it looks.

So there, standing at the edge of the forest, I saw a man waving me toward him. He had on a Hawaiian shirt.

Limbo

I KNEW IMMEDIATELY the stooge in the Hawaiian shirt was Virg. He *always* wears them. It's a sick uniform of sorts now that he's a muckety-muck at the travel agency. Virg is exactly the type of guy who eats cocktail weenies at the depressing Zany Zoo Travel Agency Christmas party in a Hawaiian shirt. That pretty much says all you need to know about Virg, except that he's got a huge combover and looks at the expiration dates on bottled water to make sure they haven't spoiled

"Hello, Edward."

"This is the first time I'm actually glad to see you," I said. When I glanced back, the other costumers were heading in the opposite direction.

"You are a mess," he said as I approached.

Virg also talks all stilted and proper. If he ever used a contraction it might get stuck in his throat and choke him. That's another check in the long list of reasons why Virg takes nerdism to new heights.

When I reached him I immediately sat down in a puddle to cool my terra firma behinda.

"Send me the cleaning bill. I can get my hands on some cash." So I lied to ole Virg. Wasn't the first time. Have about $10 to my name and the rent is due in a few weeks.

"Glad you are alright. I was worried after they took off after you."

"Who says I'm alright? And where were you when they were beating me over the head? You're supposed to be my band manager. Guess I get what I pay for."

"Which is absolutely nothing." Virg took his hands from his pockets. "You still got your job if you want it."

"Did I *ever* want my job at the miserable Zany Zoo Travel Agency? How many times do I have to show up late and make hand gestures to your customers before you fire me? I'm trying really hard to be the worst employee on the planet."

"I will give you a raise if you stay on."

"What, a whole dime an hour above minimum wage? No amount of money is worth standing by the road in a bunny costume and waving to people who curse at me."

"No one knows it is you, Edward."

"*I* know it's me." I stood. I popped off the head and shoved it into Virg's ample breadbasket. "Hanging up my ears for good, though I've had quite an illustrious career."

"Doubt your erstwhile band members will turn in their getups."

"Bunch of moochmongers." I yelled that back toward the forest in case any of them were listening.

"Here is what I think. You've been trying to get this band started for a number of months in this small town. How many odd jobs have you had?"

"It's for the sake of art."

"I understand, but perhaps you should learn a skilled trade."

"I'd be terrible as a welder since I now refuse to wear things over my face after the bunny costume experience."

"Maybe think about community college."

"Don't use the C word around me. You're sounding really absurd, Virg, like Mom or somebody."

I stripped out of the bunny costume right in the travel agency parking lot, right down to my boxers with barbed wire printed on them (Bea gave them to me last Christmas). Cars were honking as usual. Can't blame them. Women lust after me something crazy.

I threw the muddy pink smoldering mess at Virg and went inside to get my clothes. On the way Virg gave his usual free advice, which—as usual—I didn't care to hear. The man just can't stop. One thing he does know is the music business. Used to be an agent for a boy band named Clarity, or something embarrassing like that, out in Los Angeles. When the tots started getting all hairy and growing Adam's apples, Virg slunk back to his hometown.

Unfortunately for him the only decent job was to buy part ownership in the Zany Zoo Travel Agency. So he began managing it. Yipeekiyay itinerary for him. That was about the time Bea and I were getting started. He saw us play one of our first gigs. Pulled me aside afterwards. Gave me his card. Said we had "raw talent." I wanted to get in good with Virg because of his industry contacts. Promised to represent us someday if we amped up some good tunes. This kept me coming around the Zany Zoo Travel Agency and acting as though I actually liked the guy, which is pretty much impossible.

I took the costume job for some extra cash in between gigs, but mostly to keep my foot in the door with him. I told Virg that none of the Beatles ever wore bunny outfits. He said he thought that Ringo did in one of their movies. Being a drummer too, I had to give him props on that one.

Once inside the travel agency I noticed Virg had tossed the bunny costume in a clump on the front desk. I steered way clear of it. I think it was staring at me.

As I shut the door Virg's cellphone rang. He excused himself and took the call in his office. Despite my best efforts I was unable to make out what he was saying on the phone as he paced behind a glass block window. For Virg, this was being animated, dare I say theatrical.

––––––––––

"Virg? It's Bea. What's shakin'?"

"How's Venice?"

"Still sinking into the ocean. They should only allow skinny people to live here. I'm wearing boots that aren't as clunky as my normal models. We all have to do our part to save this great city."

"I am sure you had no trouble meeting people."

"I've developed a support group here. I met a good friend, Luci. My cousin Rachael came over, too. She's the founder of an organization that tries to assist people before they get addicted to things. Why do people with addictive personalities never get addicted to good things, only bad?"

"And Luci?"

"Found her on a social networking site. Her LightDancer

username was transcendent. Luci and I met for coffee a few times and she moved in. All three of us share the upper floor of an old palace. You should see the marble floors. The weather here is great and so is the seafood. How is Eddie?"

"Fine. I convinced him and his new band to dress up in animal costumes for an Easter promotion. Edward was the Easter bunny."

"That's hilarious. The big cottontail. Email me pictures of him in the pink poofy costume, which obviously drained the color from a kid's snow cone in Sacramento when it was created."

"Edward is lonely, but fine, Beatrice. Still trying to settle on a name for the band, which I think just broke up."

"Hate to ask."

"Purge Urge and the Models was the last I heard or was it the Beelzebubbas? Now I think he's moved on to Boy Foi Grais . . . or was that last week?"

"Uh! He's so pathetic and funny and frustrating. Don't ask me why, but in a strange way I miss him."

"And I need your two person band back in my life. The travel agency business is even more brutal than the band manager business."

"Has he said anything about me? You know, brought me up or anything?"

"All the time. Just yesterday, he said—if I can remember correctly—you were 'an espresso Sunday, rainy day Monday, think about a new tat Tuesday, weird philosophy Wednesday, out late listening to music Thursday, movie Friday, anything goes Saturday kind of rocker girl.'"

"Wow. I'll take it. So I have this plan. The reason I'm calling, Virg, is to get you to come here. Bring Eddie to me."

"To Venice?"

"As in come to . . . let's say . . . Barcelona, Spain. Eddie may suspect something if it's Venice. I can take the train there."

"Why don't you just fly back to Florence?"

"That'd never work. It's where the breakup happened behind Hard's Speakeasy. Lotsa bad vibes in Florence and probably a few warrants for my arrest. You have to bring

Eddie to me."

"But he won't go to Venice. He will know something is up."

"Right-o . . . Barcelona. Yeah. I'll take the train. I'll meet you two there. It would mean the world to me."

"I do have a few frequent flier tickets from all my Zany Zoo travels."

"Please, Virg. It's the only chance of getting the band back together."

"Of all the women on the planet you are not one to beg, Beatrice. This must be pretty important to you."

"I prefer the word entreat to beg. But yeah."

"It is import for me to get the band back on its feet or I'll never make a penny as your manager. Plus I have some frequent flier miles lying around. Okay. I'll bring Edward to Barcelona."

"Perfect. Don't tell him I'm involved or he may never come. *Capire*?"

"It has a cornucopia of possibilities."

"Thanks, Virg, but who says cornucopia besides pilgrims?"

Virg finally emerged from his office. I could tell his wheels were turning under the long strands of swooped over hair. He immediately says to me, "Perhaps you need to take some time away and decide if you really want to pursue this whole band thing. It is a tough business. Florence is a very small town. Ever thought of a trip to Spain? It would be so fun just the two of us."

"You're creepin' me out, Virg."

"Oh come on. Cut loose for a few weeks? You need it after today. The Mediterranean is nice this time of year. The people are wonderful."

"So is Canada. Same ducks, different loons and I can drive there. Where am I going to get the cash?"

Virg explained, in his long winded fashion, how he had a couple free tickets. "We can talk through matters of the band and next steps."

"I swear you're more shrink than manager—and move

that bunny head offa that desk. I can't stand those pink googley eyes."

Virg grabbed it up by the floppy ears and placed it on the floor with the rest of the costume. He got out his keys and twisted a lock on the administrator's desk. He pulled out the center drawer.

"I've really got to go. I need to ice down my bruises."

"Hold on. Hold on." Virg extracted a blue pocketbook that I had never seen before. He punched a few keys on the computer. "A flight leaves for Barcelona tomorrow. It connects through Washington D.C."

"Good. Bea's in Venice or some other country with no good rock bands."

"Uh, Venice is a city not a country."

"I don't care if it's a communicable disease. There are still no good bands there."

Virg finished typing in his information. He printed out the e-tickets and handed mine over. "These are first class, my good fellow."

"That's the only way rockstars travel," I reminded. "You're paying for food, too."

"Deal," said Virg.

"And the hotel." I started to head out the door of the Zany Zoo Travel Agency and swung back. "I've never really flown before."

"Find your passport that we got for the Crimson Tour that never happened," Virg reminded. "You were the one who demanded it without us having one gig booked outside of the States."

"The passport was psychological. A confidence booster."

Virg walked over and put a hand on my shoulder. "Don't worry. I'll be your guide every step of the way. I'll swing by at nine in the morning."

I went to leave a second time and swung back again. I roundhoused the pink head on the desk with a combat boot.

Misty Region of Weir

VIRG SHOWED UP at my apartment promptly at nine (because that's the kinda guy he is) on Good Friday. I got little sleep because I was thinking about the trip; so much so that it still felt like the same day.

I threw my duffel bag into the back of his pickup and slid into the passenger seat. "That's the ugliest Hawaiian shirt I've ever seen and you've got some real winners in your closet."

Virg cranked the engine without answering. He was used to my shirt comments.

"Don Ho in a pickup truck, that's how you roll."

"Leaving at this juncture, we should make it to the airport in plenty of time."

"Hades! I could still be sleeping? I try not to get up before ten if I can help it. My body has to get accustomed to living the rock-n-roll lifestyle."

Virg pointed his elbow at the center cupholder. "I got a coffee for you. It should help. You'll get breakfast on the plane."

We turned out of my apartment complex sipping away. After a few minutes on the service road we headed onto the main highway (if you could call it that) cutting through our tiny town of Florence. The city was abuzz in Easter decorations. Egg hunts were planned later in the day at various businesses and churches. I was happy to get away from it all. Maybe Virg was actually right for once in his life.

I turned on the radio and classic rock came on. It's the only classic rock station we have in Florence. We have a whopping five radio stations: Rockin' Good Time Oldies (self explanatory); Sparkles & Spurs, which plays Country (don't get me started); there's a classical station (no idea of the name of that one); Andromeda is the Modern Rock station (my fav); and lest we forget, Dimensions plays Easy Listening/Smooth Jazz/New Age/Any Other Music That Doesn't Rev Anybody's Monkey.

Over the music, Virg said, "I'm really glad you've agreed to take a vacation of sorts. The agency is happy to give you this gift. You were our Bunny Brigadier."

"I heard that last part."

"You have not been yourself since the breakup with Beatrice. I know it must've hurt."

"Yeah—for her. It's not like she dumped me. Okay? It was the other way around and don't tell anyone otherwise."

'Silly Love Songs' by Paul McCartney came on. I flicked off the radio out of frustration. Silence overtook the interior of the truck as we drove past a few more apartment complexes and strip malls. I detest silence and bunny heads that stare at me.

"You are really scratching," Virg said.

"I'm chaffed from the costume, okay? You don't have to comment. Yesterday was so terrible I would rather talk about Bea than about getting chased through the woods."

"Sure you don't still have feelings for her?"

"Geez, Doctor Love, focus on the pavement. I didn't mean that I actually wanted to talk about Bea."

Two miles down the road Virg still had his eyebrows raised and the corners of his mouth tucked into his ample cheeks.

Finally I said, "Aw Virg, if you want me to get all sentimental and stuff, which I know you do because that's the kinda rotten guy you are, my love life right now feels like a bar of soap."

"A bar of soap, Edward?"

"You know, one of those shaped like a heart you get at some cheap motel in the Poconos. Those ones that smell like a mix of cheap perfume and anti-freeze. It's so used, my love life—this bar of soap—it's taken on the shape of a cumquat instead of a heart. It has been lathered up and rubbed on so many stinky body parts that the point has been rounded into the shape of a cumquat. And now it's been dropped in the bottom of the shower. That's where it is right now. Bea's the one who did it. She really did. And my love life has just been sitting there for months, right on top of the drain cover, right at the low point of the shower. Nobody bothers to pick it up, not a single dirty person. What little is left of it—this overripe cumquat of my love—just melts, melts away into nothing until all that's left is a slick red spot on the shower floor that everybody slips on and that used to be my heart. Does that make you feel better, Virg? Huh?"

"No, Edward. It makes me feel sad for you."

"Well you should."

"That chokes me up. Do you really feel that way?"

I paused for an intolerably long time. The buildup was killing Virg.

"Naw! Don't try to get all sappy on me. Next you'll be handing me tissues and want a good cry like we're on one of those miserable daytime talk shows."

"I thought you were being truthful."

"That's why I'm going to write some great rock ballads and you never will. E. T. Nad is a man in touch with his emotions."

Virg pinched his lips together before scolding me with the very mention of my name, "Edward!"

I shrugged. "Hey, if Bea ever gets the guts to call me I will tell her the same thing just to make her feel bad—not that she dumped me or anything. I observe a lot of things in this world and I have a tendency to point them out to people. It's just my personality. I have an opinionated and active mind. That's all."

I took another sip of joe as the road started fading away and we began our descent down a steep embankment that skirted a large hill lined with pines and poplars.

Virg shot a searching glance at me. "You look pale. Don't be nervous about your first flight. It will be fine."

"Puhhhlease. I'm not nervous," I lied. "It's just that it's really warm in here." I unzipped my jacket.

Virg dialed down the heat. He then announced that fog had settled into this "misty region of Weir."

"Virg, sometimes I have no idea what you are talking about. With you it's the 'misty region of weird.'" What I did know is the fog had formed vapors that sat in the upper boughs of the pines and cypresses. The sun was having a difficult time beating it back. Because of this the Florence airport slowly came into view as we descended; first the air traffic controllers' tower, then an outcropping of hangers and buildings that included the main (and only) terminal. Virg told me it offered mostly regional jet service with occasional flights to D.C. and LaGuardia. Like I cared.

We drove on and on and on. Virg was going exactly the speed limit. Eyes focuses on the road. Hands at ten and two on the wheel. I told him he drove just like his personality. I was secretly glad we were going slowly to avoid getting on the plane.

Minutes later we both noticed that the heat in the truck would not stop. We cracked our windows and stopped drinking our coffees.

Down, down, we drove; mist roiling along the windshield. The tops of the conifers and poplars disappeared entirely. Virg dialed on the fog lights. He had me check the Internet on his phone. The airline reported no delays for our departure.

Virg shrugged. "It just *seems* like the fog is increasing now that we've traveled to a lower elevation."

"One thing I do know, it's hot as fire in here. Blazes, Virg, I'm sweating. You don't want me all sweaty for an international flight."

"Especially since you are sitting by me in first class."

"You can move to the back of the plane. I won't get offended." I flicked on the air conditioner. "Is the temperature gage in your pickup broken?"

He shrugged as we drove through the entrance to the airport complex and gradually wound our way toward long-term parking. There we angled into a parking spot.

I slid out of the truck and got my duffel bag from the back. Sure enough, a boring carry-on, which only a nerd would carry, was under it. I slung the duffel bag over my shoulder and Virg daintily lifted his suitcase out. On the sidewalk he extended the handle and began wheeling it behind him. We headed inside with me just shaking my head.

It felt warm outside, too, and the infrared heaters that were blasting a wall of heat down across the sliding front doors as we entered didn't help matters.

"Welcome to the Bacheron Airport of Florence," a young lady said with a triangular hat and a silver airplane pin on her lapel.

"You mean Hades," I informed her.

Virg and I trundled past, into the vestibule, and were met by a copse of music and golf apparel stores, restaurants, ATM machines, magazine stores, and one that offered strange-looking massage tools. A fountain danced in the middle of the open space and a few kids were throwing coins into it. There was a bank of shoe shiners camped out at the food court entrance. Being early for our flight by a couple hours (thanks, Virg), I sat down in the first shoeshine chair and Virg scampered off to once again check flight times.

I said to the guy manning my chair, "Can you fan me? It's scorching in here."

He just gave me a toothy smile.

"Charge extra for combat boots?"

"Standard boot price."

"Fix me up, Professor Polish. I *always* travel with shiny stompers."

While the guy went to work rubbing and buffing, I watched the travelers hurry to their gates. They cracked me up. A lady scuttled by with cornrows that were so swirly a space alien must've landed on her head and made crop circles. Some large guy kept yanking up his pants with one hand while he pulled his luggage in the other. It was actually a rectangular box or container he was dragging. There must've been fifty stickers and labels across it from all the places he'd been. His boarding documents were in his mouth and his eyes were nervously scanning the place. A few marine types strode by in full military garb, on their way to the Middle East, no doubt. They had fresh buzz cuts and combat boots much shinier than mine.

The shoeblack finished up with a snap and another smile. I extracted my money clip and paid him.

He quickly reminded, "Tip? Fifteen is keen. Twenty is plenty."

"How about: Zero's a hero?"

He kept his hand outstretched, fingers extending and curling back toward him. He glanced down at my duffel bag like he was going to snatch it and run if I didn't cough up a tip. His cohorts gave me the same nefarious looks.

I added a buck to his palm. "Nobody tips *me* after a rippin' set. Why should you get tipped for doing your job?"

The guy just laughed.

"I've been looking everywhere for you."

It was Virg.

As I turned toward him, a loud commotion issued through the high-ceilinged terminal. The large guy had dropped his suitcase with all the stickers and it had sprung open. He was panic-stricken. He immediately tried to get it shut—all belly and sausage fingers—but it was too late. Way too late.

A swarm of wasps began streaming out the gaping mouth of the suitcase. Instead of stinging tub-o, they huddled in the air and rushed over toward the shoeblacks and Virg and me. Hands and arms went flying. In the commotion we got pushed to the ground and started crawling. It's amazing how fast you can crawl in combat boots. Now I know why the military uses them.

Ten yards off Virg and I got to our feet and began swatting and waving. I jumped around and yelled in much the same way I had planned to end my gig that past weekend, if only I had had one. Virg's combover was forging new territory in the scientific field of whiplash physics.

I shook.

Virg shaked.

The large guy was trying to shut the suitcase with one hand and keep his pants up with the other.

Gradually, over what seemed like minutes, we stopped flailing only to view a crowd of gawkers staring at us. A couple little brats were laughing their guts out. Across the terminal the wasps were chasing the shoeblacks around in endless circles. It was the strangest thing. The insects must've had an attraction to the polish or at least the scent of it. That was the only explanation.

I turned to Virg. "That dance of yours had to be the most embarrassing dance I've ever seen."

Security was gathering. Their batons were useless against the buzzing enemy. They had taken to swatting with their caps. One guy was blowing his whistle as if the wasps were just going to fall in line and march off. This was all taking place under a Hot & Cold banner near the foodcourt.

To this day I don't know how long it went on. I gathered up my duffel bag, and Virg his suitcase. We headed over to the airline counter in another wing of the small airport. I tried not to let on that this was my first flight to the attendant who checked my Id and printed out my boarding pass. Virg was an old pro at everything since he travels a lot. He even had elite status on the frequent flier program for the airline we were taking.

We made our way to security.

Across the way the shoeblacks were still participating in their impromptu track meet. The wasps were still dive-bombing them. Security was still totally useless. The crowd was still gawping, gawping. A couple of shoeblacks were splashing in the fountain to no avail. I am certain they would've been scrounging for coinage if the wasps weren't on their case.

"You shouldn't have held me for tip ransom," I called over to them. "That's what you get! Wasps. Wasps I tell you!"

We angled into the security line with all the other stiffs. A lady in front of us had the biggest hair ever. It made it hard to see the front of the line. Virg called it "a beehive" and thought he had made a funny given recent events.

The line was taking forever. This may come as a surprise, but I'm not exactly a wait-in-line kinda guy.

Above the security area was a Welcome to Bacheron Airport sign. The place was named after some long dead politician. Why do we name buildings after slimeballs? They should be named after rockstars. The Ozzy Observatory. The Cobain Train Station.

The line moved faster than I expected. It suddenly split in

two. One path was for first class flyers (that would be Virg and me). Three stiffs were standing there checking Ids and boarding passes. The one in the middle was an old guy. He was all boney and white-haired with a long beard. His eyebrows were snowy and even the tufts of hair growing out his ears. He took my passport. After comparing the photo to my face, he compared the name to the one on my boarding pass. So I did the same to him.

His nametag read C. H. Aron. It sounded like a bad Vegas stage name for a cross-dresser. The poor wanker.

"Too bad about *your* name," I told him. "As you see, I'm in the same boat. My parents gave me the sorry name of E. T. Nad."

"Frequent flier, Mr. Nad?"

"It's his fir—"

"Would you let me speak, Virg? First time actually," I said to Mr. Aron.

C. H. Aron didn't take kindly to me. Perhaps it was my rock-n-roll hair or he was jealous of my neck tat. Then, for no other apparent reason he decided to personally escort me through the first class line and the security scanner. He even snatched me by the arm.

As we passed under the Welcome to Bachereon Airport sign, I noticed one of the letters moving. Rocking. The top of the B swung down into a pair of sunglasses. Next it fell off.

It hit me square on the head. For some reason I thought it was the exact location where David hit Goliath with the stone. Conflagration, it hurt. The others in line began to float and *divide*. My legs gave out.

One of the last things I remember is looking up from the floor and noticing that the sign now read Welcome to achereon Airport.

Everything faded to black, which is actually my favorite Metallica tune.

The Poets

WHEN I AWOKE, a bunch of stiffs were standing around. Virg and the lady with cornrows and the bearded guy were fanning me.

I felt loopy for a couple seconds and a clap of thunder was going through my head worse than any reverb I've ever experienced on stage. I blinked my way through the pain and the patterns on Virg's shirt, which at first made me feel like I had been captured and placed in a kaleidoscope.

The B was lying next to me on the floor. I held up the culprit. "That's no way to treat first class passengers."

C. H. Aron nodded. He pointed to the next available security scanner with a long, bony finger.

I slowly got to my feet. "Watch out for falling letters," I called to the back of the line. "Abandon all hope ye who enter here!"

After warning everyone in line, I requested a discount from C. H. Aron or a free drink coupon or something. All I got in return was a cut to the front of the line where a TSA agent checked my passport and boarding pass *again*.

Virg went right ahead of me to show how it was done. He placed his cellphone, shoes and keys in the bin and squirted right through the security scanner.

I got a plastic bin and put my shades and belt into it. There was no way my silver skull belt buckle was going to pass through the scanner undetected. Since everyone else was doing it, I jostled off my combat boots (being careful of the shine) and placed them into the container along with the belt.

I turned to the lady with the cornrows. "The Shoe Bomber, in my humble estimation, was by far the most successful terrorist of all and he didn't kill one person or blow up anything. What he accomplished was to make hundreds of thousands of Americans take their shoes off every day at airports around the country. *That* is terror."

"Done got that straight."

"Thank goodness there hasn't been an underwear bomber yet."

"Uh-huh."

"What if everybody had to take their skivvies off and put them on the belt?"

"Dat's low down. Sure 'nough."

"Think of all the wasted time the Shoe Bomber caused us." I tapped Virg on the shoulder. "How many passengers fly every year in the US?"

"I think it's around 650 million."

I turned back to Cornrows. "Okay. Let's say a delay of a minute each per passenger in taking off and putting on their shoes. That's 650 million minutes per year or over 60 million hours. Now I'm no math major, but that has to be more time than it took to build the Empire State Building."

"Almost ten times as many," Virg said out the side of his mouth.

"Think of all the decisions people have to make about what socks to wear when traveling. Think of all the apprehensions by those without socks about getting foot fungus when stepping on airport floors. Think of all the businessmen who take off their shoes and an arch support gets lost. Think of the twisted ankles from people trying to balance on one foot as they take each shoe off. Think of the slips and falls. Think of the smell. The *smell*. If that isn't terrorist success in spades, I don't know what is."

"Dhatphlumphat," came the incomprehensible mumble from Cornrows.

I slung my bag onto the conveyor belt behind the plastic bin with the rest of my stuff. It pulled my items into the x-ray machine. A TSA guy was sitting at a monitor, watching the glowing items pass through. I saw him jerk out of his seat. My skull belt buckle frightened him. His thoughts must have been pretty much like this: *curling iron, cellphone, cellphone, yet one more laptop computer, cellphone charger, a skull!*

I went over and stood on a yellow line.

A much bigger guy was standing on the far side of the security scanner and waved me through. He was all muscle. On his forearm was a tattoo of a three-headed dog.

I stepped through the U-shaped scanner and waited for a loud beep. No sound was made and I found myself right in front of the burly guy. His breath was bad.

"Nice tat," I offered.

"Boarding pass."

I searched everywhere and finally found it in my back pocket along with my passport. I handed them over. I thought I saw one of the dog heads on his arm snarl at me while I was doing it. I really did. I blamed it on the letter B that hit me on the noggin.

The guy looked at the boarding pass, glanced me over once or twice, and nodded to another guy standing off in the corner.

"Step over there," he barked.

I walked over to the other guy. In his gloved hand was a big wand. He told me to spread them and stick my arms out to the side. Then he moved the wand over my entire body. Next he patted me down.

"Ooh-hey-ahh-watch it-ouch-that's my-you wish-no way to treat a rockstar, buddy-hardly know you."

He finished and let me go.

"Was it good for you too?" Virg asked. He was standing at the end of the conveyor belt, smiling.

"I may have lost my virginity."

"Somehow I doubt it."

"And you didn't tell me I'd have to take off my boots or I would've wore a nice pair of socks."

"Like you have any," Virg said. He had gotten his paraphernalia already. I got my stuff on and began walking.

Virg trundled his prim-and-proper, look-at-me-I'm-a-whoopdeedoo-travel-agent suitcase on wheels behind him and I lugged my duffel bag after waving my goodbyes to Cornrows who flashed me a mouth of gold teeth.

The concourse opened into a large circular area that formed a hub for waiting planes. The hub fanned in all directions. The area was floored in that obnoxious multicolored and multi-patterned carpet that can only be remotely possible in airports and nursing homes. Way above the obnoxious carpet was a glass dome spreading bright sunlight throughout the hub. I flipped down my shades. A rockstar always has to have his shades, especially indoors.

"There's our gate," Virg announced. "A9."

Out from one of the jet ramps streamed a bunch of losers who were deplaning. Right away I could see they were tourist agents—just like ole Virg—dressed in their sorry tourist agent outfits, tour books tucked under their arms. They were sporting sunburns that matched the carpet. They had on televangelist grins. They even had nametags. The unbelievable thing about it was how they immediately recognized Virg. Their voices were trumpetlike.

"No way," a foreign guy name Lucan said.

"It really is him. It's the guru of greater Florence travel!" a guy named Homer shouted.

Some dude named Milton gave Virg a big hug. "You trained me at the Zany right out of college."

Apparently the *really cool* travel agents in Florence call the Zany Zoo Travel Agency just "Zany" for short. Didn't I say they were losers?

One of them was wearing a T-shirt: *I celebrated Mozart's 250th birthday*. Way I figure, Mozart wrote the rock music of his day. I wonder if 250 years from now they will print T-shirts on Edward T. Nad's birthday. It's January 30, 1992 if you want to get me a gift next year.

This reminded me that once Bea and I rolled around in the grass at a symphony playing Mozart. Let me tell you something, that girl puts the *art* in Mozart. She used to rub my earlobes when she snuggled with me. It drove me crazy. That was way back last summer. A very long time ago in rockertime. Bea says it's about the same as dogtime. One year of rocking, ages a person seven years. In rockertime I feel thirty-five, not twenty-one. Bea's been gone over four months now. That's almost two years in rockertime.

"Hey Virg, what if Rockmonanov came back and played 'Rock Lobster'? Or Vivaldi jammed out 'Viva Las Vegas,' and

Mozart composed 'Money for Nothing'? That would really be something."

"What are you talking about, Edw—"

"Thou art the man," interrupted a guy named Poe.

They were welcoming Virg like . . . well, like a rockstar. I was a bit jealous.

"Next they'll want your autograph," I said.

It was just then that the one with the *I celebrated Mozart's 250th birthday* T-shirt, held out his arm for Virg to sign it. Virg turned to me and smirked. "What can I say?"

I rolled my eyes.

Virg's fans finally left after praising him some more. Disgusting.

"Those were strange groupies," I told him as they trailed away. "Can we go now? We have a plane to catch."

Virg had forgotten all about it.

After a few gates we located our waiting area and took a seat. Among the hustle and bustle of fliers trying to get upgraded to first class and ladies checking baby strollers that would not fit in the overhead compartment, I thought of the first song Bea wrote for the band. It pretty sums up how we met.

Riven by Chance

Wanted to form a band called 'Fad'
Online you placed an ad.
"Hot drummer
Needs strummer."
Had low expectations
From other band vexations.

Riven by chance
Riven by chance
Cha-ya-ya-ya-ya-yaya-yance!

Outside the coffeehouse took a glance
Saw you were cute and gave it a chance.
Sat down at your table

Right then I knew you were able.
We talked for hours
Then sprinkles turned to showers.

Riven by chance
Riven by chance
Cha-ya-ya-ya-ya-yaya-yance!

Gave me your coat to cover my head
Ran out remembering all we said.
A week later, our first practice session
We didn't need lessons.
We rocked all summer
You the drummer, me the strummer.

Riven by chance
Riven by chance
Cha-ya-ya-ya-ya-yaya-yance!

Bea called it a sonnet, whatever that is. We made that 'sonnet' into our first hit of sorts when we got some local radio play. Bea turned out not only to be a great guitar player, but she could write songs like blazes. That's pretty much how it all started between us. Bea penned the songs and we both put them to music.

Sonny and Cher? Captain and Tennille? Meg and Jack? Sid and Nancy? Try Bea and Eddie!

It Howled

VIRG AND I sat there listening to the flat screens drone on overhead. A one-hour-of-news-shown-twenty-four-hours-a-day program was on. Just once I want to watch a news program without text scrolling along the bottom of the screen and popups flashing in the corners telling me what show is on next week. That's why we all have Attention Deficit Disorder. Newscasters are so boring they have to throw in a bunch of spinning, whirling graphics. Let me just watch one program without having to read across the bottom of the screen that some famous fathead gained ten pounds or fathered a love child while on a beach in the Bahamas.

Thankfully the overhead speaker announced our plane was boarding to Washington D.C. where we would get our connection to Barcelona. I was just happy to leave the limbo land waiting area of Who Cares News. We both got in line– Virg with his wimpy suitcase and me with my duffel bag. A hip hop song was playing through the overhead speakers.

"Remind me to never use the words 'shorty' or 'booty' in any of my songs."

"As your manager, that's a deal."

A gate attendant named Minos stopped us. He didn't look Greek with his blonde hair and high cheekbones and nose that wouldn't stop, but I figured he was from his name. He looked a tad unfriendly. I found this strange since we were first class passengers.

Minos scanned our boarding passes and then gave a terrible stare at the ground. "Those will never do," he said in reference to our luggage.

"Easy there—"

Virg cut me off. This was clearly his territory. Without saying a word, Virg lifted his suitcase, moved it over the luggage-sizing box, and lowered it inside.

"What's the problem," he said. "As you can see it will fit perfectly in the overhead on the plane."

"Really?" Minos wondered aloud. "While the width fits, you can see that the height of the suitcase is above the container. It will have to be checked."

Virg leaned against the counter Minos was standing behind. Virg glanced back at the growing, discontented line and said, "I am sure you're familiar with the FAA rules under Title 14, Sections 23, 25, 121, and 135 of the Code of Federal Regulations that limits the size of any carry-on bag to 45 linear inches, which, as I am sure you are aware, is the total height, width and depth of the suitcase."

Minos turned sheepish and when Virg whipped out a retractable ruler he had clipped on his key ring, Minos's eyes grew large.

"You see," Virg informed as he measured the sides, "I've got another five linear inches if needed."

"Snap!" I said.

"My apologies, sir."

Virg trundled forward. When Minos gave the evil eye to my duffel bag, I informed him, "Don't even think about it or he'll get the Code of Federal Regulations out and beat you with it."

"Very well. Have a good flight, sir."

"Bet your bongos I will." I winked on the way past.

Virg stood waiting for me at the top of the jet ramp. "Never thought I'd say this, Virg, but you were awesome back there. Can't believe how difficult it is to travel these days. A person has to have a personal travel agent with them."

"Why thank you, Edward. I take pride in my work."

"You're still a nerd, Virg, and don't forget it."

We entered a dark tunnel that formed the jet ramp leading down to the plane. The walls were thin. The sides of the tunnel prattled and groaned from the heavy winds outside. Our footfalls pounded and echoed along the way. Combat boots are loud in tunnels.

"I'll have to email the airline a Thank You card when we get back, if you know what I mean," Virg said. "That's no way to treat customers."

"Bea used to send Thank You cards when somebody gave her a gift or let her borrow a cup of flour. She *wrote* them with a real pen, ink and paper. She put the card in, like, an envelope, stuck a stamp on it, walked outside and mailed it . . . like in the *mailbox* with the whole open door, insert envelope, close door, put up red flag and wait for the mailman to come. She had issues."

As totally bizarre as this behavior is, if you knew Bea this would not surprise you. You would know that she despises email. Thinks it's impersonal. Thinks it's digital and run by computer algorithms. Can you believe her? She's got some major issues. That's why I kicked her to the curb.

"The way you keep bringing Bea up, it sounds like you miss her," Virg said as we continued down the tunnel.

"Yeah, right. We'll be a lot better off on this trip if you get it straight once and for all. I really don't miss her. She's the one who skipped town."

"You can still miss her. Just tell me if you'd like to see her again. I know I do."

When I was about to slap Virg in the back of the head, a line formed at the end of the jet ramp with the other first class passengers and "those with small children or who may need assistance boarding."

An old lady and man stood in front of us and we stopped directly behind them. They turned and looked at us in a rather funny way. It appeared as though they wanted to speak to us. I understood being a rockstar and everything.

The elderly man was sad, but affable. His puffy eyes were rheumy. The lady's skin had no elasticity. White and limp. Fissures ran down her cheeks.

I asked the man if he had ever attended a Led Zeppelin concert back in the seventies and he said no as if that was some strange question to ask.

Virg questioned if they needed any help boarding.

"Oh no, kind sir," the lady said. "We are flying to Italy because the most horrible event has occurred. I shudder to relay it."

"Looks like none of us are going anywhere," Virg said. He must have felt sorry for the elderly couple since they were traveling alone to a foreign country.

The lady bent close. Through cracked lips she uttered, "There has been a double murder in our family. Two bloody deaths."

Virg and I had no response to this. Saying "I'm sorry" or "That's too bad" would've felt trite. What I really wanted to do was to walk away, but we were trapped in the dark tunnel with a line stretching to the rear. The wind made the cheap walls around us tattle and moan in a chatty metallic way. The temperature rose in the stifling confines and, much to our dismay, the lady went on with her story.

"My name is Francine and this is my partner, Paul. Many years ago I was to be married to a young man from another village. Our Italian family is very—how would you say it in today's terms—of the old or traditional school when it comes to matters of the heart. Which is to say, my parents arranged the marriage. The dowry my parents offered consisted of the first pick of Tuscan grapes from our family vineyards for as long as we were married. Our Chianti is renowned.

"Just a few weeks before the marriage, the young man to whom I was betrothed was burned terribly in a fire on his parent's estate. From all accounts an animal kicked over an oil lamp in the barn where he was napping. When he awoke, he was engulfed in flames. The burns were mostly to his face and neck. They were not life threatening, but his appearance was hideous. This fact was hidden from me by his parents who sought the lucrative dowry from one of the finest wineries in Tuscany and to gain marital relations into one of its prominent families."

As Francine was telling the tale, I noticed a tear spring from one of Paul's rheumy eyes. "He was my brother," Paul said, shaking his head. "I refuse to mention his name to this day." It was all he could do to choke those few words from his mouth.

"A cruel turn of play was devised by his family—"

"My family," Paul uttered, shaking his head as though he were ashamed.

Francine went on. "Instead of telling the truth and giving my family the option of release from the marriage bond, they hid the truth from all. Unbeknownst to me, I was introduced to the young man's handsome brother at the wedding ceremony."

Paul squeezed off a wan smile.

"It was the first time I had seen either of the brothers. All I knew was they were dark-haired and handsome. The wedding ceremony was a lavish affair. My parents spent what would be considered a year's wage to most of the working class people in the village. Dignitaries and high-ranking military personnel from surrounding villages were in attendance. The celebration lasted deep into the night, dancing and merriment and endless wine. That night I fell madly in love with Paul, the person to whom I thought was my new husband.

"The next morning when I awoke, however, his scarred brother lay next to me on the pillow. I had never seen him in my life. I flew out of bed in fright. He jumped up and tried to slap a hand over my mouth. I broke free and yelled for the servants. Just as quickly he grabbed me by the wrist and swiped a parchment off the dresser. Before the servants arrived he showed me the marriage certificate with his name on it and told me the awful truth. Under law I was helpless. The marriage bond had been formed."

"Marriage bond," echoed Paul in a haunting voice.

"My feelings of betrayal and isolation grew exponentially. I hated the very sight of him. He treated me harshly, even brutally, and was a demanding husband in more ways than I can relate. At all times he guarded me. It was his disfigurement that caused his rampant jealousy.

"Shortly after our fraudulent marriage, he left to start an olive oil trading business on the Amalfi Coast. I immediately had the servants track down Paul and bring him to the villa. He rushed into my arms and we embraced for an hour without letting go. Under guarded watch by my closest and most confiding servants, Paul stayed with me for three days and nights. We were madly in love. He confessed that his domineering parents and brother forced him into the debauchery."

"When I took one glance at her," Paul confessed, "I fell

hopelessly in love."

"I could not fault Paul for feeling deeply sorry for his deformed brother and for trying to help him with only good intentions," added Francine. "Paul had never met me before the wedding, either. After the ceremony he could hide the truth no longer and he told his brother he was about to confess all. When Paul took a break outside to get some night air, a sack was placed over his head and he was carried off into the night."

"I was beaten and thrown onto a cargo ship that sailed to Spain that night. It took me days to get back. I had very little money."

I glanced at Paul and more tears were dotting his cheeks. The couple was obviously still together after all these years. Just as I was about to tell him to be a man, (less womanly than Boy George, but less manly than the Indigo Girls) Francine went on with the ending of the story.

"Paul's brother returned abruptly from his business venture after being unable to locate a shipping partner. Paul was having breakfast in my room when I heard his brother call for me and try to open the locked door. In a panic Paul tried to escape out the singular garret window, but it was too high off the ground. I pulled back a center rug and showed Paul a trap door that led down to an excess-wine storage room. 'I'll be right there,' I was saying to his brother who heard the commotion inside and was asking why the door was locked. I heard the alternate jangling of keys and pounding of fists.

"Paul tried to escape down the hatch, but his housecoat got caught on a board. The door burst open and his brother immediately saw us. He unsheathed a rapier strapped to his belt and ran at Paul. Just as he was about to plunge the blade into Paul's neck, I stepped in front of him. The rapier went through my midsection and into Paul's neck."

'Enter Sandman' is another favorite *Metallicasongof—*

―――――――

"Edward, wake up."

The next thing I know Virg was patting me on the cheeks and yelling at the stewardesses to get me some water from the plane.

I managed to prop myself up on an elbow. "What happened?"

"You passed out again, Edward."

"I did not. How long was I out?"

"Two or three minutes."

"I doubt that, Virg."

The bottled water came and I struggled to my feet. I rested against a railing in the tunnel as the other passengers gawped at me. I blamed it on the B that fell on my head to whoever would listen. I blamed it on the close quarters and the time we had to stand there and wait. I blamed it on anything but the story. I chugged down the cool water. The line still wasn't moving. Once again I was the entertainment for everyone.

When I had finished the bottled water, I asked, "Where's Francine and Paul?"

Virg spun around to search for them. We both looked puzzled. Everyone else standing near us was in place and accounted for. They acted like they had no idea what we were inquiring about. We called for them up and down the line and got nothing but crazy stares. The elderly couple had vanished.

"Where did they go?" I asked Virg.

"If their heart-wrenching story was true, Edward, they died four decades ago."

The walls prattled and shook. Outside the wind howled. It howled.

Three-Headed Dog

AFTER MY LITTLE swoon the line began slowly moving. We continued down the rest of the jet ramp, crossed the little bridge and walked onto the plane. A light mix of rain and sleet was falling outside, which is common for Eastertime in Florence. I looked at the weather nervously and Virg told me not to worry. They would de-ice the plane.

"And this news is supposed to put me at ease?"

As we made our way toward first class the weather caused shadows to dance and play inside the plane. I was still on the lookout for Francine and Paul, but they were nowhere to be found. In my recovering state I saw shadows in the form of a three-headed dog that resembled the one tattooed on that security guy's arm.

You should've seen all the tubs of lard at the front of the plane. First class fatsos aplenty! Never having ridden in first class (or any class for that matter), I envisioned the passengers would all be rich and thin—not necessarily in that order. Was I ever wrong in spades. For a moment I thought we'd stepped into an all-you-can-eat buffet at a glutton convention. I puffed out my cheeks for Virg.

"Please. Let's just take our seats."

We stored our luggage in the overhead. I chuckled when I saw the three-headed shadow eating the tubos. Two heads were munching away on the ears of one guy. The other had a lady by the nose.

Virg and I took our seats. Virg rode shotgun by the window and I got the aisle.

This is strange. When I buckled my seatbelt it reminded me of Bea. I felt compelled to tell Virg about it. "That's another thing about Bea. She's always trying to make the world a better place. Little Miss Do-gooder. As if she could actually *change* anything. One of her pet projects is to try and convince the FAA to upgrade the seatbelts on airplanes. There are no shoulder belts on airplanes, only lap belts.”

“I’m well aware of that, Edward.”

“One time she explained that if a plane ever gets in an accident everyone’s upper body will snap forward. I told her if our plane drops out of the sky—like when our band is famous and we’re squirting around on our private jet with Monk Monkeys or Mormonkeys, or whatever cool name we decide on, emblazoned in huge letters on the outside—then we have bigger problems than whiplash.”

“That’s just Beatrice, Edward. She notices things like missing shoulder belts.”

“Come to think of it, Seatbeltless would be an intriguing name for a rebellious band. I just thought of that out of nowhere. Same with Monk Monkeys. Really I did.”

“I thought we were talking about Beatrice, Edward.”

“That’s one of your many problems, Virg, you always bring up Bea.”

“I didn’t—”

“So when Bea sees ways to make the world better, she just goes off like some popinjay about the lack of safety until I finally tell her to work on song lyrics or some new riffs or something. I don’t know what she is doing without me in Venice to keep her straight. She’s probably all a mess.”

Virg wasn’t listening. I adjusted the stream of air piping down from the overhead. It was still hot despite the falling sleet out Virg’s window. Across the aisle I noticed a fat guy in a dark suit. He was trying hard to look the part of a serious businessman. The newspaper in his hand contained a bunch of stock numbers that ran down the page. In his lap was a leather folder with the letters CIA-CCO stamped across the front.

The Fed, I thought. Next to him was another stooge in a black suit so I listened in on their conversation in the hopes of learning a few national secrets or at least who killed Jimmy Hoffa.

“We gave 110% . . . gut check win . . . all heart . . . left it all on the field . . . gutsy performance . . . hit that one out of the park . . . the last yard . . . fourth down . . . take the ball and run with it . . . ninth inning . . . free kick . . . stay in the batter's box . . . overtime . . . down field . . . out-of-bounds . . . three strikes and you're out . . . threw me a curve . . . home stretch . . . no harm, no foul . . . TKO . . . fourth and goal . . . the final mile . . . step up to the plate . . . at the bell . . . eye off the ball . . . down the field . . . slam dunk . . ."

Everything they talked about was couched in disgusting sports metaphors. I almost puked. They didn't even mention one game or team in doing it. It was just how they talked. It took them twice as long to discuss any point because of the sports lingo sprinkled in at every movement of their tongues. I really wanted to hurt those guys.

"There's no I in team," one of the Feds said.

"There's no I in team, but there is in win," CIA-CCO said with a big smile.

"And there's two Is in idiots!" I yelled across the aisle.

Under the glare of the Feds, the stewardess approached.

I asked her if they had packets of those peanuts.

"You must be thinking of *another* airline. We have never given out peanuts."

She shrugged. Asked if we needed anything to drink and stuff. "Perhaps a coffee or orange juice?"

I spoke up. "Did you know that no word in the English language rhymes with orange?"

"I guess not. What can I get you, sir?"

"And when you think about it, no English word rhymes with sphincter. Believe me, I've tried. SphincterTown would be a stupendous name for a band if you ever want to dump this whole airline thing and get a real job."

For some reason the stewardess seemed offended.

Virg leaned across me. "Thank you, miss. We would both enjoy a coffee."

She headed toward the tiny serving area at the front of the plane. She was a bit huffy.

Didn't care. So I went off and told Virg the top three rudest service providers:

1. Airline stewardesses;
2. Cable television service reps;
3. Driver's license clerks; and
4. Grocery store greeters.

When the stewardess returned with our cups of joe I said, "You know, if the airlines really want to reduce weight on planes to save gas, reduce emissions and help the environment, they need to stop getting rid of lightweight items like pillows and blankets, and instead get rid of those bulky, solid metal drink carts. If you can't get rid of them, at least transition to recycled plastic drink carts that weigh one tenth as much."

The stewardess was nodding. Virg was nodding. The Feds were nodding. The three-headed dog shadows were nodding. When I preach, I preach the truth, brothers and sisters.

"You could easily get rid of a couple hundred pounds a trip. And besides, aren't those heavy drink carts dangerous if they become dislodged during flight?"

"Our drink carts are not dangerous, sir," she offered. "That must be another airline."

"What we need is a fat, ugly, greasy guy to film a documentary about the dangers of drink carts. We can get a bunch of strongmen to wheel him on a cart right up to the front door of a major airline headquarters with video camera rolling. He can confront the CEO when the doofus arrives in the morning. We could have our pick of fat greasy guys from any of these people in first class. We really could. It would rake in millions."

I introduced myself to the stewardess / flight attendant / whatever to make up for offending her with all the sphincter talk.

"From the moment I stepped on the plane you recognized me as a rockstar, didn't you."

"Actually, no. But your name is quite interesting."

"Okay," I said, "so I s'ppose you're wondering about my sorry name. Listen up because I'm only going to say this once."

"I really have to serve the other passengers," she told me.

"Just listen for a sec. I come from a long and distinguished line of Nads. There were the Nads of New York, the Nads of Nantucket, and before them the Nads of the Netherlands. I would be Edward Nad the Younger if my middle name (Theodore) had matched Dad's (Charles). My name is bad enough without Junior tacked on the end.

"Dad is a banker and Mom sells a line of all natural washing detergents called Eco-Stain-Able (ESA for short). I call them both 'money launderers.' They could afford to send me to private schools and did, what with me being an only child. I was glad they got it right the first time. I mean, who wants a sibling? Not only was I the first and last kid in our family, I was sickly. Raging allergies in junior high. Never was I so ill as when I attended Our Lady of Infinite Health. This may come as a surprise, but I got beat up a lot there; never as much as in high school at Our Lady of Perpetual Peace. Now *that* was a very violent school."

"The customers. I have to—"

"It was in high school that I turned to music and started ripping on the drums in my parents' basement. I played the stretched skins for hours every night. They let me get some aggression out. A few of my early bands failed due to lack of talent by the other members. First the Encumbered Cucumbers turned rotten and then Scratch Monkeys fell to earth and died. It wasn't until I met Bea that things started getting off the ground in a hurry. She is my very *former* girlfriend. Well . . . we got local play on a radio station in Florence for a couple months. The fans were crazy about a two person rock band with a hot chick at the mike. Then Virg, here, took us on as our manager, and then . . . well . . . we had creative differences and Bea skipped town for Venice. It's in Italy."

The stewardess gave me a look as though I had given her way too much information. She didn't even ask for my autograph. Can you believe her?

"I really must serve the other first class passengers now," she said firmly.

"Hey, do you have any nice stewardesses on this flight?

Oh, sorry, that's another airline."

Virg slugged me in the arm.

The final passengers finished boarding and one of the stewardesses closed the front door to the plane. She then shut the metal cockpit door and the pilots locked it from the inside so that terrorists could not access it.

The lead stewardess got on the microphone and read the warning card about what to do in case of an accident. She went on and on. She offered no tips on what to do without shoulder belts in the case of accident.

It made me even sleepier. The coffee had little effect. Like I told Virg, I wasn't used to getting up much before ten . . . preferably noon if possible.

The lead stewardess made one final check of the seatbelts while the plane rolled backwards. We taxied toward the runway and then stopped. We sat there for a few minutes while a couple other planes shot into the sky. I gripped the armrests tightly as our plane took off toward Washington D.C., where our connecting flight to Barcelona, Spain awaited us.

Section II

Et Tu, Plutus?

THE FLIGHT TO D.C. was bumpy on takeoff. I kept asking Virg if that was normal. He said it pretty much was. I said he was pretty much a liar. But once we got above the cloud cover everything smoothed out. Within ten minutes one of the stewardesses came on and let everybody know it was now safe to turn on electronic devices.

Virg told me it was now safe to let go of the armrests.

A half hour later one of those heavy, metal carts was wheeled out. The stewardess passed out trays that contained a stale-looking biscuit and a plate with a glob of orangish spinach and a gelatinous egg mixture speckled in spinach. A few wedges of wilty fruit were off to the side. Virg immediately tore off the plastic and began eating the stuff. Like he was famished.

"Whuttt?" he shrugged after noticing my stares. His mouth was full.

"You have no shame."

Eventually I picked at the casserole, ate a couple of fruit wedges and took a few bites of the biscuit. The best part was the coffee, which I quaffed.

After that I scanned a shopping magazine that was in the bin in front of me. I listened to the CIA-COO guys for awhile. I played with the window shade and the air vent. I smiled at the lead stewardess. I turned to Virg. "That coffee is going right through me."

"Me too."

We both glanced forward and saw the first class bathroom was occupied and a few gluttons were in line for it next. Virg and I had to use the one in the back of the plane. I mean *way* back.

We unclasped our seatbelts, carefully slid from the row without spilling our trays, and began walking toward the rear of the plane. The bathrooms felt like they were a city block away. I was surprised at how many people were asleep already.

Around row fifteen or sixteen we had to stop because some lady, who was dripping in jewelry, popped up in front of us and reached for her luggage in the overhead.

At the same time a guy near her jumped up, too. Half-eaten food wrappers spilled from his lap. Magazines fanned out of his seat bin. Newspapers and plastic bottles were everywhere. I just knew they would never be recycled. Everything about the guy spelled waste.

They were now both blocking the aisle, oblivious to us.

Before we could push through them, the jewel-encrusted hoarder yanked her carry-on from the overhead with such force she could not control it. It slammed into the cranium of Sir Waste-O-Plenty, which bent him over his seat in an awkward way.

Wadded up cracker wrappers fell out of his pockets and he cursed, much to the chagrin of two young mothers sitting nearby who tried to cover their kids' ears. It was too late. Light travels faster than sound and sound laced with curse words travels faster than hands (except when I'm playing the drums).

The guy's face turned red. As soon as he righted himself he grabbed the lady's carry-on and threw it down the aisle. It landed with a thud and broke open. Some very large undergarments flopped out that may have been fabricated by a hot air balloon company. I was just glad there were no wasps.

Bap. The lady slapped the guy across the kisser.

The waster looked surprised and confused all at once. When he got his wits about him, he shoved the lady. Just pushed her full on. She toppled backwards over the armrest of her seat. Those in the surrounding rows began screaming and those across the aisle got a glimpse of the hot air balloon underwear in action.

A guy sitting next to the lady climbed over her into the aisle. He announced, "I am Plutus," and then beat his chest while adding, "and you have insulted my wife."

Another Greek, I thought.

Suddenly Plutus clocked Sir Waste-O-Plenty right in the nose. Jowls quivering, the guy toppled into the pile of trash on his seat. Blood trickled across his cheek.

As if that wasn't enough, Plutus rolled up a beauty magazine and started beating the guy on the legs with it. "Don't mess with Plutus!" the husband barked.

"Or with Texas," I added.

The brute must not have liked my remark because he turned to me with baleful eyes and raised the magazine. As any great rocker would do, I dove onto the floor.

More people got in on the action.

Soon Virg leaned down and started berating me for leaving him in the heat of battle. I didn't listen. When do I ever listen to Virg?

Feeling my way along the floor my hands felt a soft, frilly material. I knew exactly what it was. I saw that Plutus's cowboy boot was standing on it.

I tightened my grip and yanked the undergarment harder than when I used to give wedgies (got quite a few, too) at Our Lady of Perpetual Health. His leg went out from under him and he crashed to the floor but not before whacking the side of his head on an armrest.

He lay in the aisle and didn't move.

When I was *sure* he was knocked out—I mean, like really sure—I stood and stuck a combat boot on his stomach and raised my chin in victory. The crowd was cheering. I held out my arms in a flying formation. "That's how we glide!"

Virg tapped me on the shoulder.

"What, Virg? What? Can't you leave me alone for one second so I can enjoy this?"

"Do you realize you have that lady's underwear hanging from your ear?"

I snatched them off and held them up. "We're the panty police and this is a raid."

There was more cheering and fist bumps, especially from the guys.

Plutus began to snap out of it as Virg and I strolled over him. He uttered nothing more than a wheeze as I walked across his face.

"*Et tu, Plutus?*" I couldn't resist. I fist bumped a few more people.

Another fifteen rows and we finally reached the back of the plane.

"Never underestimate the power of panties, Virg."

"Blue chiffon is a good color on you."

There was no wait for the johns at the rear of the plane. Virg went in the skinny door on the right and I took the one on the left. I did my business and beat him back out. I'm sure he has a bathroom ritual, like how to use the john in fifteen simple steps. He's soooo slow and deliberate about everything. I can just see Virg washing his hands over and over with that antibacterial soap and looking all happy at himself in the tiny mirror. And then after drying his hands (very thoroughly, mind you), I am sure Virg smiles as he smoothes down his hair then smoothes down his Hawaiian shirt, checking all the buttons, but first ensuring that the T-shirt underneath is tucked into his tighty whiteys. And finally, I imagine, he makes one last pass at his teeth to ensure there is no spinach caught in there from the sorry first class casserole he devoured.

I waited for him to emerge. "Any longer, Virg, and we would be in D.C. Keep your eyelids peeled for Plutus as we walk by. I don't trust him."

Virg chuckled. "He has your boot print on his shirt."

"And face."

Quickly we made our way down the aisle. Lots of glances were shot our way, but no one said anything. They didn't dare. I whispered to Plutus on the way past that his wife wore granny panties.

He reached for me but I was already in the first class cabin with Virg, as we took our seats. The stewardess had cleared our trays of the rubberized casserole we had to endure.

No sooner had we sat down than some kid a row up, stood. I could see his T-shirt from my aisle seat. MARSH OF STYX was stamped across the back. From what I could make out, bunches of angry people were fighting in a swamp. Fire was engulfing them. A red-faced guy with a pitchfork was dancing around and laughing. The people on the shirt were kicking and biting each other.

These kids nowadays. They just don't have good fashion sense like me. When he sat back down I looked over and noticed that the CIA-COO guys across the way were asleep. I leaned my seat back and tried to do the same.

"Wake me up when we get there," I said to Virg. "And I thought flying would be boring."

Phlegyas

WHEELS SLAPPING AGAINST pavement awoke me from a deep sleep. My legs and arms flung into a long-jump pose.

"Geez, I thought we had crashed."

Virg chuckled. Then he said I had drool on a corner of my mouth. I told him to shut his trap and wiped it off with his sleeve. There was no way I was going to ask him for a tissue.

The flight attendant welcomed us to Chantilly, Virginia and Dulles International Airport. She asked us to fly again soon with the airline.

"What kinda guide are you? Thought we were connecting in D.C."

"Dulles serves the greater District of Columbia area, Edward."

I repeated his snippety response to myself in mocking fashion. When the seatbelt icon went dark, I was the first in the aisle. I got my duffle bag from the overhead. A sharp pain raced up my leg. The CIA-COO guy had flung the heavy part of his seatbelt over his armrest and clocked me right on the knee. Man did it hurt.

"Thanks a lot," I said as I grabbed my bag. "Go win one for the Gipper."

The guy offered some phony sports apology about tripping over the base while rounding third. I ignored him. The guy'll obviously never be in a rock band. I let Virg into the aisle and snatched his suitcase down for him. In deplaning we said goodbye to the captains who were standing just outside the cockpit. They were smiling like Broadway actors at curtain call and obviously looking for compliments.

"Nice glide," I told them. The flight attendant gave me a sour look. She was the one who got tired listening to my story about Mom and Dad and how I grew up. Secretly, I think she wanted me.

We stepped out of the plane, made our way over the jet bridge, and up the tunnel to the main terminal. Windows surrounded us on both sides. A mix of snow and fog swirled in all directions. Mist rolled and frolicked across the tarmac. Visibility was very poor across this macabre landscape of fading lights, mechanical beasts and orange tentacles. We had landed in a foggy swamp that was supposed to be the nation's capitol or somewhere near it in another state.

Virg was surprised the pilots were able to land the plane. That failed to make me feel any better about flying. Suddenly a look of concern flashed across his face. He darted over to a bank of Departure screens that displayed the city, time of departure, status and gate. I followed right behind though limping a bit from the meeting of seatbelt buckle and kneecap.

Our mouths fell open when we saw the same word streaming down the rightmost column of all Departure screens—Cancelled.

"What does that mean, Virg? I mean, I know what it *means*. But what does it really *mean*?"

He didn't answer but instead charged straight for the service counter of our airline. The lady behind it ("Mary, Team Member") verified that our connecting flight had been cancelled indefinitely and that no flights were scheduled to depart Dulles International Airport until the following day. Virg put out his hand as though he was about to run into a telephone pole while standing still.

He launched into a big dissertation about us being first class passengers and how much business the Zany Zoo Travel Agency gave the airline on a yearly basis. He could pull up many of the receipts on his phone. He really could. Mary had never heard of the agency—which made him mad—and she didn't much care.

Only Virg would try and argue our way out of the weather.

After punching a bunch of keys on her keyboard, Mary found a way to book us on the next available flight the following day. It left at noon for Barcelona. Noon! Virg thought it was too late. I thought it was too early. I didn't even want to get up until then.

Out of frustration we put our backs against the counter wall and slid down to the floor. Elbows went to knees and palms to chins. We even sighed at the same time.

"So?"

"So?"

"Whatdawedonow?"

"Idunknow."

"So?"

"So?"

After a few minutes of blank stares I questioned, "What kind of tour guide are you?"

"I can't control the weather, Edward. Let's catch a cab and get a hotel room for the night. Tomorrow we'll come back to the airport and make our connecting flight. This will give us more time to hang out and talk."

"Oh, I feel tingly all over."

"Let's get moving. I have a feeling the D.C. hotels will be filling up quickly and it's not even lunchtime. Forget about staying at one of the airport hotels. I'm sure they are already full."

In our perturbed state we followed the signs to Ground Transportation with the rest of the stiffs. On the way Virg made a call back to the office and learned there was a vacancy at some place called the Trident Hotel downtown. As we came down the escalator to Ground Transportation, we noticed a long, snaking line waiting for cabs into the city.

"Flabby Cabby would be a good name for a band," I said.

"The line must be an hour long," Virg warned.

Right there, half way down the escalator, I had a moment of genius. "Forget the cabs. We're riding in style."

As we got off the escalator a group of limo drivers, most dressed in dark suits, were holding plain white cards with names printed on them. A long-faced driver with sideburns to match was holding a card that read Edward Nathan.

"Follow my lead, Virg."

I took out my driver's license, put my thumb over the D in my last name, and flashed it to the limo driver.

He barely took a glance before tipping his cap. "Good day,

Mr. Edward Nathan. Can I get your bag and that of your travel companion?"

"Sure, but it's not like we're . . . you know," I made clear.

"As you wish."

"Feel free to call me Edward." I gave a Cheshire cat smile to Virg.

Virg looked amazed at the scam I'd pulled off.

When the driver was a good three paces in front of us, I said, "I always wondered how those limo drivers actually *know* they are picking up the right person. Anyone could walk up and say they are Fred or George or Susan. I bet half of them, just like our guy up there in front of us, don't have a clue who they've picked up. They are driving around people who just want to get to their destination in style. I mean look at the banking crisis of 2008. We already know that the people in the backs of limos are frauds. I bet half the limos in D.C. have frauds in the back seats. . . even some who aren't politicians."

Virg gave me an anxious look. I could tell he was uneasy about this.

"Limo Bimbos would be a fine name for a glam band."

We trailed our limo driver, with the basset hound face, out into the fog that had gotten thicker during our walk through the airport terminal.

The driver pointed to his limo and we followed him twenty yards down the sidewalk where the rest of the limos were parked. All the while the halogens overhead gave off a sickly blue-yellow light that barely cut to the ground. The sun was nonexistent. Visibility was thirty feet, max.

The driver opened the rear door and Virg slid in first. Once I was inside and the door shut, he took our luggage around and placed it in the trunk.

From the backseat I noticed the driver's certification mounted to the divider wall. His name was Phlegyas. There was no telling if this was his first or last name. It may have been the name of his cold medicine or the sound of him coughing. I discerned two things from it: First, you had to get a mouthful of phlegm to say it correctly and second, it was of foreign origin no doubt. Just once I'd like to see someone born in America driving a taxi or limo. I really would. Now that I think about it, that would be a fine business idea. American Taxi Company—our drivers were actually born here!

When the driver got behind the wheel I could tell from the rearview mirror that he seemed a bit sour—perhaps at the weather or the impossibly long face his creator gave him.

We slowly moved out into traffic. To break the ice Virg asked Phlegyas if he'd been driving limos for long. In a thick accent he said he was actually a boatman by trade. A boatman!

I made some crack about canoeing on the Potomac that he didn't appreciate.

We exited the airport onto the freeway and drove until a sign pointed us to Washington D.C.

When I suggested that taking the side streets may be quicker than the freeway, he just shrugged at me.

"Whatever floats your boat," I said.

At the bottom of the exit ramp we stopped at the first traffic light. Face pressed to glass I peered into the bleakness that had become our nation's capitol. D.C. was a blackened moist smudge of a city. It seemed like it had been this way for a couple years. Maybe four. I tried to identify various landmarks, but to no avail. Heck, I could barely see the car next to us.

Silence overtook the limo and fog roiled down the sides of the glass in cascading sheets. This was much worse than the mist we experienced in Florence on the way to the airport—Virg's 'misty region of Weir.' This was real, unlike the fog machines I use at gigs.

Lit by the dashboard electronics and the stop light overhead, I saw in the rearview mirror the face of Phlegyas grinning in a pulled-taffy, sinister way that curled the corners of his thin lips.

I heard my heart knocking.

Time slowed. It had to be the longest traffic light I had ever experienced.

I tried to blink. I tried to breathe.

Abruptly my window shot down into its metal casing. Mist

spilled into the limo and licked my face. I shot toward the middle of the back seat to get away from it.

"What on earth!" I screamed. I was trying to swat the fog off me as though a toxic cloud or swarm of wasps at the Bacheron Airport. "Make it stop. Make it stop!"

That's when I heard the laugh of Virg's squeaky little voice. The flowers on his shirt were bouncing up and down next to my face. "I pushed a button on the center console," he confessed.

I swatted him in the arm and returned to my seat. "I oughta throw you out right here and make you walk to the hotel."

"Edward, you should have saw the look in your eyes. That was hilarious!"

"What's going to happen to the band if I die at a young age of a heart attack? Huh? Ever think of that, smartmonger?"

I had no sooner finished chiding Virg when an arthritic, muddy hand reached through the open window and latched onto my T-shirt. It tugged me toward the opening with surprising force.

"Put the window up! Put the window up!" I yelled at Virg.

The hand twisted my shirt into its clenched fist. The knuckles were big as walnuts. Whoever was attached to the other end of it had putrid breath.

"Drive!" I screamed to the front. "Drive!"

"The light is red," Phlegyas informed in all calmness. "I can do nothing."

"Run it if you want anything resembling a tip. Run it!"

"The window, Virg. Now!"

My eyes followed from the hand to the arm to the body to the face that was now only visible. What appeared to be a beggar was standing outside the limo. Tattered rags covered him. His skin was fish-fry grimy. "I am Filippo Argenti," he announced.

"I'm going to filippo you off if you don't let go of me!"

"Look at you all, driving around in such opulence. Such lavishness of lifestyle. This only feeds my anger. Cast your eyes upon me. See how destitute I am. Feel my rage. It is the rage of nations."

"That's a pretty Fuld statement to make about our money," I said as I felt his grasp tighten. His yellowy fingernails were like talons and they were digging into my neck.

I tried to jerk away. I tried to get my boot high enough to kick. "Do something, Virg!"

The window began slowly moving up. I used all the leverage I could muster to twist free of Filippo's grip. Just as I felt an instance of safety I started berating him. I was surprised when Virg joined in.

We alternately called out to Filippo through the remaining inches of open space, "We're not rich . . . God helps those who help themselves . . . Think I got money from working at the miserable Zany Zoo Travel agency of greater Florence? Do ya? How much you think a guy in a bunny costume makes?"

As the window closed, the light changed. Phlegyas stepped on it.

Filippo ran next to the limo for as long as he could keep up, clawing, grabbing, trying to get a finger hold. Twenty yards later he stopped. All that remained was a drumstick–shaped line of mud across my window.

I looked back and Filippo Argenti was waving his arms in a mad fury and doing a dance of insanity in the middle of the street.

After the run-in Virg apparently realized he had forgot to tell the limo driver that we did not want to visit whatever destination Phlegyas had been instructed to take Edward Nathan. Instead Virg told him to take us to the Trident Hotel near the White House.

"*Black* House in this weather," I commented.

"Bleak House," Virg said.

I told him he needs to pay attention if he wants to repeat what I say.

He said I was full of the Dickens.

After taking a bridge or two, we entered the city proper. A sign read THIS IS YOUR CAPITOL. In the pervasive fog, it appeared to say DIS YOUR CAPITOL. I referenced it and lamented that we had become a hip-hop nation.

Soon Virg pointed out the Washington Monument. The airplane avoidance light on the top of it made the upper portion look like a red spike floating in air (or a lighter held in the air at one of my concerts).

When we got into the heart of D.C., Virg referenced a cluster of historic hotels and Phlegyas angled to the curb. He got out and pulled open our doors. He then removed our luggage from the trunk.

When he returned, Virg tipped him.

I had no idea how much, but I informed Phlegyas that "It would have been more if you had been a little quicker with the gas pedal at the red light."

Phlegyas gave me an angry glance and got back in the limo. That's when it got really bizarre, like something from an Andrew Barger novel (not that I've read any).

I watched Phlegyas put down his window and stick his umbrella outside. Not in the normal way. He stuck the pointed end down and began *pushing off* with it in the fog like he was in a canoe or gondola. I swear. Which only made me think of Bea in Venice.

The Boatman.

The limo began moving slowly up the street, lurching forward with each stroke. I thought I heard an eddy of water. There was no engine sound.

I referenced the limo and stuttered. Virg was already walking toward the hotel. He didn't hear me. For a minute I stood there stuttering and pointing. I blamed the vision on the bad airplane food as the limo bobbed and floated away.

Room 1313

I CONTINUED WALKING in front of Virg—rather fast (not that I was frightened in the fog or anything)—up to a historic hotel fronted by a large, wrought iron gate. Stanchions jutted from the concrete walls high above. There were gargoyle heads that peered down from the fog. Above them we could see no further. The sun was a blotted orb. Afar off angry voices—perhaps three of them—were yelling toward us or at us. We could not tell. They were, however, coming from high up in the nether regions of the fog. I thought the voices were saying something about Medusa and stone. They were shrill and kept on as we reached the front door.

"Great hotel, Virg. Let's get inside."

"I'm with you."

We reached the massive glass front doors that resembled a gate with their patchwork of curved metal and large handles.

Virg pulled at one in a useless way. The door merely rattled. He tried to push with his shoulder and got nothing. The distant voices called out. He thought they were saying our names.

"You need to start pumping iron. Stand back."

I tried the adjacent door, then both at once. They would not budge for me, either. On the final try I put some back into it. I applied my combat boot to the doorjamb and tugged. The door still would not budge.

From the foggy nether regions we peered through the metal and glass into the lobby of the Trident Hotel. We saw no one. So we began knocking frantically—Virg on one door, me on the other—until our knuckles were sore. The voices from above were getting louder. *Closer.* I half wondered if they were coming from the gargoyles watching overhead.

Just as we were about to give up, a doorman appeared in

a white tux. He was the personification of calm. He nodded to us and reached toward one door. I heard a latch pop. The doorman swung it open. He apologized for the inconvenience, blamed it on some teenagers run amuck in the fog, and welcomed us to the hotel.

He offered to assist us with our luggage, but we refused as we entered the grand lobby. It had marble floors and posts that Virg called "pilasters." They supported a ceiling inlaid with tin squares. A gift shop off to the side was called THE SIXTH CIRCLE. It was so mod sounding.

A long desk awaited us in the lobby with smiling clerks all eager to check us in.

We steered toward a perky lady who looked young—not as young as a Chinese gymnast mind you—but young nonetheless.

"Hello, gentlemen. My name is Jennifer and I will be assisting you."

Virg took over. "I have a reservation. It should be under Zany Zoo Travel Agency."

"Separate rooms," I blurted. "We're not . . . you know."

Jennifer smiled and punched a few keys on the computer terminal in front of her. She looked puzzled and tapped a few more.

Next to me it appeared Virg was saying a silent prayer.

"I am awfully sorry," the young lady finally said. "It appears we only have one room available under the reservation. The weather has grounded a lot of travelers in the city."

"Tell us about it," I said.

"The room is number 1313, but unfortunately it is not ready yet."

"We'll take it," Virg said, handing over his credit card and Id.

"Very well."

Looking around I noticed a bunch of people coming out of a long hallway lined with rooms. They were sleepy—clothes ruffled—and might have been the dead rising from their graves or else they had been out clubbing all night.

After Jennifer was finished with the particulars, Virg gave

our luggage to the concierge for storage, and we took a seat on a high-backed sofa in the lobby. It had squiggly wood designs that Virg called "Elizabethan."

"Never heard of this Elizabeth designer, Virg. You are probably just making it up. And I don't care anyway. Now listen, not only do we have to share a room, but you got us Room 1313, which means its room thirteen on the thirteenth floor, of all the miserable double bad luck. And you've gotten us stranded in Washington D.C. We can't even get into our unlucky room and besides all that, we haven't had lunch yet. Traveling with you is like traveling through Hades, Virg. It really is. Hades! Virg? You paying attention, Virg?"

When I got his attention Virg tried to calm me down with some kinda psycho-baubledeegoop about how it would be worth it when we got to Europe. He suggested we grab a bite to eat while they got our room prepared.

I told him he was paying. He agreed and asked me to get us a table at a sandwich shop he had seen across the street when Phlegyas dropped us off. He said he had to make a call back to the office. That's when he wandered off down the hall the stiffs came out of.

"Beatrice! Thank goodness I caught you. We've been waylaid in D.C."

"Eddie's alright, right?"

"We're both fine. It just puts off our arrival in Barcelona for another day."

"The best way to keep Eddie safe is to keep him out of the mosh pits."

"Don't worry about a thing. We've got ourselves a hotel room, but they only had one so we have to share a room."

"Ha! I can hear Eddie complaining about it now."

"You haven't forgotten a thing about him."

"So whatcha got planned in the big city?"

"We're grabbing a sandwich for lunch. Probably just the normal stuff," Virgil said. "As Edward will tell you, I lead a rather bland life."

"You live a vicariously wild life through your shirts, Virg. You've now got Eddie in your life 24/7, and that certainly is not bland. When you think about it, every life is extraordinary in its own way. I don't believe for one minute elderly people who claim they've had a humdrum life. Getting an education, feeding yourself every day, working a job, it's all spectacular. Anyone who has gotten from point A to point B in any walk of life has had some near misses with the Grim Reaper and some great accomplishments along the way. From what I understand, just raising a kid is a monumental accomplishment. Just to live through every day is quite remarkable. We all have extraordinary lives that we're living, it's just that some people don't recognize it because they're too caught up watching everyone else's lives."

"Beatrice, I love the way you look at things. It really is refreshing."

"Perspective is everything."

"How's Venice?"

"I am gondola gonzo. I may never drive a motorized vehicle again."

"Not even Edward's meter maid car?"

"There's not a chance he would ever let me get behind the wheel. Besides, you are making a huge assumption that something with three wheels that looks like a wedge of cheese going down the street can actually be considered a vehicle, Virg."

"You almost made me snort."

"Get here soon and be safe. I can't wait to see Eddie."

"What about me?"

"Of course you, Virg. You're the best manager a band's ever had. Eddie feels the same."

"I am not so certain."

"Remember, don't tell him our secret, Virg."

Habitually Latté

ON MY WAY to the sandwich shop I stopped at the intersection as I waited for the light to change. The insane voices had stopped overhead, but it was still foggy as pea soup. I stood in a thicket of businesspeople. Most were jabbering on their cellphones or listening to music. Much to my dismay, an Italian guy who said his name was Uberti struck up a conversation. There was something about him that told me he was a big goober.

". . . about as many as there are dark, hairy guys in New York City," I was telling him. Uberti had turned the conversation to politics. We were in Washington D.C. after all; yet this did little to change my thinking that politicians are a bunch of stooges. Mom always told me to never talk about the three Ps in public: Politics, the Pope, or Personal bodily functions. Throughout the years I've honored her advice on at least two of them. Bea can tell you how bad I've been on the third.

"I care not if the bill is sponsored by republicans or democrats," Uberti exclaimed. "I just want bills passed."

"Bills?" I thought for a moment as we stood there on the corner. "You know, the Duckbilled Platypuses would rock as the name for a girl band. Now that would get attention."

Uberti just stared at me. I don't blame him. I realized the guy had never heard such a fantastic name for a band. I told Uberti how I was in a band (and the only member of it at the moment). I went on to tell him that any future band members would be screened really well. I didn't want any more chicks skipping town, *à la* Bea, or lads turning out feminine. There's no place for that in a rock band.

The fog was not lifting. The diffused light finally signaled we could walk. As we bumped and knocked our way across the intersection another Italian gentleman, only much older, butted in on the conversation.

Cavalcanti was his name. He was all bug-eyed and crazy looking. He asked where I was visiting from and if I was traveling with anyone. I told him I was from Florence and left off the part about it being in New York. Thinking I was from his homeland, he perked up. As we stepped over the curb at the other side of the street I said I was traveling with Virgil, which the old guy mistook for "Guido." Can you believe him? It must've been his hearing aid. Cavalcanti asked why Guido wasn't with me, to which I responded that he kept getting me into grave situations. At hearing the word "grave," old Cavalcanti thought Guido had died on me or was near death, and took off down the sidewalk in apparent horror.

"Later, weirdo," I told him.

Uberti started back on the whole politics thing right where he left off. Bills, bills, bills. I told him the only thing I knew about them was that they had to be paid on time. This is especially true at Guitars & Grunge in Florence or they won't let you buy any more equipment. Believe me, I know.

I gave Uberti good riddance and spun into the sandwich place. I searched for a table. A waitress pointed me to the back. I headed over to a circular one in the far rear corner. Virg came in in a few minutes, looking absurd in his Hawaiian shirt among all the business suits. I waved him over.

"Hey Virg, Habitually Latté would be a classic name for a coffeehouse, don't you think? Or Thanks a Latté, or Casting Lattés if you wanted to open a Christian coffeehouse. Since we're in D.C., we should trademark the names."

"You are unflappable," Virg responded.

"Unlike your hair. And what have I told you about using big words?"

At the counter the lines were seven deep with customers. When we at last got to the front, Virg ordered soup in a bread bowl (since that's the kinda guy he is). Trust me, if you go into any sandwich place and see a guy in a Hawaiian shirt, he will always, always, always order soup in bread bowl. This is one of the most concrete scientific facts in the world. If you're ever in Venice and run into Bea, just ask her, if you can get her away from her gondolier long enough.

Virg said he was paying for both of us.

"Not that we're . . . you know," I stated to the blue-haired kid behind the counter. I then ordered a turkey sandwich with red onions and caso cheese. I got the blue corn chips on the side. I was feeling so patriotic in Washington D.C.

"Anything to drink?"

"Black coffee," I announced.

This really threw the kid behind the counter into a tizzy. He scratched his head for a moment. I realized he didn't know how to make black coffee. His face was pinched up and confused. It was too *simple.* If I had ordered up a Grand-Mocha-Frapa-Moon-Unit-Zapa with foamed vanilla soymilk, the kid would've whipped one up in no time. It's hard to order just a black coffee these days. That's the kind of miserable world we live in.

We finally got our food and went back to our table.

"So who'd ya call back at the hotel?"

"Uh, just the travel agency. I wanted to see if there were any other flights out. No luck."

I pointed at my cup of steaming joe. "Let me just tell you one more thing about Bea, Virg, and then I'll shut up about her. She claims the best coffee beans come from some place called Sumatra. Who's ever heard of that? I doubt it even exists. She may've gotten it from *Karma Sumatra* that old India book about love and stuff. Unlike me, she has an active imagination."

Virg was nodding up and down, then side-to-side.

"Once Bea told me slow-witted people have fat thoughts. Fat! She went on about how all thoughts have mental calories associated with them. People who keep thoughts to themselves and hardly speak or write anything should go on mental diets because they are not burning enough mental calories. That's the way she sees it. Books with great literature are veggies for your brain—low calorie and high in mental fiber. 'It keeps your brain bowels loose,' is what she said. Brain bowels! I asked her if watching a lot of TV makes your brain retain water and get bloated. She told me not to be silly."

I took a bite of sandwich and when I had finished munching on it, I continued with the story as Virg slurped away at the bread bowl. Embarrassing.

"Bea would order skinny lattes when we used to go to the coffeehouse. Says it keeps her thoughts 'slender and skinny.' Slender and skinny! Don't even get her started on the different types of fats for thoughts like monounsaturated and transfats. She'll go on for hours. It will make your head explode. I told her she was eye candy for *my* brain and that I wanted to suck on her. She loved that."

Minutes passed. We continued eating and looking out into the suffocating fog that had taken over the city. The businesspeople with their briefcases and serious looks were specters disappearing and reappearing in the mist. I finished my sandwich while Virg slurped away methodically to get every last drop. I began to realize that any trip is long when traveling with Virg.

I felt my cup. The coffee had cooled enough where I could drink it. I added a packet or two of sugar, at which point I said to Virg, "After the success of the band, if you want to branch out and manage girl bands or something, Refined Sugar would be a decent name. Think it over. That's free of charge since you bought lunch."

Virg tried to speak but I cut him off.

"Bea puts a butterscotch candy in her coffee to sweeten it. Sometimes she acts all European coffeehouse artsy on me. It's too much for a guy to take. At Christmas she would stir in a candy cane. Bea said it gave the drink the 'essence of the season.' I just liked to watch her lips when she would take the candy cane out and suck the end of it. Bea's crazy with that kinda little stuff. She calls them 'nuances.' I call them annoying."

"I thought you were going to stop talking about her?" Virg questioned.

"I am, I am going to stop talking about her. And let me tell you something, it's very embarrassing to sit at a table with you while you munch on the side of a bread bowl in public like you've been on a hunger strike for the last thirty days."

"No one knows us here."

"And that's a good thing for me since I'm with you."

Virg's comment about me talking about Bea all the time really had me ticked off. "Okay, so you think I talk about Bea a lot. Right now am I talking about Bea? Huh?"

"Actually, you are."

"Yeah right, Virg. Tell me how I am talking about Bea right now. What am I saying about Bea?"

"You just said her name again. Twice actually."

"Do I need to beat you down right here in front of all these people? I'll slap that bread bowl right outta your mouth. Don't think I won't."

"Speaking of Bea, do you remember these, Edward?"

Virg got out his wallet and flung on the table a set of lyrics Bea wrote early in our relationship.

Beautiful Rocker Boy

Inked neck;
Hair a wreck.
Those boots, that steel;
It's bliss I feel.
Dark clothes of passion;
Forget Paris fashion.

Beautiful rocker boy!
Beautiful, beautiful rocker boy!

Rippin' gigs on Saturday nights;
Your music takes me to new heights.
We'll get matching tats;
What's wrong with that?
Hey you, yeah you, don't be coy;
I'd love to make you my toy.

Beautiful rocker boy!
Beautiful, beautiful rocker boy!

"This doesn't make me miss her, you know."
"Why are your cheeks getting red, Edward?"

"They are not. Now, if you are finally finished with Bea I will change the subject. So what's there to do in Barcelona when we get there anyway?"

"Well, we can see Antoni Gaudi's modern church. We can stroll down La Rambla, the most famous street in Spain or spend time at Parc Guell. It has many unique sculptures and it might spur your creativity."

"Great, Virg, I was hoping there would be something fun to do."

CAFC

WE MADE A right out of the sandwich joint and crossed the street at a different intersection a block down. Construction crews were at work busting up the sidewalk. Rubble lay in heaping piles on the misty lunar landscape, roped off by a thin yellow ribbon. Amid the loud knocking of jackhammers we carefully skirted the area.

Further down the sidewalk, where we could actually hear each other speak, Virg stopped me and pointed to a manhole cover. I remembered I had told Bea Womanhole Cover could be a name for our band, but I realized that it would be a spectacular title for a female cover band that could play weddings and graduation parties. I didn't tell Virg. I knew he wouldn't understand.

"See that?" he asked. "The Metro subway runs under it. We'll have to take it while in town."

I leaned over the manhole cover. A putrid smell was rising from it and I flinched back. "Not if it stinks like that! They keep dead bodies down there? Dead politicians? Is it some kinda subway sepulcher?"

"I'm not sure what that smell is."

Next to the cover I noticed someone had dropped a religious button that read POPE ANASTASIUS. Never heard of him? Yeah, me neither.

I left it there in case the owner came searching for it. I realized the moniker Dope Popes would sell a lot of music for a hip-hop act. Again, I didn't waste this one on Virg.

We made a left and headed back up the street to the Trident Hotel. Inside we paid a visit to Desk Clerk Jennifer. She was perky as usual, and so was I now that I'd gotten caffeine. A few keystrokes and she once again informed that our room wasn't quite ready. Virg thanked her. Jennifer suggested that we take a walk around D.C. and we decided to take her up on it.

Outside, cars raced down the avenue, parting the fog just enough to reveal a block or more of pavement. "Check that out," I told Virg. "Look at all the manhole covers in this section of town. I count at least seven. Seven circles."

He shrugged. He was useless as usual. Down the sidewalk he started going on and on about ethics in the travel business and who got first class upgrades from the airlines and who did not. Like I cared.

In a few blocks we spotted a government building that sat gray and imposing on its concrete moorings, which pretty much describes every government building now that I think about it. Above its metal double doors was inscribed FEDERAL COURTHOUSE and under that COURT OF APPEALS FOR THE FEDERAL CIRCUIT.

In an effort to get Virg to stop rambling about heretics in the travel business, I suggested we have "a looksee into the judiciary." The inside was government issue to a boring fault, imposing with its symbols and flags and grim stone carvings.

Burly guards immediately waved us over to a security checkpoint. The line was ten deep with attorney types. Can't miss them. They were either fat and bald, or trim and fit to a fault. All suits and splendor, pulling at their cuffs and straightening their ties. I figure attorneys try way too hard in most areas of their lives. They try so hard at work I've heard many of them get divorced and have no social lives, which is probably a big reason why they get divorced.

We watched them emptying out their many pockets of communication devices and car keys. They removed metal clips from their ties and cufflinks from their sleeves. Their briefcases were gingerly laid open on the conveyor belt. Tablet computers were extracted and also laid on the belt. They carefully placed their buffed wingtip shoes in the bins. As I well knew, buff jobs are very important when it comes to footwear. One guy had a nervous twitch and this other guy had a hole in his dress sock. They tried to look *very* important.

Attorneys crack me up!

"Let's go through it," Virg offered as he shrugged in a way

that said: We have nothing better to do.

"I can tell you don't have a girlfriend, Virg, because of how much you want to get frisked."

The line moved quickly. Thankfully we made it through without me having to step to the side and have some dude with dog tattoos explore me.

After reading a placard to find some place interesting to explore, we took an elevator up a couple floors. When the doors opened we stepped into a non-descript hallway that smelled dingy and looked strikingly similar to the insides of a hospital.

Clerks were filing past us with sheaths of paper. Virg and I made a right down the hall and were dumped out into a waiting area defined by chairs set in an L-shape. A few of the attorneys were camped out there waiting for a clerk to call them into the courtroom for the Court of Appeals for the Federal Circuit.

We sat down and waited to enter with a pretty junior attorney who was sitting next to an older attorney. He had that I'm-trapped-in-my-profession-and-I-can't-get-out look about him. The old guy had to be (drum roll please) a *senior partner*. He looked groggy. The bags under his eyes were puffy gel packs. Fissures of wrinkles checkered his cheeks. He kept looking at his wristwatch.

"Hey, Virg, old attorneys never die, the Grim Reaper just gives them new timesheets."

The pretty associate next to him wasn't much over twenty-five. She told Virg that the CAFC was the only court in the country for direct appeals from the Federal District Courts on patent matters.

"Don't bill us for that," I told her in a whisper. Realizing she was nervous and that this was likely her first trip before the judges of the CAFC, I let her know that Band Garage would be a rippin' name for a band.

She gave me a smile and let me know she was not musically talented. I reminded her that no attorneys are. She said her name was Amber.

I said we'd come in and watch her arguments to offer a little support and that we could applaud when she got finished speaking. To which she confessed that Senior Saddlebags would be doing the speaking.

"Try to keep him awake," I said.

Virg and I sat there for a few moments when I began to feel the black coffee running through me. I excused myself and headed into the john. When I swung open the door I couldn't believe it.

Let me just tell you that the strangest thing you'll ever see in your life is the urinals in a government building. Hey all you joes and janes, tour the johns next time you're in D.C.! There is nothing more patriotic. Nothing more ancient and historic in D.C. Forget paying lots of money to go to the Smithsonian or tour the White House. A porcelain parade of antiquities await.

Standing in a long row were the glory days of potty time. The pee-pee days of yore. The commode abode. The ancient world of wee-wee. A bippy brigade. The Ivory Coast of incontinence.

Puzzled, I looked at them for a long time. From the side, the urinals were the spitting image of Ben Franklin or Alfred Hitchcock. Take your pick. From the front, the devices resembled giant Ls with the base and drain built right into the tile floor.

Forget this, I told myself. *Too complicated and weird.*

I immediately headed for a stall. I was beginning to break out in sweat from all the potty stress. After I had shut the door, I turned around and found what looked like an upside-down porcelain saddle. For a moment I thought the toilet must be under construction or perhaps an alien had planted it there to sample human DNA. Thankfully it did not glow when I stepped toward it for inspection. Searching. Peering. Looking. *There is no way to flush this!* On the wall I searched for a manual on how to operate the device.

Maybe it's automatic. Maybe Virg will know.

I stepped back waiting for a gush of water and nothing happened. I noticed a foot pedal down by the tiles. A foot pedal! I didn't want to drive the toilet, just flush it. I expected to see a steering wheel, stick shift and horn.

I ran out of the stall. I was out of breath and hadn't gone

anywhere.

I strolled back to the bank of urinals and grudgingly angled into one. After undoing my skull belt and jeans I began doing my business. It felt as though I was tinkling on my combat boots since the receptacle was way down on the floor.

Suddenly I heard the door to the bathroom open and the dull click of fine wooden soles across the tiles. I glanced back just as Senior Saddlebags was making his way into one of the stalls. Amber must have woken him up to get ready for court. By the pace of his steps, he was obviously in a rush. People are always in a rush in D.C., especially lawyers and Congress people. So why on earth can they never get anything accomplished? No bills passed. No decisions. No nothing but a bunch of hot air being passed around. I just don't understand it.

Standing there I heard the senior partner yapping away in the stall. Something about "You SPQ." Of all the things I've been called in my life, I've never been called an SPQ before . . . or even a PQ for that matter. In high school, at Our Lady of Perpetual Peace, I once considered Inspector Q for the name of my band. That's about the closest I've come.

Why is the guy calling me names? I thought. There were these long pauses. I didn't answer. How does a person respond to an esquire calling you an SPQ? From the *other sounds* he was making I was about to call him a PU when I realized from a beep he was on his cell. That's right, he was doing his business and talking on the phone. That's the kind of people lawyers are. They're the kind of people who call you up while they're doing their business on the john, and they're billing you the entire time. No joke.

Having had enough of this (and being finished with my own business), I went over to the sink to wash my hands. There was one giant sink against the far wall that is best described as a long trough. I expected pigs when I stood in front of it.

The soap was another issue. I was searching for it when another Suit rushed into the bathroom. You want to know what he did? He stepped up and started doing his business right in the trough. Now I was really, really confused. Suddenly a giant rush of water came flooding in one end of the trough. I thought I was going to get whisked away into the foul sewers of D.C. It scared me to death.

Without washing my hands I got the heck out of there. I darted past the bank of strange porcelain urinals, each one going off automatically as I rushed past. *Kersplush, kersplush, kersplush . . ..*

I got a 21 urinal salute on my way out. Everything is so military-patriotic in D.C. Thankfully I escaped with my life mostly intact.

Seventh Circle Holdings, LLC

"FIRST, WHATEVER YOU do, don't go in the bathroom," I said as I reached the chairs. I was bending over, panting like a dog. "Second, don't shake my hand."

"Get hold of yourself, Edward. You are very flushed."

"I was just flushed 21 times. I really was." I began pointing behind me. "There was this giant porcelain trough and—and the urinal salute and—and Senior Saddlebags was on his cellphone and this guy pulled up to the sink—" I stopped abruptly when I saw Amber snickering at me. I shot her a wink. It made me feel good that I at least gave her some levity before the big legal argument.

"Give me your phone, Virg. I should call Mom and let her know I'm okay. Not that I call my mom very much." I said that last part to Amber. I stepped down the hallway.

———————

"It's your favorite son."

"Hi, Eddie. I came by the apartment around lunch and no one answered the door."

"I was out."

"But I made lasagna for you."

"I mean way out. I'm in D.C. with Virg."

"Virgil Hance? That guy who was managing the band?"

"Right-o. We're going to Barcelona. He's buying. Not that we're, you know. Anyway, we have a layover in D.C. so I'm calling to let you know."

"That sounds odd, Eddie. Well be careful. Did you bring your multivitamins?"

I found myself pushing against the wall as if I could hide in the cinderblocks. "Mom."

"And plenty of clean underwear?"

"Mom."

"I learned at a Webinar that Eco-Stain-Able is the best all

natural washing detergent for cotton. Isn't that neat. My company had an independent survey conducted. Let me know if you are running low."

"Mom, I have to go."

"Wear a coat, Eddie. I'll freeze the lasagna for when you get back. When *are* you getting back?"

"Bye, Mom. I'll give you a call from Barcelona. I'm hanging up now."

"On Easter. Don't forget. I'll have a basket for you, too, when you get back. The bank gave your father a chocolate piggy bank just for—"

Back down the hall I was giving Virg his phone back when the clerk of the court slipped out between two oak doors that led into the courtroom.

"Oral arguments for the case of HereTech, Incorporated versus Seventh Circle Holdings, LLC and Round One Corporation will now proceed!"

Virg and I hung back while Amber and her senior partner, who had finally emerged from the bathroom, went in first. It was unbelievable the amount of folders they lugged inside the courtroom along with a couple laptop computers.

The bailiff had a nametag on that read MINNY TAUR. She gave me the once over when she noticed my messed up 'do, combat boots, shades that I had flipped down for court, T-shirt and skull belt buckle. I'm sure the tat on my neck didn't help either. Remind me some time to let you know what the tattoo on my neck is. Really, you should.

From her scowl, Minny sure didn't care for my type. As she stood there in her face-pinched anger, Virg pulled me past her through the double oak doors.

The courtroom was not as lavish as I imagined. The paneling was red oak with a dark stain. Under the soft lights it appeared bloodwashed. Straight ahead, the judges' three seats sat high above the audience at a semicircular table. Placed next to their microphones were crystal glasses and pitchers of water.

A United States emblem, made of wood and brass, hung below the judges' table on a cheap-looking partition. Behind the chairs were three separate curtains of crimson, which only added to my eerie feelings. Portraits of past judges, long in the grave, lined the oak panels, each of them holding a thick book to make them look important. In the future, judges aren't going to appear as smart holding ebook readers in their portraits. That's the truth, so help me God. Judges have the creepiest portraits made of them that you will ever see. I mean, why not statues instead of portraits? At least on a statue your eyes aren't all glassy and fish-big as though they're getting ready to fall out of your head like they were in the judges' portraits. Their eyes seemed ready to roll down one of the deep channels of material in their robes and then onto a desk where their gavels would smush them. *Phtaht!*

Virg and I took our seats. There were plenty of open chairs.

"Hey, Virg, when I get rich from the band I'm going to have a statue made instead of a portrait. I'll ensure my neck tat makes it on the statue. I think that would be cool, a white statue with a black ink tattoo as the only color."

"Very well."

As I continued to scan the courtroom I noticed that under the portraits was a single row of chairs that had young, smart-looking people sitting in them. Most wore little thin glasses. A few had laptops. Virg said they were law students getting court experience. I said they were "LERNS." Law nerds.

There were no windows in the courtroom. The air was stale and locker room smelly because of all the sweaty attorneys who argued their cases in there. And it was hot. For some reason it just kept getting hotter the longer I was on the trip with Virg.

Amber and the senior partner were arranging their documents on one of the front tables. They only got little plastic cups to drink water from. You would think a government that spends $700 on toilet plungers and obviously no money to update its bathrooms into the last century, could buy a set of drinking mugs for the lawyers practicing before its courts. You really would.

The crowd was sparse and I assumed this meant it was

not a very important case in the grand scheme of patent law and blowhard fatheads.

Just as I put my boots up on the back of the chair in front of me, the opposing attorneys came knocking into the courtroom. They were all business and determination.

One of them wore a cowboy hat and boots to match. Tex sat down with another imposing attorney at one of the nondescript tables in the front. Their brows were pinched and they had candlesnuffer noses.

Off to the side was a court reporter, hair tied back in a ponytail, fingers at the ready. The show was about to begin.

Minny Taur walked down to the front of the crimson courtroom. A handgun and jangly keys were attached to her belt. On her other side was a baton that almost looked like an arrow. At the front she gave one of the attorneys a glare and he immediately removed his cowboy hat. Then the bailiff stepped up to the platform where the judges sit. "All rise for the Honorable Judges Herea, Altez and Rodriguez for the next session of the Court of Appeals for the Federal Circuit. God save the United States and its esteemed courts."

When we took our seats, three judges came out of the individual curtains like mini Wizards' of Ozes. They came out at exactly the same time in such an orchestrated way that I was searching for a puppetmaster holding crossed sticks and strings. The judges were dressed in flowing black robes fabricated of a lightweight nylon or rayon material. Not a wrinkle could be found.

They sat behind their brass nameplates. Herera began studying the thick set of documents in his hand as though a schoolboy cramming for an exam that was about to start. I had doubts whether he had read the court briefs. Judge Altez looked straight ahead at the cowboy lawyer (Tex) who was ambling to the podium that sat six feet below the judges. It was as if the attorneys were arguing from a casket to the funeral procession above ground. Judge Rodriguez, the third and final judge, leaned back in his chair and stared at the ceiling as if he had never seen one before.

The judges were hyper-engaged, bored or studious. I couldn't tell which. What they all had in common was that they were mean-looking, ornery. It struck me that the only people who hate their jobs more than lawyers are judges. Thank goodness Tex took his cowboy hat off *before* the judges came in or he would have lost his case straight out. I am convinced of that. These were not judges you wanted to show up by grandstanding.

I stuck my shades on the top of my head.

Tex only got half a sentence out when the judges began grilling him with questions. "Your Honors, as you see from independent claim one of the patent—"

"Is that language really in the claim, Counselor?"

"Are you relying on the Doctrine of Equivalents?"

"What of prosecution history estoppel?"

Tex blurted, "I have searched, Your Honors, the file history of this patent and—"

"How do you reconcile your position, Counselor, with this court's ruling in *eBay*?"

The interruptions went on and on. Now I knew why there were no windows in the courtroom. It was so members of the audience didn't jump.

Even Rodrigues fired a few questions but he never took his eyes off the fascinating ceiling to do it. I figure he had a few questions lined up before he appeared from behind the Wizard of Oz curtain. He must have done his homework unlike Herera who was still fumbling through the papers in abject confusion.

By the judges' last names I was surprised any of them could speak English. Have I told you that hardly anyone speaks English in America's headquarters? They really don't. Washington D.C. is the most foreign place you will ever visit. You could hear more English on a Peruvian bus headed back from Spanish class, if you want to know my opinion. And if you don't, you're going to hear it anyway. And besides that, I don't care if you don't want to hear my opinion. I'm a rockstar.

Judge Herera kept looking at his watch, which he wore backwards. By "backwards" I mean that the face was under his wrist. He looked so goofy every time he kept sliding up his robe sleeve and looking at it (and boy did he always keep looking at it, as if the government paid him by the glance) like he was checking for a tan on the belly of his arm or poison ivy or something. Never trust a guy who wears his watch backwards.

Speaking of time in the courtroom, these judges had this goofy light system they had come up with. It had all the professionalism of a junior high science project. There were three colored lights mounted on a plank of varnished wood. They weren't even high-efficiency light bulbs. Talk about a waste of tax dollars.

The judges gave each attorney 15 minutes to speak their case-in-chief and then 15 minutes for the rebuttal from the other side. That was green light time. Woohoo! The final minute was yellow light time. When the red light came on the judges would cut them off mid-sentence and tell them to sit down and pretty much insult the lawyers' mothers and first born. It was great! I think the judges enjoyed it too. The colored lights appeared to surprise poor Amber and they kept her jumping and scrambling for papers. By the interest of the judges, and the way they perked up when the red light came on, I bet they only became judges to yell at lawyers. That was their only gratification in being judges. The only way it could have been any better is if a giant hook came out of the wall and jerked the lawyers from their podium or a trapdoor sent them sliding down into a garbage bin like a game show or a large hand encased in a rubber glove slapped the fire out of them. Take that Esquire-for-Hire! *Bap!* And *bap* again. And *bap* a couple more times after that just for good measure.

Virg and I were elbowing each other.

Everyone should be able to tell a claptrap lawyer to pipe down at least once in their lives. Now *that* revs my monkey. I could make some money off that idea. I could hire lawyers just to talk about some legal nonsense and people would pay me a ton of money just to tell them to shut up. People would line up for this down the block. Think of the game show or reality TV it would spawn. What would be really great is to make those car accident lawyers who advertise on daytime TV, get berated on my show. The Bar Association should have that be a requirement for all lawyers who embarrass the profession with those ambulance chaser commercials. They really should. Those lawyers should get wacked upside the head on TV.

When I returned from my reverie, Judge Rodrigues was still counting invisible sheep on the ceiling. I was glad he didn't snore. He obviously thought being a judge was the most boring job in the world. Let me tell you, after I heard the lawyers bellow for forty minutes, I was completely ready to agree with him. From the look Amber gave me as she walked out of the courtroom with the senior attorney, she agreed too.

Virg and I stayed behind and heard a few more cases. Apart from when the lawyers got yelled at, the rest of the cases in the afternoon were boring, too. A government contracts case and more patents.

Right when an Indian attorney was arguing about some land rights to a patch of desert in Arizona, I yanked Virg by the arm and we got up and left.

I didn't care if the law clerks lining the walls or bailiff yelled at me. I was sick of being bored to death.

Harpies

WE DASHED FROM the CAFC building. The dower cases were too much to take, even for a boring guy like Virg. On the way out I searched for Amber, but to no avail.

The elevator was not crowded and we landed on the first floor without stopping at any other. We moved quickly past the security line and the officers standing guard. I told Virg about how I wanted to patent my Lawyer Shut Your Trap game since we were in D.C. and the Patent Office is located nearby. I told him the income from it would help me pay for my world tour.

He rolled his eyes.

"What? You need to be more supportive if you want to be my manager, Virg. We are in D.C. and we have nothing better to do for the next couple hours. The hotel may not even have our room ready yet. In fact, I am pretty sure they don't at the rate they are going."

Virg coaxed me into visiting the U.S. Patent Office Museum instead. He stated that I would learn more about the patent process there by watching how-to movies and thumbing through books than I would at the actual Patent Office. He said it would be very educational.

"Hey, I got plenty of education up through high school, thank you very much. BTW, Academentia would be a fine name for a college band."

Once through the double doors of the courthouse building, Virg led me down to the Metro subway. The smell was not as bad as I imagined when I got down there. It smelled much better than the steam coming from the manhole covers on the street and it was certainly better than the locker room stench of the courtroom.

In the concrete underground Virg studied a map encased in glass that was mounted on the wall. He did this with the intensity and circumspection (if that's a word) that only a tour guide can possess.

While he traced his finger along the multicolored lines, I noticed a group of female harpists setting up their large instruments in a nook of sorts where the cinderblock walls had been painted into a forest scene. Strange faces were peering from it in a *Mid-Summer's Night Dream* atmosphere. The trees had grimacing faces on them.

As strange as it was to see harpies in the subway getting ready to play in the oddly painted nook, I walked over to them to take a listen because any kind of instrument fascinates me. I am a musical genius, after all.

They were a bunch of young ladies, this is true. All prim and proper. I slid over and began talking to them as they unpacked their instruments. One had a small harp like one of those you see in Renaissance paintings of the angels.

"What's shakin'?"

In all their hurry they were paying me no attention.

"I'm in a rock band. It's down on its luck right now, but not for long. I've been trying to figure out a great name for it. What's the name of your band?"

One responded that they did not have one since they had only recently decided to get together and practice in the subway in the hopes of getting a few tips. They were university students.

"Ever thought about The Lacsidasies as a name for your group? What about the Harp*she*chords? How about Aire on G-String? Think of what you could do with your outfits."

None of them seemed to appreciate that last one. I thought for a moment, tapping my boot as a subway train rumbled by. They kept unpacking and setting up.

"Okay-okay, I got it. Go with the name Angels and your first album can be titled *Up in the Aire Harping on Something.* Naw. That one's a bit long."

The harpies were unappreciative of my awesome names. Luckily Virg walked up and I immediately warned them, "Be careful, ladies, he's the manager of my band and he'll try to sign your band, too."

"Really!" said the one on the small harp.

"Oh, now you come alive," I said.

Virg tried to be modest. "Unfortunately, ladies, one band at a time for me."

The harpies were deflated. They finished setting up and shuffled into place. They raised their instruments. I asked them to at least give us the name of the song they were about to launch into, which they said was "Andrea Vigne da Siena."

After a few tuning strums they began. I must say the music was all the more beautiful and melodic in the dark, subterranean vault where we stood. The acoustics were surprisingly good and the haunted woods background did wonders. Standing there listening to them in this environment, I missed the gnawing rasp of a good electric guitar and the knocking of a kick drum, but the stuff wasn't bad.

After the first song I elbowed Virg and motioned to an open case on the ground in front of the harpies. He dug out a few bucks and tossed them inside. They smiled.

Virg pointed to his wristwatch in an anxious way.

"Okay, just let me tell them something. You need a good smoke machine! Some thigh-high boots wouldn't hurt either! Think red patent leather! Think stilettos!"

Who knows if they heard me, but they didn't look very appreciative for the advice.

Virg and I waved and headed off to catch our Metrorail to the U.S. Patent Office Museum.

"They didn't even wave back, Virg, and you tipped them."

In two shakes we reached the tollgate for the Metro. To access it, Virg handed me a plastic card. He went first and inserted his card into a reader that sucked it in and spit it back out. I did the same and we both made it through the turnstiles. We shot down an escalator and one of the Metrorails was waiting for us. Once inside the subway car we took our seats. In a few moments an audible warning sounded and the sliding doors closed.

Virg finally informed me that to get to the U.S. Patent Office Museum we had to go to another state—Virginia no less. I told him that sounded like too far of a trip and that we had a plane to catch at noon tomorrow.

Virg just laughed and said he thought the music of the harpies was heavenly.

I said there needed to be more rasping and grinding of instruments, and it sure wouldn't hurt sales if they wrecked one of the harps by smashing it into a wall or jumping on it or lighting it on fire.

"You really make me laugh sometimes, Edward. The large harps cost as much as a new car. I doubt they could wreck very many of them before going out of business."

The Metrorail rocked into motion.

"Even without violence the harpies' music was heavenly. What is heaven to you, Virg? You religious? Mom and Dad raised me Catholic."

He raised his eyebrows.

"I mean, how do you think of heaven?"

"Well, we know there will be mansions there and streets of gold."

"Yeah, and if there's mansions, there must be music halls and clubs with amplifiers and the biggest drum set you've ever seen." Virg seemed to be losing his attention. He was looking at the painted scenes on the tunnel walls. I tugged on his beflowered sleeve. "Ask me what my view of heaven is."

"Okayyyy. What's your vision of heaven?"

"Glad you asked. To me heaven is never having to say goodbye. I've had enough goodbyes in my life and not a one of them has been *good*. They should call them badbyes. Know what I'm getting at? Heaven is forever. No goodbyes. You can play a rippin' set for 100 years and never play the same songs again for 1000 more and no one can copy your songs and put them all over the Internet in heaven. Best of all, you can spend 10,000 years laying down tracks with the greatest rockers of all time."

"Do you really think a lot of them will make it to heaven?"

"Wow. That's the first good point you've made on this trip. So anyway, no one leaves heaven and you never, ever have to say goodbye. That's what heaven is to me."

"Like when Beatrice said goodbye?"

"No, Virg, I wasn't referring to her. I really wasn't. I don't even think she said goodbye now that I think about it. She got into the cab and that was that. Bea broke up the world's greatest band. She should be put in jail. It was worse than when the Beatles broke up."

"The Beatles? Really, Edward."

For a couple minutes we sat in silence as lighted murals flitted past the windows. I noticed a dreary one that was similar to one painted on the wall behind the harpies. It was another tree scene of writhing figures. I flinched away, tired of the nightmarish murals.

I looked around inside the tube. The D.C. Metrorail was surprisingly clean. No one pays any attention to you on the tube. You could be a living tree and no one would pay attention. For instance, if you were homeless you could ride it all day and all night to avoid the cold winter air. Free heat and a free place to sleep. The homeless live a pretty good life in D.C. Congress has a good life, too. They work less than the homeless, go to lavish banquets, and never get anything done for the country. The only person who doesn't have a good life in D.C. is the President. I would never want his job no matter how much you paid me. Half the people in the country get mad at him no matter what decision he makes and everyone gets mad at Congress no matter what decision they don't make.

The overhead announced that our stop was next and the Metrorail began to slow. A line of passengers stood waiting, all detached looking and ready to get back to their families after a long day of work. There is no way I could hack a nine-to-five. I would be miserable at it. The rockstar lifestyle is in my blood.

In front of us the doors flew open and we exited the Metrorail with a bunch of other riders who pushed and shoved us. People know you are a tourist when you travel with Virg.

At a map station he searched for the street we needed for the U.S. Patent Office Museum. Once he found the King Street sign, he pointed to it over the heads of the marching people trying to get in or out of the subway. We snaked through the crowd with all the grace of a couple water buffaloes.

On street level the fog was still hanging around. Virg rotated a few times to get his direction. There were a few more turns and squinting and scratching. He appeared lost.

Some tour guide.

Section III

Shoeboxes

THE U.S. PATENT Office Museum is a national secret. I'm sure of it. More secret than the Pentagon or Area 51. If Virg hadn't stopped to ask directions about a thousand times we never would've known it was in the Madison Building.

Inside we spent a bit of time in the lobby checking out the souvenirs, then entered a room of sorts framed by black curtains. There was a flat screen TV and we watched a short film along with about ten others, most of whom were sitting on the back row of chairs.

Virg called the movie a "vignette." I warned him again about big words and let him know that Bea once showed me her vignette. When Virg raised his eyebrows I let him know it was her first rock video. "Just her on stage, Virg. At the very end she kicked over the mike stand. It rocked!"

During the movie Virg and I learned there are millions patents and that a new state-of-the-art Patent Office was being built to house all the patent examiners and other technical government types and the museum, which was moving, too. Inventors were shown at banks of computer screens viewing digital patents in Arlington, Virginia. A strange shot had them bunched together and huddling in the rain for some kinda group picture.

I whispered to Virg, "Maybe they should invent a way to find the Patent Office Museum."

We learned there are patents on everything imaginable. A segment displayed odd patents from goofy toilet inventions to ways of forming cow dung into useable items like golf tees. Who knew there are so many manure entrepreneurs in the world? The movie showed how the current Patent Office was located in Crystal City. It sounded Wizard of Ozish to me and I guessed it was near the CAFC with its Wizard of Oz judges that hid behind curtains and berated the lawyers when they came into the courtroom.

Apparently the old search room housed narrow aisles of wooden cabinets from which the dudes were pulling out wooden shoeboxes. Shoeboxes! All those shoeboxes took me back to last year when I was helping Bea organize her boots in the closet. She has a wall of boot boxes. Not stacked in the horizontal, coffin way. Oh, no. She stacks them vertically with the tops off so you can see every tall boot at once. "The Banana Republic way," as she calls it.

"Why so many?"

"Please. I'm just getting started."

"But they're all black," I informed her.

"The heels are different. Some have zippers. Some have buttons. Some have lace—Dad?"

I saw Bea glaze over right that instant. "Bea? You okay?"

"I've done alright for myself," she was saying to the wall of the closet. "It's harder without you, but I'm making it."

She reached her arms into the air and did a hugging motion.

"Uh, Bea?"

"Eddie. I'm so sorry. It was my dad."

I glanced around the closet. "Where? I didn't see anybody."

"He's dead."

"That's what I hoped you wouldn't say."

"This is the fifth anniversary of his death. I miss him so much. Please don't think of me as a weirdo. I am sane. The ghost, or spirit or entity or whatever you want to call it, of my hippie father just pops in to check on me once in awhile."

"That is a bit different. My mother checks in on me all the time and she's still alive."

"At first I thought I was crazy. As a teenager I paid monthly visits to whatever head shrink Florence High School had on staff. They always said I wasn't crazy, but I knew better. I thought I was crazy, too, until Dad began telling me things about Mom I had no way of knowing since she passed away while giving birth to me. I learned she was colorblind and that she always drank from a can with a straw and won a pineapple eating contest on Maui the year before I was born."

That was the first time I had been around Bea when she had a paranormal encounter of the parental kind. Throughout our brief but torrid (that means, hot) relationship Folco Portinari would appear to Bea at random times: in the middle of a movie (got told to keep quiet by the lady behind us), during the middle of Mass (that was embarrassing) once at the Florence Fair (people thought she was one of the mimes), and you know about our gig at Hard's Speakeasy.

I flashed back to the shoeboxes on the screen. Each one in the old Patent Office was filled with moldering, dusty old paper patents. The patent edges were yellowing and I half expected them to crumble when patent searchers picked them up. It was as if they were at the edge of a forest (or what used to be a forest). I thought of an old song by The Cure.

The video camera began moving down the giant cornrows of paper stacks. Miles and miles. They seemed to never stop. A bespeckeled man with an official searcher badge was busy at his harvest. By the look on his face, he was pleased with his crops. He didn't even stop to look at the camera as it brushed by in the thin aisle.

Of all these millions of patents, inventors still cannot come up with a way to cure the common cold or to prevent syrup from spilling out of those fruit cups when you tear off the lid. That's probably why the searcher wouldn't look at the camera. He's freakin' embarrassed.

"Hey Virg, I want to see the patent for electric drum pads. That would be a riser!"

Some lady in the back shushed me. I rotated and stuck my tongue out at her. When I turned back to the screen I got beaned with a hard candy. Then one skimmed my ear. There was no question that the members of the audience were violent against nature, art, God and certainly me.

"I'm not taking this anymore. I'm a rockstar."

I stood and faced the enemy crowd. I stuck a finger in the air and began to pontificate on the social injustice of getting hit in the head by hard candies. "I just want all of you to know that when Iggy Pop was—*khaphft!*"

"Edward, are you okay?"

A butterscotch candy had landed right in my throat. My eyes bulged. I couldn't breathe. I collapsed to my knees. Before I knew it Virg was grabbing me around the chest from behind in a very embarrassing way. He clasped his hands together and began pulling and lifting.

"One. Two. Three."

"*Tfhpahk!*" The candy made the reverse sound coming up. It knocked once on the tiles and lay there before me in an orange-yellow sticky ball.

I struggled to a standing position and tried to gain my rockstar composure, which is much swankier than normal joe composure. I took a couple deep swallows and said to the entire back row, "Thanks a lot you buncha reverbmongers!"

After I had set the back row straight I pulled Virg by the sleeve to get out of there. It took me a few tries to find the slit in the black curtain and I heard snickering from the back row.

When we finally got outta there I stuck my head back inside. "And I'm not picking that candy up, either." That's when I stuck my tongue out at them.

We learned a lot at the museum as we strolled around. In one corner we found out that patent attorneys are the only attorneys who have to have a technical university degree (engineering or the sciences) to sit for the Patent Bar. If they pass that *and* the regular state bar exam—along with three full years of law school after the university—they can practice before the U.S. Patent Office as a registered patent attorney.

I stood there next to Virg reading the display and feeling rather stupid. I remarked, "I'm not against education. I really am not. It's just that so much of it is wasted on attorneys."

"I'd say patent attorneys are double nerds."

"Yeah, nerds squared," I responded, head down, rotating the display.

"Both engineers *and* lawyers! They were a double whammy of nerdishnous."

"Squirt straight!" I said.

"Gearheads and gavels!"

Virg's voice sounded a tad strange and so did his humor that was actually funny. I turned and said to him, "Got a sore throat?"

"That wasn't me," he said, motioning behind him.

We both turned and found an elderly man standing there. Gray curly hair danced on his head. Permanent lines of joy were etched into his olive complexion.

"I'm George," he said. "I'm visiting Washington from Greece."

"What city?" Virg asked. "I've been there twice."

"The ancient city of Crete."

"Sorry D.C. is having such bad weather."

"I've been inside, mostly," George said, "browsing through its many government buildings. I spent most of the morning in the Smithsonian."

"They have any good rock bands in Greece?" I questioned. "I feel really embarrassed for you if that's where Yanni guy is from."

"I am afraid I only listen to classical music," responded the old man of Crete.

I extended my hand. "I'm Edward and this is my manager and part-time travel agent, Virgil. Be on the lookout for my band. I would tell you its name but I'm having an awful time trying to come with it. Not that I don't have tons of names. It's just that I'm having a hard time picking one. And now that I met you, standing right here, right now, I'm considering The *Geek* Gods instead of The Greek Gods."

The old man smiled. "I wish you the best in your endeavors and travels, gentlemen."

With time to kill, Virg and I continued to wander around the Patent Office Museum. There were charts of patent registrations over the years and old photos of past heads of the U.S. Patent Office. We learned a bunch of useless information, such as you can actually get a patent on a plant and that George Washington signed the first patent in 1790.

"Did he patent the cherry tree?" I asked Virg.

"Good question."

In a room off to the side were odd looking parts and

strange items. Most were constructed of wood. As we wandered inside to get a closer look, we learned that in the past inventors had to submit physical models of their inventions to the Patent Office for evaluation. A plaque to my left said a fire at the Patent Office destroyed over 75,000 models in 1877. Today the Patent Office requires two-dimensional drawings. It made me wonder why the Patent Office doesn't mandate digital three-dimensional drawings for mechanical inventions so that they can be rotated and evaluated by the patent examiners. Anyway, what do I care? I'm a rockstar.

Virg and I moved on to another display case. From above, spotlights shown down on lacquered wood fittings and axel joints.

"I wonder how Henry Ford wheeled his working car into the Patent Office?" I said.

"I think the motorized carriage was invented after the Patent Office stopped requiring physical models of inventions. There were the fires, too."

"If the museum doesn't have a model of the first toilet because it burned up, all they have to do is rip one out of the john in the Court of Appeals for the Federal Circuit. And don't say, 'That's *patentably* absurd,' Virg. I bet the ladies at the counter hear that 50 times a day. Now please stop smudging up the display glass. Let's get back to the hotel. They have to have our room ready by now."

Virg agreed and we made our way out of the working model room, through the main display area, across the lobby, and onto the sidewalk. The fog had burned off a little. I at least could see more floors of the tall buildings. We began tracing our steps back to the hotel. Before too long I broke the silence by remarking, "For my Lawyer Shut Your Trap game I thought you just had to file a one page form to get a patent. Did you see all those pages and drawings? And then the film said you should hire a patent attorney to write it all for you and to prosecute the patent application at the Patent Office. And it takes about three years. I'll never get my game patented."

"It is both costly and time prohibitive for the individual

inventor to get a patent these days."

I mouthed what Virg robotically said in mocking fashion as we reached the Metrorail station.

Ser Brunetto

THANKFULLY OUR ROOM was ready when we got back. Due to the Trident Hotel being at capacity for the night, the lobby was full with businesspeople jabbering on their cellphones and looking aimless and stupid as they tried to look important.

At the front desk we were given our plastic cards to the room. Virg handed over our baggage claim ticket and a busboy soon emerged from a back room toting our luggage in each hand. He was about my age, but nowhere near as cool.

"This it, gentlemen?"

"We pack light," Virg said.

"Very well. I am Brunetto," the busboy announced.

I took one look at his shock of dyed blonde hair and said, "You sure about that?"

He showed us the way to the elevator. Once inside the marble-floored car, he pushed button thirteen. I had forgotten we were stuck in Room 1313. Though I am not superstitious, this left me feeling uneasy.

On the way up I noticed in the mirror that the busboy's nametag said SER BRUNETTO. I figured Ser couldn't be his real first name. I figured it must be a typo and that it meant to read SIR.

To break the silence—especially since I couldn't rely on Virg to say anything that would resemble human conversation—I said, "From your name I gather you're Italian."

"No, sir. Latino."

Have I commented yet that no one in D.C. was born in America except maybe the president and people aren't even sure about that.

More silence ensued as we moved up. Floor 7. Floor 8. Floor 9.

"I know it appears funny that we're staying in the same room and all, but it's not that we're . . . you know," I clarified. "The hotel's full and we could only get one room."

"Very well, gentlemen."

More silence ensued as we moved up. Floor 10. Floor 11. Floor 12. Virg looks so funny in a mirror. He really does.

A ding let us know we had made it to our unlucky floor. Ser Brunetto held the doors open for us as we exited the elevator.

We made a left and then a right down a long corridor lit by cheesy faux gold sconces. The walls were hung with paintings of foxhunts and giant pheasants. All of them had frames painted in faux gold. Who was the Trident Hotel trying to fool? And, of course, that same obnoxious multi-colored carpet was back that I saw in the airport.

"Hey, Virg, I don't want any of this kind of carpeting in my dressing room at concerts. Got it? If the venue has it laid down, they'll have to rip it up or I won't play there. And I want lots of coffee in the dressing room; both hot and cold, like over ice. And Scottish butter cookies—"

The busboy's eyes lit up and he interrupted me. "So you're in a band? What's it called?"

"Here we go," Virg said in a huff.

"Thanks for asking," I responded. "I'm leaning toward Smoking in Bed. The hotel vibe brought the name on."

"Oh, so you are just deciding on a name?"

"When is he not?" Virg stated.

"I'm serious. Smoking in Bed would be a classic name for a rebellious rock band. Not only do they smoke, they do it recklessly. Now *that* is cool." I held out my hands. "Don't worry, neither of us smoke and if we did, we certainly wouldn't do it your fine hotel."

"I prefer Latin music," Ser Brunetto disclosed.

I almost laughed. I held it in.

At Room 1313 the busboy started explaining stuff before we entered. He showed us how to insert and remove the plastic card to open the door (like, duh), and then launched into a dissertation on a metal knob mounted in the middle of the door.

"Inside you will see a plastic bag by the bed. Simply place your shoes in it and hang the bag on this knob. During the night your shoes will be taken and cleaned for you. In the morning you will find them buffed and hanging back on the knob."

With those instructions Ser Brunetto popped open the door and we strolled inside our room. On the immediate right was the bathroom. Ser Brunetto flicked on the light.

"You will note, fine gentlemen, the tile and glass shower. Behind the door is a bathrobe and slippers. You will notice the hotel crest on both the robe and slippers. I am afraid, however, there is only one. If this is any inconvenience I can—"

"Don't worry about it," I said. "Virg can have the bathrobe and slippers because that's the kinda guy he is. Rockers don't wear bathrobes and slippers."

"Very good. On the ample Italian marble sink you will find custom soaps in the shape of our hotel crest, which of course is a trident."

"Sure it's not Lucifer's pitchfork?" I asked.

"On the sink you will also find a shower cap, mouthwash, cotton swabs, and a hair dryer. Above the shower is a heat lamp that is operated by this switch."

I noticed the bathtub drain was closed in anticipation of a nightly bath as if *anyone* takes a bath in a hotel tub that you just know is crawling with foot fungus compliments off all kinds of nasty people.

Next to the tub, beside the sink, I noticed one of those small mirrors secured to the wall by an armature. It had a circular light around it. Given the angle, the mirror was magnifying Virg's face like a circus funhouse. Believe me, you really don't want to see Virg like that. As I backed out of the bathroom, I figured the small mirror was only good for shaving, tattoo inspections, or popping zits. That was pretty much it.

Ser Brunetto quickly showed us the queen-size bed we would share in the main room.

"Like I said, we're not, you know," I told Brunetto. "Just business associates trying to save a buck."

Brunetto issued a halfhearted grin.

As I turned around I hit my head on a chandelier hanging right in the middle of the room. "Oy!"

Virg laughed while Brunetto steadied the light, which had what appeared to be little tarnished devil faces on it and that's probably why it hurt like the devil.

"Don't let your hair get caught up in that chandelier, Brunetto, or you might never escape."

He seemed pleased that I noticed his 'do. "I look forward to downloading music from your band," he told me. Then, for an uncomfortably long time, he just stood there smiling.

I whispered in Virg's ear to tip the busboy even though Brunetto liked Latin music. I was getting tired of the *grande tour a la Latino.*

Virg did his thing and Brunetto nodded under his shock of blonde hair. In a few shakes he had left the room and Virg immediately began hanging up his clothes on the few wooden hangers in the sliding-door closet.

I flopped onto the bed, boots dangling off the edge. "Hope this ugly chandelier doesn't fall on us in the night. It gives me the creeps."

A few moments of silence ensued. I don't like silence.

"Hey, Virg, you listening?"

"What? I mean, yes, Edward," came his voice over the squeaking din of hangers grating along the metal rod.

"Besides a rickety chandelier with devil heads hanging above my bed, here are twenty-five other things that really creep me out in no particular order: (1) People who say at every presidential election that this is our most important election in history. (2) Anyone who leaves voice messages and says their telephone number so fast you have to play the entire message over three times to write it down. (3) Sports. (4) Yuppies. (5) Yuppies who like sports, which is every Yuppie. (6) Valentine's Day, but not St. Valentine, he kicks A. (7) Cats. (8) People who write or read stories about cats. (9) Authors, especially the one writing this. (10) Hip Hop crap. (11) Chicks who wear tight shirts with things written across the front so when you try to read it they give you this dirty look for looking at their dingleberries. (12) Country music. (13) Hollywood stars who comment on politics as if anyone cares what they think. (14) The urinals in D.C. (15) Fog that traps you in D.C. (16) Fish eggs that pop in your mouth two hours after you eat sushi. (17) Did I say 'Country music'? (18) Those little bathing suits the male platform divers wear in the Olympics. (19) Democrats. (20) Republicans. (21) People who talk about Africa like it's one big country. (22) People who don't wash their hands after using the john, especially if they've just spent time at the urinals in D.C. (23) The Suits. (24) Staying in Room 1313, or in any room on any floor of any hotel with you, Virg. (25) Girlfriends who move away and break up bands."

I Tre Italiani

VIRG FINALLY GOT his clothes hung up. His Hawaiian shirts lit up the dark interior of the closet something fierce. I could see them from the bed where I was lying and realized there would be no reason to leave the bathroom light on that night.

"Let's get some grub," I said. "This afternoon wore me down at those government buildings. From what I've seen they've got excellent Middle Eastern food here in Washington D.C. I mean, where else would one go in the headquarters of American than for Middle Eastern food? We can get some humus and grape leaves and spiced meat and pita bread."

"Fine with me."

"You strike me as the kinda guy who likes babaganosh, Virg."

He emerged from the shadows of the closet. "Actually, Middle Eastern food doesn't always agree with me. I was thinking more along the lines of Italian. Some nice, hearty pasta would serve me well."

"I'm too hungry to argue."

When I got up I hit my head on that blasted, bedeviled chandelier. This was the second time.

"Stop laughing or I'll wash your mouth out with the pitchfork-imprinted bar of soap."

Let me tell you, chandeliers should only be allowed in dining rooms and lobbies. That is it. There should be a law against them being any place else. They don't belong in elevators or in hotel rooms, especially if they will cause a rocker to knock his head against them getting off the bed.

We made quick work of the long hallway and got the express elevator that did not stop on any of the floors below us. In the lobby we said "hey" to Ser Brunetto who smiled as I warned him to avoid Salsa music.

The *concierge*—which is Virg's fancy name for the dude who stands behind a desk all day and draws on maps—recommended an Italian restaurant within walking distance called *I Tre Italiani*—which was the *concierge's* fancy name for The Three Italians.

As we turned left out the gatelike double doors of the hotel, nodding to the doormen in white, I noticed Virg sticking his finger in the air. He brought it down, inspected it, licked it, smelled it, then put it back in the air. I realized, after being embarrassed for half a block, that he was checking the fog. What a dork. His odd travel agent behavior didn't even dignify a comment. Sometimes it's best to leave weirdoes alone.

Outside the hotel dusk had fallen hard on the city. Long shadows toppled across streets and crashed through alleyways. Most of the buildings' lights had illuminated. Because of this it made it difficult to tell whether the fog had lifted.

For the next block we got stuck behind a rather wide man who was smoking as he strolled leisurely down the sidewalk. We could not get around him. He was looking up at the buildings and the people, ladeeda, out for a leisurely stroll in D.C. This guy was so slow he was even driving Virg nuts. You may find this hard to believe, but I never go anywhere leisurely. Bea says I need to relax more. Bea has issues.

I could not believe it when I saw the man in front of us—who should've had one of those WIDE LOAD signs on his back—smoking backwards. That's right, *backwards*. This is not to say he was walking backwards or even turning around while doing it. Rather, the cigarette butt was sticking out the *back* of his fingers as opposed to the other way around. When he took a drag he kissed the back of his hand and when he brought it out, it was like he was waving in beauty queen fashion.

From our vantage point he was no beauty queen. *Lard king*, came to mind for just a brief second and I forgot about my hunger.

The way he put his hand up, I thought he was going to get melted by a ray gun or attacked by crows, and was shielding his face.

At the first ray of dusk filtering through the fog, we jived and shimmied around him. It had been nearly a block of getting smoke blown backwards in our faces. It had been nearly a block of coughing and gagging. I felt as though I had just played a gig.

A block and a half later (that felt like an hour and a half) we finally turned. Virg led me into *I Tre Italiani* where a dark-haired, almond-eyed hostess met us at the front.

Virg gave her the name on the reservation, which she checked off in an appointment book opened between a bowl of chocolate mints and a multicolored lamp sitting on an ornate table.

The hostess snatched our menus from a bin on the wall and led us into the restaurant, which only had one main seating area. Off to the side was an open-air kitchen and the smell from it was incredible. In the back of the restaurant was a tall, but delicate waterfall that appeared out of nowhere from the ceiling and disappeared into nowhere in the floor.

As we snaked our way past the candlelit tables, I began feeling underdressed. I was the only one wearing combat boots in the entire place. I really was. This feeling of being underdressed happens to me a lot in public. Virg looked a hundred times more out of place. He was the only stooge wearing a Hawaiian shirt.

As soon as we took our seats he leaned over. "Here's a trick I have learned traveling to nice restaurants over the years. If I'm traveling alone, to check out a new hotel or city that the Zany Zoo is pushing, I dress to the nines."

"A Hawaiian shirt is not the nines, Virg. I don't know what the nines is exactly, but it is not that. You're dressed to the point fives, maybe. The ones would be pushing it."

"When I am seated at a fancy restaurant, I immediately take out a pen and note pad, scan the restaurant, and act like I'm taking notes."

"Let me guess, they think you're a food critic."

"Right. I get the world's best and fastest service."

"Didn't think you had it in you, Virg, but that's pretty

cool. When I want fast service I try to avoid fast food restaurants. Those are some of the slowest places you can ever eat. To top it off, when you get your food the order is usually wrong. They should call them slow and wrong food restaurants."

"Not that I'm a success every time, Edward. Sometimes they see right through my disguise or don't even pay attention."

"Hey, every U2 has their *Zooropa*."

Our waiter came by with a basket of breadsticks and questioned if we wanted anything to drink. We both ordered water. Virg got his with lemon in it. He's so swanky!

As the waiter left I asked, "Why can't anyone drink water anymore without lemon in it?"

Virg brought his shoulders to his ears.

We made our way over to the waterfall to pass the time. The lights focused on the tumbling water gave it a romantic and eerie appearance all the same. No matter how close I got to it, I could neither see the top nor bottom. Behind the water was a tile mosaic of a beautiful woman standing in a bed of flames. BELLA DEI DIAVOLO was stenciled beneath her.

Virg tossed in a coin and it quickly disappeared into the bubbling abyss.

"What'd ya wish for?"

"Oh, it's a secret, Edward. Well . . . actually two secrets."

We made our way back to the table and sat down. It felt like everyone was looking at us.

From where I was sitting I had a perfect view of three rotund chefs with tall white hats. They were cooking away in the open-air kitchen. From the circular area where they stood I could tell they were three in the round or "round three" as Virg called it. Whatever.

I could tell they liked their butter and cream, if you know what I mean. They were very jovial Italian fellows and obviously loved their jobs. From one of their skillets shot a burst of flames and the chefs gave a triple shout of *fuoco torrefatto perfezione!* When translated from Italian it means, "One of the three fatsos almost caught fire."

When the fire had gone down, I noticed the names of the chefs stenciled on the brims of their hats: GUIDO, JACOPO, and TEGGHIAIO.

"I know those guys, Virg!"

"What? The chefs?"

"Yeah, they're from Florence. I went to high school with them. They were best friends. The only Italians in our class. After graduation they took off for culinary school in New York City and I lost all track of them."

I got up from the table and walked over to the open-air kitchen with Virg tagging behind. *"Ciao!"* I said in a voice loud enough for them to hear me over the sizzle of food and knocking of pans. Since that was about the extent of my Italian, I waited for a response.

Tegghiaio squinted through the steam rising up from a bowl of tortellini he was draining. He tapped Guido and pointed.

I waved. Smiled.

They put their utensils down and stepped closer.

"Remember me? Edward T. Nad of Florence. Our Lady of Infinite Health? Used to always be tardy for history class. Now I'm starting a band that I may call the Re-tardies. Isn't *that* a coincidence?"

Guido's eyes lit. "Yeah, yeah, Eddie. The black T-shirt guy. Sat in the back. Used to get beat up a lot by the jocks. You were always trying to get a rock band going." He thought for a second before remembering. "Scratch Monkeys. That was the name."

"No. It was the Encumbered Cucumbers," blurted Tegghiaio.

"Actually, both," I verified. "Yep, that's me."

"Un vecchio amico!" they both shouted as Jacopo walked over to join them.

Before I could move I had six hairy Italian arms around me. This brought with it the smell of garlic that I figured would last the rest of my life no matter how many times I showered with a little bar of soap imprinted with a pitchfork.

Everyone in the restaurant was rubbernecking. Before we knew it, Virg and I were wearing chef's hats. While we stood there talking to my old acquaintances, one would duck away to finish a dish he was preparing, only to appear again and continue the conversation while another darted back to the bowels of the kitchen. They asked about Florence and we told them nothing had changed. Jacopo asked if I ever got hitched. I told him the story of Bea and how she took off and that she broke up the band. Low and behold I glance over my shoulder and Virg is shaking his head from side-to-side. When I turned back Jacopo gave me a big hug again.

It was great seeing the fellows. They felt the same.

Over the course of our dinner we received special little plates of food items the chefs were trying in the kitchen that night. Cold cut meats here, fancy cheeses there. All of them were fantastic. I had to remind Virg to put down the bread and try them. "How many loaves of twisted garlic bread can a man eat?"

His shoulders went to his ears again.

For dessert two martini glasses arrived with the best crème brûlée Virg has ever consumed. It was my best too; since it was the first time I had tried it.

When the check came all it had on it was a big smiley face—no price or anything—and best wishes from Guido, Jacopo and Tegghiaio.

"I'll pay this one, Virg. You get the tip."

Gerry

WE WAVED TO the three jovial chefs on our way out of *I Tre Italiani,* offering many thanks for the great dinner and promises to give our best to certain mutual acquaintances back in Florence.

"I like those guys. I really do."

"Me too. It's good to see a few locals doing well."

"Yeah, just like me. Whoa. Did I just see you roll your eyes, Virg?"

"It must have been the lights from the passing vehicles."

"I'm successful, just not mega-successful yet. You, on the other hand, work at the Zany Zoo Travel Agency, which is one step above the guy who hoses goose droppings off the sidewalk at the Florence Municipal Park."

Virg looked dumbfounded as we walked along. "Beatrice says that success is all relative, like wealth. Beatrice told me that you are successful if you truly believe yourself to be successful. Nothing else is needed. In other words, success is what you believe, not what others think about you. Furthermore, Edward, you are the one who dressed up in a bunny costume."

"'Furthermore, Edward,'" I repeated in mocking fashion. I was sure to crinkle my nose as I said it. "Okay, so maybe I did for one weekend, which had to be the worst time of my life. Let me tell you, it's hard work waving at traffic for eight hours. My arms killed at the end of the day. I couldn't play the drums when I got back to the apartment. Plus, the lining in those costumes really chaffs in all the wrong places. A woman approached me with her little brat kids and wanted me to give them rides on my back right on the front lawn of the miserable Zany Zoo Travel Agency of greater Florence, New York. I told the lady to get lost and then you got all mad because you received an irate call from the husband. So yes,

I remember it very well and I don't like you much for giving me the rotten job or for bringing it up. And, and, and now you brought up Bea again. What is it with her?"

We tried to cross the street and were greeted with the blare of a taxi horn as the cabbie made a right turn. We jumped back on the sidewalk just in the nick of time.

"Watch it you jerk," Virg blurted. It was about the worst language I had ever heard him use.

I spotted a department store built into the lower floors of a tall building. We decided to pay it a visit to waste some time.

From outside I didn't see many people milling around. Inside were high ceilings and shiny chrome racks of clothes that looked pristine. On the lower floor the only people I noticed were a security guard and two ladies checking prices on scarves.

We headed up the escalator and right for the big screen TV section where a bank of glowing flat screens greeted us.

"Look at that big-haired guy," I commented to Virg in reference to a rocker being interviewed on the TV. "He has way too much gel in his hair. I can still remember the days when MTV actually played music videos."

"As your manager, I'll try to never let you do anything stupid like that. It's career wrecking."

"Uh, you did let me wave to traffic in a bunny outfit as if that's not career wrecking in itself. I'll never let you forget that, Virg."

"Oh stop it. No one knew it was you."

"Hey, there's the videogame section."

We hustled over, but first had to make our way through the stuffed animal paradise that was the children's section. I could tell Virg was enchanted by it all.

I asked him, "Ever wonder how Tigger and Roo got in *Winnie the Pooh*? Like how did a tiger and a baby kangaroo get in the Hundred Acre Woods anyway? Where did they come from? Maybe India for Tigger or a country in Africa? Roo may have come from New Zealand or Australia. I can see Pooh Bear and Piglet and Owl (A. A. Milne sure was creative on that name) making it into a forest, and maybe even

Eeyore if he escaped from a farm or something, but not a tiger and baby kangaroo. If they floated across the ocean on separate rafts—"

"Your mind never ceases to—"

"The Pantsless Poohs would be a swinging name for a band, Virg. Now *that* makes sense."

On the other side of the children's section we located the videogame area. A couple flat screens invited us to play the latest title.

We each grabbed a controller and started clicking away. On the screen was displayed an eerie landscape of mountains, lumbering clouds, spewing fire, jagged cliffs. Ravens and falcons gyrated and cavorted among the peaks. Crosshairs appeared before us and we began firing digital bullets.

"Got one!" Virg exclaimed a little too loudly for being in public.

Down below I glimpsed a cargo boat and squeezed off a few rounds into its hull. The boat started to sink into a fiery lake. Military types jumped off and a lifeboat was dropped over the side. A monstrous arm reached out of the water and pulled the lifeboat below the surface.

It had to be a half hour we were standing there getting our game on, when Virg started complaining that his feet hurt. I did not want to stop. I was beating him royally. I told him he needed to get a pair of stompers. They are the most comfortable things your feet will ever wear.

Back in the children's area I spotted a giant stuffed dragon. I clicked the pause button on the controller and ran over and grabbed the creature. His collar said his name was Gerry. His face was benign, almost happy looking, as stuffed monsters for kids sometimes are. Gerry had a forked tail curled like a scorpion (or Bea's eyelashes). The dragon's front arms were hairy and for a moment I thought of being hugged by the three Florentine chefs an hour ago.

I struggled with the huge beast, yet somehow managed to pull, drag, push him over to the videogame area after toppling a 24-hour sale sign and crashing over a pyramid of sock cubes.

The clerks were gaping at me . . . as if I cared.

"Here we go, Virg. Take a seat on Gerry the Dragon."

Virg sat on the front of him and I mounted the back, which had circlets and knots tied on it.

The game continued. I was up half a million points on Virg and loving it. A few times I had to ask him to lean to the side. It was hard to see on the back of the dragon.

Demons were flying everywhere and my digital rounds clipped their leathery wings at a machine gun pace. A few tried to climb up the side of a mountain. I vanquished them and called out for more.

Soon we entered another level of the game and were forced to fly in a helix pattern around a high waterfall that made us both dizzy. The droplets of water that splashed onto the screen were very realistic and so were the demons. I shot one in the face. *Bha-lam!*

"Stop rocking," Virg said, "I am missing my targets."

"I can tell by your embarrassing score."

Looking away, Virg noticed the congregating assembly of store clerks. He got nervous.

"We had better go."

"Are they going to put us in the videogame gallows? What could they possibly do to us?"

"Let's go, Edward."

I reluctantly hung up the controller and dismounted the dragon. Virg quickly did the same. Both of us headed toward the escalator.

On the way past the clerks I shot them an uppity glance. They thought they were above us. Umpf!

Shapushashasuh!

A BLOCK DOWN from the electronics store we followed a street along the backside of a few prominent buildings. Under anemic street lamps blowing trash played at our feet. The pavement was riddled with grave-size potholes. A rat skittered out of one, darted over the curb and into an alley. One of my boots splashed in a fusty puddle. Graffiti was everywhere. The street was as crooked as a Chicago politician. At the most we could see half a block in front of us. We began to hear thumping rhythms and saw the faint glow of a neon sign up ahead.

"I don't like this."

"Me either lest you forget you're the tour guide."

We noticed cars with shiny chrome wheels that were parked in front of the building. They were luxury cars made to look *street.*

"Maybe I should get spinners on my meter maid car."

"Shhh! Keep your voice down. This isn't the best part of town."

"Like I didn't know that."

Excited voices were echoing through the night. Phantasmal ladies moved in and out of the front door with faces painted in white and crimson. In a few more cautious steps we were at a fronting angle that enabled us to read the sign overhead: THE EIGHTH CIRCLE PRESENTS THE MALE BOLGE REVIEW.

"What kind of a tour is this? You've led us into a bad part of town right in front of some male review club. Disgusting!"

"I thought it was a shortcut to our hotel. We should head back the other way."

"Deuce straight. That shirt you've got on'll attract a lot of unwanted attention. It might even get us shot. And I don't appreciate that."

More dark vehicles with even darker windows rolled past. We headed back toward the department store. We alternated glancing behind us to make sure no one was following us. Once safely in front of the department store I wanted to check if anyone was trying to beat my high score on the videogame but Virg wouldn't let me.

Twenty minutes later, after stepping over a homeless panderer or two, we safely arrived at Room 1313; but not before walking past the hotel lobby staff with their fake smiles. Did they actually believe that we believed that they were glad to see us? The frauds.

In the room Virg took off his shoes and began rubbing his sausage links. I unlaced my boots and popped them off. I tied the laces of the boots together and headed for the door.

"What are you doing?"

"You heard our man, Ser Brunetto, free shoe shine. All I have to do is hang my boots on this knob out here. I need to get the grease off after that terrible part of town you took me through."

I opened the door and slung the tied laces over the special knob. They twisted and rocked to a standstill. I hoped the cleaning people wouldn't mind the scuffs on the beige door. I'm a person who makes a mark in this world in many ways.

Back in the room I noticed a Hawaiian shirt slung on the chandelier, shoes next to the bed and a flop of hair on the pillow. Virg had already snuggled down. Man, a queen-size bed never looked so small.

I unhooked the ugly shirt from the chandelier as I thought it might frighten me in the night, flicked off the lights, and slid into bed feeling mongo creepy. I lay there with arms tucked into my sides as tight as they could be, legs pinched together. I was being as small and skinny as possible to avoid touching you know who.

"I am sooo tired," Virg complained.

"Me too."

"You never did tell me what happened when the band broke up. Was there a final straw for Beatrice that made her leave?"

"Don't want to . . . talk about it."

"I see. That is pretty much what I expected."

I yawned. "Then why'd you ask?"

Outside the Trident Hotel, the honking of horns and the occasional blare of a police siren purled into the night. The pillow was too soft, bed too hard. I bunched up the pillow under my neck and realized it was going to be a restless evening.

"Hey, Virg, how come nobody yawns or sneezes when they're asleep? Answer that one. When you're sleeping is when you're the most tired. You should be yawning a lot then. And don't you think pillows with their dust mites would have you sneezing a lot when you sleep? Think about it. No yawning. No sneezing."

"Uh-huh."

The reflection of a distant sign flashed incessantly on the wall across from my bed. Colors dreamily moved across the chandelier only to pause and hide behind a crystal, then emerge another color. The wall told me in waves that there was a coming art show by artists named Alessio, Thais, Venedico and Jason. Lying there I had to admit that the last name didn't sound very artistic. The artists were having a Christmas show at Easter, complete with ornamented trees and presents. The whole concept was something about birth at death or melding Christ's birth with his resurrection at Easter. A mouth swallowing a tale.

I got up and shut the curtains. "Ya know, Virg, I'm tired of groups banning Mary and Baby Jesus from courthouses and parks at Christmas. What I should do is start a religion where the sacred symbols are Hawaiian shirts so they will be banned from any public-owned land or building in America. That would make the world beautiful and eliminate most of your wardrobe."

"*Shapushashasuh.*"

He was out of it. I slipped back in bed and turned over in the direction of Virg; fluffed my useless pillow again. "My love life right now feels like one of those calendars the day after Christmas. I just feel that Bea has slung it into the half-off bin. 'Come get cardboard Eddie, all stiff on the backside with a glossy paper front!'"

Virg mumbled something. He does that a lot.

"But it's almost not worth having Christmas because of the joy hangover. People ask you if you had a good Christmas as if anyone in the annals of time has ever responded, 'Why, no, I had a *terrible* Christmas,' except me now that Bea's gone. I get so depressed the day after Christmas when I realize my late Christmas cards will be arriving in the mailboxes of relatives I don't really like very much. So I slunk out of bed to the fridge where all I find is crumbs left in the fudge pan, a petrified turkey leg on a miserable Santa plate and a carton of old eggnog with only a few drops in it. I shake it in the hopes more eggnog will magically appear but it doesn't, which only makes me think of Bea and her love of 'skinny eggnog' for 'lean minds and bodies' that we will never share together again. I slam the door to the fridge and stagger past the cranberry-imprinted plastic cloth stretched over the kitchen table—on which we made out after a hellacious gig last year, mind you—and continue into the living room where I spend the next two hours taking down the artificial tree that has no presents under it from Bea, just a year's supply of Eco-Stain-Able from Mom and a new toaster from Dad's that was a left over from the new checking account promotion they had, along with a digital music player I gave myself, which only causes me to think of Bea more because she used to claim all my Christmas presents to her were really gifts to me), and I am reminded how everything's so small these days that it's hard to get any presents of substance under the tree like when I was growing up and you couldn't even see the tree skirt because it was piled with such big gifts."

"*Shapushashasuh.*"

"Now everything's so miniature that it strikes me while dismantling the artificial tree that there are only three things getting bigger in this world: waistlines, TV screens, and vehicles. The rest is going Lilliputian in a hand basket, which makes me detest people all the more who ask me if I had a nice Christmas. So I grind on this for an hour and then try to jam the tree into the *Klauset* while it pricks-pricks my arms to heck and jabs-jabs me in the face, which only makes me utter creative cuss words while racking my brain trying to figure out where Aunt Ethel got those plastic ice tongs she gave me so I can return them for a pack of gum or maybe a guitar pick. This makes me think of Bea *again* and the moving art she made when playing with any guitar pick on any guitar. Then I finally get the tree wedged in there—poked and bleeding, reeking of artificial pine scent—in that dark closet where I won't see it for another eleven months, when I glance down and notice fake pine needles all over the cheap area rug that was made in Asia by some guy named Wong who has never celebrated Christmas and probably never ever will and who certainly didn't have a nice Christmas while he was sowing up Easter bunny costumes, one of which would be used by the abysmal Zany Zoo Travel Agency of greater Florence, New York. So I reach for the vacuum and immediately realize that it's now buried behind the miserable artificial Christmas tree in the dark closet, which forces me to realize no matter how long I vacuum and no matter how thorough I am there will always, always, always be a couple fake needles left in the weavings of the Asian rug and that next year's Christmas won't be quite as good as this miserable one because of all the fake needles that fell off the tree this year."

Virg's lips flapped. I wasn't sure if it was a response.

"One Thanksgiving I had the idea of coming up with Thanksgiving songs for the band since there are a billion Christmas songs and not one Thanksgiving song—not one—and Bea says, 'Who's going to buy the album, pilgrims?' And remembering that comment only forces me to roll over onto the cheap area rug and curl it up around me, a big stinking holiday burrito of Asian chemicals and eggnog-tainted perspiration, where I fall asleep with the lights still on, and fake pine needles scratching the back of my neck. That's when I hear the chiming of a 'Jingle Bells' ornament that I forgot to take off the artificial tree buried somewhere deep in the closet. And it goes off nonstop for the next day until it runs out of batteries about the time when my late Christmas cards arrive."

"*Shapushashasuh.*"

"Know what I'm saying, Virg? You been there? Bet you never even had a girl of your own to break up with on Christmas or any other holiday."

A lip smack and then a gentle snore rose from the other side of the bed. With the sheet wrapped tightly around his fist, Virg rolled over, taking half the covers with him and leaving me exposed to the atmospheric elements of Room 1313.

I yanked them back. "You kill me. Really you do."

My breathing slowed. The digital clock resting on my nightstand anemically glowed 11:59. The drone of street sirens waned. The heater cycled down—down . . . the pillow . . .

The Um in Umbrella

"SIMON SAYS, 'THE beast is hungry and needs a sacrifice lest it consume thee. Whack the tray of cookie dough into its mouth.'"

Wearing my apron with stitched flames running down the front, I slid the tray inside and swung the oven door closed.

"Simon says, 'Poke the beast in the eyes.'"

I set the timer for eighteen minutes and stepped back toward Bea. She was perched atop the kitchen counter in her tight jeans and poofy chef's hat with matching flames that I was supposed to be wearing if she hadn't swiped it while we made the chocolate chip cookies. If you're in the kitchen with Bea she'll take it upon herself to sit up on the counter in some crazy hot outfit, which is usually just jeans and a tight T-shirt, that makes it looks as though she is not trying at all to be the blazes of Hades; but she's absolutely smoking. The surest way for a woman to be sexy is to plop up on the counter in jeans, kick her feet here and there, smile, and talk about anything. Bea sure does it. Bea is all about sexy. She's bringing it back in spades and aces. She doesn't even try. That's just Bea. She can say anything she wants when she's perched up on the counter and be spectacular doing it. Like when I have to play Simon Says just to put a cookie tray in the oven.

"Simon says, 'Insert spoon in bowl used to make the sacrifice and gather the remnants.'"

I scraped the remaining cookie dough from the bowl. When finished I had a heaping tablespoon of the chunky, sugary mixture inches from my mouth. My tongue got juicy.

Bea had me standing there for at least a minute—a minute!—before giving the final instruction. "Eat the remnants!"

I plowed the entire mixture into the trough that was my

waiting mouth. The mixture lit my senses. By the time I had extracted the spoon Bea was busting up laughing.

"I didn't say Simon says."

"Hughfph? Geezth. Canfth balk wid ma moth phfthul."

Wasn't mad in the least, though. She won but I had the cookie dough in my mouth, so really I won. Couldn't take my eyes off her as I chewed.

You should've seen her up there on the counter jiggling and laughing and crossing her legs, jade eyes enlarged and bright, wavy brown hair springing on those shoulders, driving me crazy. Near the top of her T-shirt it read BLONDES NOT BOMBS, which was crossed out. Below it read BOMB THE BLONDES.

I walked over toward her and she squeezed me between her legs. "You are such a Simoniac!"

"I think I've been insulted," Bea said, "but thanks. Realize we have a utopian relationship. The one who makes the cookie dough gets to lick the batter."

"Licking Batter may work as a title for our band."

"I like it, but it's not tough enough." She flexed her biceps in that crazy T-shirt.

"Look at those pipes. Now that's tough."

Before I could proffer another name for the band, the chef's hat was stuffed on my head right down over my eyes. Blinded, I knocked and struggled around the tiny kitchen. I heard the bowl rattle on the countertop. I felt my knee whack the edge of the cabinets. Finally I yanked the hat back up where I could see. Bea was gone.

"Come out, come out wherever you are."

I started searching for her but not before taking another spoonful of goodness from what was left in the bowl. I began with the kitchen cabinets and moved on to the bathroom.

"Simon says, 'Stop hiding right this minute.'"

I got nothing.

The bedroom was empty of hot rocker chicks. I didn't waste my time looking under the bed. It's a breeding ground for dust bunnies. Bea knows better.

Finally I found Bea after realizing the Christmas tree stuffed in the closet was not her. Her arms are much less prickly. Anyway, this all took longer than I expected in the one bedroom apartment. She was sitting cross-legged behind the sofa. Lying in front of her was a ringed binder. She climbed over the sofa (me watching every move) and placed the binder on the beat up coffee table. I glimpsed sketches, color swatches, copious notes written in the lithe handwriting of Bea.

"I'm ready to make my pitch to Florence's all access cable TV station."

"The one we watch after our gigs and laugh at? Those Canadian ladies are hilarious. 'This is how you tap the maple tree. Notice the angle of the spout. It is very important to clean the end to remove any sticky substances before insertion. Real maple syrup tastes much better than agave nectar. Bring the camera in closer, eh.'"

"The sappy programming is about to change. The owner has a slot he needs to fill. Like I told you yesterday, he'll give it to me for free just to get advertising money during the commercials. I have to sell him on the pitch."

I dropped next to her on the sofa. "You mean *we* have to sell him on the pitch. I can see our first TV gig now. We'll set up in a field and play background music to the Canadian maple syrup ladies."

"I'm serious, Eddie. I've got a rippin' idea for the show. Go with me today to meet with the guy."

"Can you give me a hint?"

She closed the ringed binder that apparently had her notes dispersed inside. "I don't want to let any sunshine out of the bottle yet."

"His name again?"

"Nicholas the Third." Bea said this with a grin.

"Why not Nicholas Thrice? It's a bit more artful—"

"And a bit more nice," Bea rhymed. She can do that to you if you're not careful. She'll just cut you off and rhyme all over your fat amp. That's why she puts the words to our songs.

The smell of baked cookies filled the air as we sat there and thought for a couple minutes without saying a word, teasing our hair, inspecting our tattoos like any respectable rocker couple does when they have down time.

Outside rain pricked at the thin walls and spotted the cars in the parking lot of the apartment complex. The trees began to blur. Wind pressed its will against the metal casements.

To break the silence I began a drum solo on the coffee table. I have to practice somewhere and playing my drum set in the apartment got the cops called a number of times. They call me "Mr. Nad" when they show up. It's all I can do to keep from snickering—so I do. "Is something funny about this, Mr. Nad?" I shake my head and bite my lip. "What is so humorous about disturbing the peace?" I tell them, "Nothing at all." Finally, after snooping around, they leave.

Bea socked me in the arm before I was through with one song. Hand drumming drives her off a cliff.

"The all access cable show is fine and all, Bea, but we have to find a way for them to pay us so we can stash away money for our tour. Florence can't support one rocker let alone two. Hey, we could auction some of our signed memorabilia."

"We need a name for our band first."

"I'm working on it."

"Besides, your idea of auctioning me on the Internet didn't work."

I issued a sheepish look. "Sorry 'bout that. Hoped you wouldn't find out."

"When did you suppose I would find out, when the guy who paid a million dollars for me showed up at the door?"

"He didn't actually make the payment. The winning bid was technically a million and one dollars. That's awesome considering I started the bidding at one penny. You were listed with great shipping terms."

"Yeah, 'easy pick up.'"

"Don't be sour. You're worth more than a million to me. Just trying to raise money for the band."

In an instant her arms were around my neck. That's another trait about Bea. You blink and she's got those strong guitar-playing arms wrapped around you, whispering something hot and breathy in your ear.

We rolled on the sofa for a while. Arms flailed. Legs twisted. She's tough to pin, believe me. In the middle of it Bea reminded, "We have to get over to the cable station. We can't be late like we are for most everything else in our lives. I'm really into making this work."

"A few more minutes longer?"

"That would be N-O."

"But you are my passionista."

Bea laughed as she wriggled away from me and slipped on her coat. She tossed my leather jacket over and then checked herself in the bathroom mirror.

"You look fine," I told her.

"Sure? Do you mean 'fine' as in okay or 'fine' as in ravishing?"

"I mean 'fine' as if it has two or three syllables. The drawn out fine. Fa-ine-na. It's much better than just the normal one."

"Now come on already."

I took her by the arm. She grabbed an umbrella by the door on the way out. I had never seen it before. It had the markings of Bea on it. When Bea gets in one of her coffeehouse artsy moods she begins painting things. Not canvases or wood siding, but *objects*—clothing, jewelry, flower pots, now I could tell she had taken to umbrellas in a spasm of creativity.

Walking down the sidewalk she opened it. There was a giant sunflower painted across the top. If you were looking down on it from a second story window you would be met with a lovely sunflower staring up at you in the middle of a gloomy, rainy day.

"You are the essential existential," I told her. Right there the phrase stuck in my brain craw. "Band name?"

"The Essential Existentials? Hoom. Not bad . . . but I think it's more a name for a greatest hits album if we were the Existentials for a decade or so."

"You're killing me, Bea."

Suddenly I noticed the rest of Bea's artwork. The underside of the umbrella was painted sky blue with a few playful clouds dancing here and there so that anyone under it only had to glance up to see a perfect day. Bea had brought her certain brand of cheeriness to the world—whether inside or outside the umbrella—on the dreariest of days. She will do that to you if you are not careful.

On the lip of the umbrella I noticed JUST BEA stenciled in a shade of green that strangely matched her eyes.

"That's the name for my new clothing line. Just Bea." She winked.

"I like that. You should trademark it. Just Bea. Now that's existential."

"Trying to use my little brand of sunshine to beat back the clouds one at a time."

"You put the *um* in umbrella," I told her as we reached the end of the sidewalk. "But how about sharing it with me?"

FAAC TV

WE REACHED THE meter maid car that was parked a few spaces down from the apartment door. Got it for two grand. First thing I did was trick it out with subwoofers, chrome wheels (had to buy four because the guy told me they were only sold in sets of four), and a roof rack for Bea's guitar. The back hatch is where I store my drums on the way to a gig. I mounted a skull (that matches my belt buckle) on the front bumper that I got at a Halloween store. The beauty of the triangular shape is that it doesn't take up a whole parking spot. I can park it at many different angles.

Bea climbed inside and I shut the door. At the driver's side I collapsed the umbrella and piled in behind the steering wheel. On the third try the meter maid car rumble-spurted to life.

"That was quick," Bea remarked with a look of surprise.

"In the rain no less."

"Must be my umbrella. It makes the lawn mower engine in this thing happy."

I could not argue with that, although the fifty miles a gallon it gets makes me happy.

We pulled out of the apartment complex and headed for the Florence All Access Cable TV Station, known in the area as FAAC TV.

"Can't wait to hear your pitch," I confessed.

"You're going to like it. I promise."

"I'll be there to back you up and so will the meter maid car with its bulbous fenders."

Bea tittered loudly. I like a woman with big titters.

"That's what I love about you, Eddie. Who in the world says bulbous?"

"What about triangular window nodules?"

That sent her into a laughing fit up against the car door.

At times Bea'll just curl up and laugh on you like that. There she was all hot looking in those jeans and T-shirt. I could see the faint ripple of her abs. Thankfully she quit or we would've crashed. I cannot keep my eyes off her when she's like that.

We soon reached FAAC TV. Nothing is far away in Florence. It was a ten minute drive. That's thirty minutes in meter maid car time. The place was easy to spot. FAAC TV had a gaggle of antennae and gray satellite dishes standing guard on the roof. Apart from the roofline, FAAC TV was a non-descript, red brick, single story building with few windows. In high school I mistook it for a bomb shelter.

Smiley face umbrella in one hand, Bea's waist in the other, I walked with her to the plain metal front door of FAAC TV. I was about to open it when a stream of people came barging outside.

Bea and I leaned back to keep from getting trampled.

A group of eight people streamed out. They were dressed in identical oversized business suits. The shoulders were like football pads. The sleeves extended down well past their arms. The pants were baggy. I mean flaglike. On their feet I noticed large bowling shoes. The strangest part about their costumes wasn't the material at all, rather the way they were wearing them. They had them on backwards. Backwards I'm telling you! This made it appear they were walking with their heads facing the rear.

The last one out of the door said, "Hi, I'm Michael Scott."

"The man with two first names," I said. "What kinda tomfoolery, or should I say *mike*foolery, are you guys up to?"

With that Michael Scott extracted a business card from the inside lining of his suit coat. This was accomplished with much twisting of arm and pulling of material, as he had to reach behind him.

"Be sure to watch our show: Fortunetellers, Diviners and Drive-ins. Each week we do a different segment here at FAAC TV. Our managers thought the backwards suits would be a crazy touch."

"Don't go into the music business," I advised.

Bea corrected me by mentioning an old Talking Heads

video. She thought the outfits might work in a retro sort of way.

The strange gentlemen, with Michael Scott leading the way, hurried down the sidewalk in the rain without any covering for their backward heads.

"Nice umbrella by the way," Michael Scott shouted back.

"Just Bea," Bea said. "Coming to a store near you."

"Uh, Bea, they live in Florence where there are no cool stores."

"Okay, maybe not," she responded in a quiet voice.

Inside the building we found an open reception area with an empty desk and two leather sofas that may have been beige a few decades ago. Beyond the desk was a hall inset by six rooms, three on each side. Electronic signs were mounted on top of the hallway doors. One was illuminated with the word RECORDING. The others were dark.

"I wonder if they've got sound equipment we can record on?"

Bea shrugged. "I'll ask . . . that is if they like my idea."

"Which is?"

"Push the button on the desk. Hopefully someone will realize we're here."

I did and we took a seat on one of the sofas, trying to cover up our tattoos as best we could. Have I told you yet what my neck tattoo is? No? Remind me sometime and I will.

We sat there for a few minutes knocking around band names and putting in order the songs for our next gig. Bea had only written a handful at the time so it wasn't too hard. We finally heard footfalls coming up the center hall and a lanky man appeared wearing a plaid shirt and corduroys. His beard was graying and cropped close to his face. He glanced at a clock hanging above us and apologized for being late.

We stood. He extended both hands and we shook them at the same time—Bea the left, me the right—as if you care.

"Pleased to meet you," Bea said and told him our names.

"Call me Nick. It's nice to meet both of you. Why don't you come on back to my office. From what little I know of your idea for a show, it sounds interesting."

The three of us made our way down the center hallway to the rear of the building. I tried to peek into the room where they were recording, but I didn't see much on the way past. I wondered if the Canadian syrup ladies were in there. At the end of the hall Nick opened a non-descript door that simply read MANAGER overhead. He stole behind a small pressboard desk with a faux oak grain surface. We sat in the folding chairs that fronted the desk. From a pullout drawer he extracted a yellow pad of paper and a pen. "Let's hear it."

Bea laid the umbrella across her lap and edged up on her chair. "Okay, Nick, you know the local news, right? How it's a total depression incubator? A robbery here. A murder there. 'Our top story tonight, the stock market is crashing! A flood in India. An embassy burning in Bahrain. The bailout isn't working.'"

"The record labels are ripping off bands," I threw in.

Bea continued. "I bet if they did a study, suicides are highest after the nightly news."

"No arguments from me," Nick verified.

"Well, my idea is to have a news program that only broadcasts good news. It will be the yang to the yin of all other news stations in the world."

"Let me conceptualize this for a moment," Nick said. "You will broadcast news on the weekend that is in direct opposition to the local and national news, which only broadcasts bad news."

"That's it. That's our pitch in a nutshell," Bea said.

I sat back in my chair and reminded myself for the hundredth time that Bea is pretty smart.

Nick put his pad of paper down and thought for a moment. He put elbow to desk and propped his chin on his splayed fingers while he looked us over. Finally he asked me, "Are you part of this? You look almost surprised. I'm sorry, but I'm terrible with n—"

"It's Edward T. Nad and I'm not surprised in the least. Just taking it all in."

"What do you plan to wear on the show?"

He asked the question in a way that frowned on our current outfits. What do people have against combat boots?

"We seek out clean programs if possible."

"What is this place, the Vatican?" I said. "It's not that we're going to dance naked on the desk."

Nick leaned back in his chair. "Oh forget that. It doesn't matter. I sometimes have to be reminded this is an all access cable TV show."

"Good. Because I don't remove my stompers for anybody," I confessed.

Bea added, "We saw those guys in the big suits on the way in." She looked side-to-side and whispered, "I got news for ya, they were on backwards."

Nick smirked at this. "Good point."

"Our band will do the intro music for the show," Bea offered.

"What's the name of your band?" Nick asked.

"Brilliant Ant," I said.

Bea kicked me a good one. Sheepishly (or lambishly), Bea let Nick know, "We're still getting our name hammered out."

"I understand."

"As we understand our zenlike news experience—we don't even like to call it a program—will be brought to the fine viewers of greater Florence each Saturday at two a.m.," Bea said. She has a way of clinching deals before they are brought up.

Nick held out his hands. "Not so fast. I am exploring a number of options for this slot."

"We work for free," Bea added.

"I know. I know. Can we give your pilot . . . a test run?"

"Sure! How 'bout right now if you have the time?"

"Very well then. Let's do it. Follow me into Room 5."

Section IV

Bea Excellent

NICK LED US across the hall to a small room that sat opposite his office. He flicked on the lights and not much happened. I expected the room to illuminate more than it did. The overhead canisters struggled to brighten the place by casting yellow-white lillypads on the floor.

On the walls were black cones that served as sound barriers. Long reams of black paper covered the floor and were dappled with stains that looked like blood-splatter in the lillypads of light. Nick warned us not to slip as we walked over to a desk in the middle of Room 5. I noticed that the desk was identical to the cheap one in Nick's office.

A plank bridge was suspended from ropes at the very back of the room. A speaker in the corner was playing the show recording in Room 2. The characters had crazy names like Deaddog, Pigtusk and Crazyred. I viewed what may have been grappling hooks dangling from the ceiling. The smell of fresh pitch wafted through the air. Demon masks hung from a coat rack in the corner.

Our wan faces got a confession from Nick. "The four a.m. slot just did a tribute to KISS. The rock band."

"Reverb!" I exclaimed. "Like the vibes of this place already."

"Hope it won't distract from your audition."

"Not a chance," Bea said firmly.

"Fine," Nick said, standing front and center. "Give me ten minutes of your program. Our only camera is recording in Room 2. Just pretend I am the camera and talk to me conversationally. We've found that the more natural you are on TV, the better. Either of you had TV experience before?"

From behind the desk we shook our heads; not up and down, but side to side.

"When I raise my right hand, pretend the light has gone on and we're recording."

"Follow my lead," Bea whispered.

I drummed a tune on the desk. It rocked.

"That must be the intro music," Nick acknowledged.

Bea cleared her throat and Nick raised his arm. "Welcome Greater Florence to the first broadcast of Bea Excellent Always. B-E-A is your home for the optimistic and the positive in the world at large. Let's get right to the experience. Today over three hundred stocks rose today, which includes a basket of companies with a presence in Florence. There were no reported robberies in Florence today—"

"—or hatchet murders," I added.

"Turning to Mother Earth, there has never been a recorded earthquake over 3 on the Richter scale in our city. It has now been over fourteen months since a fire was reported in town. Don't we have the finest looking firemen ever? Buy their calendar and help keep Florence a great place to live and work."

Nick was smiling and motioning for us to keep going.

"Let's turn to the weather forecast. We gained almost two minutes of sun under daylight savings time yesterday. The days are getting longer, folks, and we are one more day closer to summer and Christmas."

"Shiny, shiny—bliss, bliss," I tossed in.

Bea swallowed hard and gave me a look. "Yes, it was rainier today than yesterday, but it was a full five degrees warmer than this day last year when we had twice the amount of rain. Anyone in need of the happiest umbrella on planet earth?" Bea held her umbrella up and expanded, twirled and collapsed it back.

"A black one with white skulls would also be nice," I told the mock TV audience.

"Continuing on to our life and environment segment, two dozen maple trees were planted at the Garden Nursing Home of Greater Florence on Monday, which will remove 312 pounds per year of carbon dioxide from our air. Over twenty kids from Carlson Middle School helped out at the GNHGF over the weekend to rake leaves. Let's all applaud their volunteer efforts. Also, tests today by Florence Gas and Water demonstrate that we have some of the cleanest drinking water in the country."

"Let's all do the dance of cheer and happiness," I threw in.

"How about sports?" Nick asked.

Bea looked at me. I looked at her. I said, "Have to confess that neither of us know much about sports. We'll brush up on that for the actual show. I'm thinking of a segment that focuses on our band every week. What songs we're writing, gigs we're playing, our newest tats. Stuff rockers want to know—"

Bea tapped me on the shoulder and whispered, "Let's get on with it." Looking back at Nick, she said, "Every week we will close the show with our Top Ten Optimisms."

Nick threw up his eyebrows. "T-T-O from B-E-A. This should be interesting. Let's have it."

Bea got up and walked over to the dark wall. Its aligned sound cones reminded me of the spines of a dragon. She began moving a hand up and down it like she was displaying merchandise in a game show. I assumed she planned on using a chart to display the T-T-O on the show.

"In closing, we present the Top Ten Optimisms for the week. Number ten—You have only a one in six million chance of getting struck by lightning this year! Number nine—Seven people died today from exposure to inanimate objects and you were not one of them! Number eight—Less than one person will die from being stomped by a captive elephant this year! Number seven—"

"You were not attacked by clowns today!" I interjected.

Bea shot me another look.

"What? It can happen, people."

"Number six—You were not one of those who died as an occupant of an agricultural vehicle today. Number five—In the last week you were not one of the people who expired when a foreign body entered a natural orifice."

I busted up at that one. Fell right out of my chair. I couldn't help it. Bea can just one-off a saying out of nowhere and next thing you know you're on a floor covered in black reams of paper, with dots of fake blood on it, laughing until your side hurts. When you finally clear the water from your eyes all you see is demon masks staring down at you.

"Number four—Be thankful you were not one of the people who died this month from being locked in a meat freezer. Number three on our countdown—You, kind viewer, were not one of the two people this week who died while riding in an animal-drawn vehicle."

I was still laughing by this time, but I managed to lunge myself back into the chair.

"Number two—Nearly two people a day die after falling out of bed and you were not one of them! And now for our number one optimism of the week—"

I jumped right in. "Your band manager doesn't work for the miserable Zany Zoo Travel Agency. If he does, call me because he's got some explaining to do," I said, making a handset shape with my fingers.

"That's *interesting*," Nick said. He paced for a few moments with hands clasped behind his back. "Let's hear your signoff. You do have a signoff, right?"

I decided to take the lead. I just wasn't getting enough airtime in this gig. "I'm Edward T. Nad and this is my little cumquat, Bea here. She's cutielicious. Thanks for watching and all that stuff. We know you have a choice when it comes to a news experience. We're glad you made the right one. Keep it positive, Florence, keep it rockin' and come see our band play at Joe's this Friday—"

"No need for a self serving plug," Nick interrupted in a commanding voice.

"It's not like he's our father or something," I whispered to Bea, but I think Nick heard me. Still, I pressed on. "We're opening for PrayDown, not that we play Christian rock or anything."

"I am taking us off the air," Nick informed. "The arm is coming down. Watch it. Watch it. Off the air."

"Our name is The Disenfranchised and and and—"

Nick was approaching the table now. "That's quite enough. The camera light is out."

"I'm the drummer and Bea here is the lead singer and

guitar player. She writes the lyrics—"

"I've heard quite enough."

"If you're lucky I'll give out some autographs after the gig and—"

"Stop talking! Off the air!"

"If you tune in often you might even learn how I got the tattoo on my neck and—"

That's when Nick dove at me across the desk; palms out like he was going to choke me.

I had to roll the chair backwards to get away.

He thudded onto the desk.

Bea jumped in front of him and that seemed to jog his senses. He stopped moving forward and just lay there, arms surrounding his drawn-up knees.

She began talking to him in the most logical of ways. She said this was all unscripted. With a little practice the show would be smoothed out. Really, it would. She asked him if he liked the B-E-A moniker and even told him about the Just Bea accessory line.

A minute later I peeked my head over her shoulder. I had on one of the KISS demon masks from along the wall. I figured if Nick punched me in the nose it would hurt me less and him more.

"So listen, we're not even on the air. It's pretend, man. You don't have to get all violent on us, Nicholas Thrice."

Crablike, Nick backed himself off the table. Once standing he began straightening his plaid shirt and smoothing down his corduroys. He wasn't saying anything. He had come to his senses and his embarrassment showed.

"I take it we don't get the slot," Bea said with a grin.

"Please leave."

We headed for the door. When we had almost reached it I yelled, "Hey Nick, FAAC you!" I shook my demon face back at him and made a noise with my flapping tongue that sounded like *phlopa—phlopa—phlopa* through the mouthhole.

Bea led the way out of Room 5 and I ran after her. I was sure to check my back to ensure Nick wasn't chasing after us.

Bea was a bit perturbed at me. In a matter of speaking

the hallway wasn't big enough for the both of us and Bea said nothing as we ran.

We reached the lobby in due course. Rain streaming down the window made Bea remember she had forgotten her umbrella.

"Would you mind?" She took one look at the mask and said, "Forget it." Bea headed back down the hallway.

"What? I'm incapable of grabbing an umbrella just because I have a demon mask on?"

Kabala-la-las

AS I WAITED for Bea to come back down the hall, I peeked in Room 2. Deaddog, Pigtusk and Crazyred were going at it in macabre costumes that were as bad as their names. Arguing. Fighting. I heard the sound of frogs and saw a guy named Curlybeard sobbing in a corner.

Deaddog must have seen me through the door window. I saw him raise his snout in surprise at the demon mask. He pointed in my direction. That was my cue to get out of there.

Bea was making her way back up the hall. "Come on. The snouts are after us."

She caught up to me and we left FAAC TV in a hurry.

It wasn't until we were halfway down the sidewalk, tucked under the safety of the happy umbrella where I was sure not even a bomb could drop on us, when Bea realized I still had the demon mask on. She tore it off and tossed it in the bushes.

"What?"

"Brilliant Ant? The Disenfranchised? I don't remember agreeing to them as names for our band. In fact, I've never heard either until you announced them in front of the entire Florence cable access viewing area!"

"We weren't live. Besides, all great band names take time to grow. They are seeds planted in the mind. What about The Kabala-la-las? Would you have liked that better? It has a mystic ring to it."

"Ugh!"

"Now you're sounding like Charlie Brown."

We reached the meter maid car and I tried to get the door for Bea. She would have none of it. Before I could reach the handle she had opened the passenger-side door and was collapsing the umbrella (with my head still in it, mind you).

I extracted myself from the sunflower and got back inside

knowing I was in for a very long ride back to the apartment. For a moment I almost offered to walk.

"I want us to stand out, Bea. We own over ten thousand digital songs. It's rare that I know what band is even playing when one comes on that I like unless I've got their bumper sticker plastered on the back of my car. It's a digital whitewash. All binary ones and zeros. Bands don't stick out anymore. Our name has to command attention."

"I agree, Eddie. But the ones I've heard so far don't work for me."

"So Womanhole Cover doesn't rev your monkey?"

We pulled out of the FAAC TV parking lot.

"And what made you think about clowns right in the middle of our audition? Clowns!"

"It must've been the demon masks. Clowns traumatized me in my childhood. I'm not the first."

Thankfully Bea didn't continue the conversation until we had made it through a couple traffic lights. It went a little something like this—

"When I asked you to follow my lead, I wanted your comments to be more in line with mine. They were nothing of the sort. We lost any hopes of broadcasting Bea Excellent Always."

Two blocks of silence ensued.

"Hey, Bea?"

Nothing.

"Bea?"

"Three additional silent blocks."

"Bea?"

"What?"

"You're cute when you're mad."

"Just focus on driving."

The rain slowed to a patter on the windshield and I dialed down the wipers. Right after, I turned up the fan on the defogger. There was hot air o'plenty in the car. I was having difficulty seeing the road. Cars whizzed past us as if we were going in slow motion. This may come as a surprise, but the meter maid car is not the fastest on the road.

A billboard displayed an advertisement for an outfit called

the G Rafters. It was a rafting expedition trip to Costa Rica being offered by Virgil and the goons at the Zany Zoo Travel Agency.

"Maybe we need to get away to Costa Rica," I offered.

Bea was not easily distracted especially when she knew I did not have the money to pay for a trip to Cleveland let alone Costa Rica.

"I had a great concept for news that is positive and good. Now it's going nowhere."

"It would make the world a better place and I know you are all about that. I really do. I was hoping our music would be a way to do that."

"And it will, I just—"

"Sorry I screwed up back there."

Bea turned to me with those big green eyes, which caused me to take my eyes off the road. Her eyes are magnets. You have to look at them. You have to get lost in them.

"Remember, God loves you, Eddie, but he loves me best!" She flashed me a big-huge-I-want-to-eat-you-up smile.

"Aw Jezebel, Bea."

No sooner had I said those words than a truck horn blared at us from oncoming traffic. Bea shrieked. Time slowed. Tires churned. I jerked the slow, limbering, squat, three-wheeler back onto the right side of the road. A spray of water deluged us.

For a moment we had crash-landed in an underwater world as we peered through the windows of our triangular submarine. A Beatles tune marched through my head. Mailboxes (– Mansions – Memphistopheles) melted. Signs blurred. I hoped none of my bumper stickers washed off the back. Dead Milkmen stickers are hard to find! I also hoped the skull was still cable-tied to the front bumper. These were always my excuse for not washing the car. Bea said it was laziness.

A firm grip on the steering wheel got us righted. The windshield wipers, struggling against the torrent of water, began to make progress. Seconds later I could make out the signs of the various businesses dotting both sides of the road.

Without saying a word we rotated our necks and tried to return to a sense of normalcy, which does not happen often for us. Rain continued to beat a steady rhythm on our triangular tin can. Silence ensued for another mile, which, again, does not happen to us often.

"This has been a stressful day. Let's do something creative for dinner. I'm thinking Indian. I'm thinking chicken tikka masala. I'm thinking spicy."

"Yum. And basmati rice," Bea said.

"Why is one piece of rice pronounced the same as one thousand pieces of rice? Why isn't rices a word? Hey, I know where I can get an authentic recipe."

I took out my phone and brought up the stored number for customer service at our local Big Box store. In a few seconds I was on the horn to somewhere in India. I was exploiting a known fact. Anytime you call customer service in the United States you will be transferred to a call center in India. Mr. Gupta came on and I drilled him for his family's chicken tikka masala recipe. Bea scratched it down as I repeated it aloud.

When I got off the phone, Bea said, "You're dangerous and resourceful. Not necessarily in that order."

We stopped at an Indian grocer on the way home to pick up the ingredients, as I had none of it in the apartment. In truth, there were no ingredients for pretty much any dish from any country in my apartment unless macaroni-and-cheese counts. Bea reminds me it is not a food group.

Another two miles and we had reached the Edward T. Nad One Bedroom Palace of Awesomeness. Thunder boomed somewhere overhead. I grabbed the food out of the back hatch. There was no way I was going to try and infiltrate the dry confines of the sunflower umbrella on the way up the sidewalk.

Out of nowhere Bea snatched my arm. "You see that?"

"What?"

"That flash in the apartment window."

"Lightning, Bea. Lightning."

"Do you hear that buzzer?"

"Reverb!" The ringing was back. I hadn't heard it since

our last gig, which was quite a while ago. "Those stupid amps. We've got to get better earplugs, Bea."

She was now pointing at the bay window that juts out from the kitchen of my one bedroom apartment. "Look. Look! There's smoke!"

I stopped and turned. In the rain-dappled glass, I saw curls of gray wafting from the oven door. The mystic qualities froze me for a moment. I followed the stream of gray up to the ceiling where it joined a congregation of thickening air.

The bag of basmati rice, cumin powder, turmeric, low fat yogurt (thanks to Bea), ginger, cayenne pepper, lemons, onions, chicken, and butter crashed on the sidewalk.

We fixed on each other and said in harmony, "The cookies!" We had forgotten to take them out of the oven before leaving to visit our violent friend at FAAC TV. "Why didn't you take them out?" That was also in unison.

I rushed to the front door and fumbled for my keys that seemed lost inside the front pocket of my jeans.

"Come on. Hurry!" Bea implored.

I finally got them out and after a few shakes of the cheap lock—courtesies of the cheap landlord who doesn't even like our music—was able to rattle open the thin door.

We pushed our way inside. The smoke was worse than the circulating air at the final set of one of our gigs. The oven timer was blaring a monotonous tone. The smoke detector was not going off. It struck me I had not changed the batteries like, well, since I had last washed the car.

When I found Bea she was trying to beat back the smoke with the umbrella and looked pretty goofy doing it. She was collapsing it in-and-out, jellyfishlike. If any chick can look hot doing that, it's Bea. Seriously.

I swiped an old dishrag off the sink and ran to the oven. I flung down the door.

A cube of solid smoke blasted me. In the middle of it—in the horror of it—I thought I saw a flying grizzly. I really did.

Eyes watering, I was able to fish out the tray of charred cookies with the dishrag. I tossed them into the sink and turned on the faucet while Bea shut off the oven and slammed the door shut. She immediately pushed up the kitchen window. The smoky air began to get sucked out of the apartment.

The kitchen began spinning, but then it wasn't the entire kitchen, just the oven. My final recollection was looking—

Caiaphas

—AT THE GAUDY chandelier. That's all I could see through the smoke. From somewhere up above water was hitting me in the face. I thought I had been drug back out into the rain. The stupid oven buzzer was still going off, only it had gotten much louder. And Bea was yelling at me to get up. Yet she never calls me "Edward" unless she's mad at me, which is a lot of the time. Only, after a few harsh words, the voice was not that of my lead singer. The voice almost sounded like—

"—Virgil. Did you hear me, Edward? It's me. You have got to get off the floor. The hotel is on fire."

The stooge was shaking me and patting water on my face. "The oven," I said.

"I know it feels like an oven, Edward. That's what I've been telling you. The hotel is on fire!"

"Quit splashing water in my face. Okay? I'm awake. How did I get down here?"

"I tried to wake you, but you just turned over and rolled off the bed. Up! Up! We have to get moving."

I shot out of bed, knocked my head on the blasted chandelier, and stumbled past the end of the bed with an instant headache. The room was filling with smoke. These smoke detectors, unlike the ones in the apartment, worked. They were blaring the monotonous trumpets of Hades.

"What are you doing?"

"I'm rubbing my head and looking for my stompers."

"You put your combat boots outside the door to get polished. Remember? They are downstairs by now. Wear these."

Virg tossed me the pair of white, crested slippers out of the bathroom. They flapped against my chest and dropped to the floor. They were stamped with a trident that I was convinced, in all the heat and smoke, was Lucifer's pitchfork.

"I'm not wearing slippers. I'll go barefoot."

"Are you crazy, Edward? There will be broken glass everywhere, hot metal and wood."

"Thanks, Fire Marshal Virg." I reluctantly put them on while the sprinklers in the room splashed me across the shoulders and back.

"Now wear this, too."

That's when he threw me the hotel robe with another pitchfork on it.

"No way, Virg, I can get dressed."

"There's no time for that. You're in your boxers. Put it on! Get your wallet and passport, too. We have got to go!"

I had never seen Virg that animated. He had already thrown on his clothes and stuffed his suitcase. He stood there with his untucked Hawaiian shirt, looking even more embarrassing and frumpy than usual. I guess he did it while I was asleep on the floor and he was yelling at me. With a scowl, I slipped on the robe, all the time repeating aloud: "Rockers don't wear bathrobes and slippers. Rockers don't wear bathrobes and slippers. Rockers don't wear bathrobes and slippers."

Virg felt the door, verified it wasn't too hot, and told me to drop on hands and knees. He did the same after unlatching the lock and turning the door handle.

I checked outside and sure enough, Virg was right. My boots were no longer on the doorknob.

Crawling, we made a right out the door and started making our way down the hall. Tufts of flames were creeping up the wallpaper. One of the hunt club paintings was being swallowed by them; horses, foxes, and men with funny-funny caps.

For all the precautions of my guide, making military along the hallway floor was actually a good idea. The air was much cleaner than the streaks of gray writhing overhead. With Virg crawling in front of me, however, the view was terrible. I had no idea how he was pulling his suitcase along the carpet.

The sprinklers were on in the hall, too, and the back of my robe was sopping wet. It was getting heavier by the second. I alternated taking breaths through my nose and mouth.

People were screeching. A lady dashed by carrying a young child in her arms. Some guy in basketball shorts almost stepped on me, at least I hope it was a guy because he/she had hairy legs.

The fourth door we crawled past was canted open and an older lady was sitting outside, propped up against the wall. Her hair was stringy wet and lined in gray. She had dark streaks under her nose and at the sides of her mouth. She was hacking and wheezing for air.

"I'll be alright, Caiaphas," she kept saying to an older guy with curly hair who was kneeling alongside her.

"I am the chief sinner," he confessed. "I am the one who caused it all." Caiaphas was rocking back and forth, head in hands. "Forgive me, Ruth. If we don't make it out of here, forgive me. We have had such a wonderful life together and now this."

I peered into their room. Flames were dancing for joy on the bedcover. The lampshades on either side of the bed had turned into flambeaus.

"We've got to get the both of you out of here," Virg stated with uncommon forcefulness.

He took Ruth under one arm and Caiaphas took her under the other. I grabbed Virg's suitcase and kept crawling.

We noticed a few guys in white robes, stippled in bright silver and gold, directing hallway traffic up ahead. We were on the same floor, but it appeared we were looking down on them. The smoke was playing tricks. From it a knot of shouting and waving people were disappearing into a door on the left that had an exit sign above it. We knew the stairs were nearby.

In a few moments the four of us reached the stairwell that was dimly lit by the backup lights attached to the exit signs. We began our descent.

We immediately merged into a crush of people streaming down from the floors above us. A heavenly host of white robes. It was as if a hundred choirs had taken up lodging at the Trident Hotel and church had just let out and the buffet restaurants had just opened for business.

Being on the thirteenth floor meant we had twenty-six flights of stairs to traverse. I didn't pay much attention to Virg and Caiaphas as they struggled with Ruth. Virg was struggling under her weight. She was saying she thought she could walk, but the guys would have none of it. "One step at a time now. Careful. Easy does it." I was just trying to get down the stairs without tripping in the horrible slippers. Having to lug Virg's suitcase did not help my balance, either.

Heated voices (no pun intended) rose up the stairwell. The entire hotel was being evacuated even though Caiaphas started the whole thing on the thirteenth floor. The firemonger. Right now he was going much too slowly for my taste. Felt like an hour until we were halfway down and a half hour more until we had just a couple floors left to go.

Sixth floor. Fifth. Fourth.

The air was getting cleaner and cooler. The floor indicator numbers were easy to read now as we passed each landing. Anxious voices chattered away, their sound bouncing off the concrete walls. Virg's forehead was dappled in sweat. The drone of the alarms was giving me a headache. The chandelier didn't help matters.

Third floor. Second. First.

A guy with thick glasses pushed me as he rushed toward the bottom. He had suitcase in hand. He almost knocked Virg and Ruth down as he passed.

"Watch it, loser," I called out.

Panting and tired, we reached the lobby. Firemen were swarming across the tile floor in their reflective outfits. Many had axes in hand. Cops were directing traffic. Ruth shook off Virg and Caiaphas. This was my opportunity to make Virg carry his own suitcase.

Ruth began walking slowly as people exiting the stairwell flowed haphazardly around her. Caiaphas the Sinner took her hand. I had half a mind to turn him in to the cops, but I just wanted to get out of the burning hotel.

Outside, the firemen and police directed us across the street with the rest of the streaming rush of people. The hotel had been cordoned off by yellow tape.

Once we got across we huddled on the corner with the

rest of the hotel guests. My ankles felt cold. I was used to having them encased in leather. A bank sign informed us it was near freezing. This struck me as bizarre as I watched flames shoot out the building on the thirteenth floor. All of us were still sweating from the escape.

One room blazed much brighter than the others on the unlucky floor. Virg nudged me and said in a hushed voice that he thought it was Caiaphas's room. A fire truck soon arrived to the applause of the crowd. Firemen hopped off in workmanlike fashion. Two began unraveling the firehose while two took an end and began hooking it up to a hydrant. They started blasting a constant stream of water into Caiaphas's room. It wasn't doing much good.

At this point I noticed a couple bald guys standing next to us in brown robes. The men were laughing and cutting up. Everyone around them, from the dower looks, found this to be inappropriate behavior.

"Where did you get those robes?" I questioned. "You look like two jovial friars—if I may be so bold—which I usually am."

The chuckling man next to me said, "That's exactly what we were just commenting on. We're bankers."

"So is my dad," I said.

"I doubt if they care," whispered Virg.

"Our flight was grounded. The hotel was chock full when we got here. All they had left was the penthouse and they gave that to us at no additional charge."

"Why didn't we get the deal, Travel Agent Virgil?"

"In the penthouse you get chocolate brown robes. Go figure. Combine that with our bald heads and we are surprised no one has asked us for communion."

We all started laughing. The people in the crowd scowled at us.

"Forgive me Father Friars, for I have sinned," I said.

"All we need is a Bible and a rope for a belt," one of them offered.

"Bet you make good cheese and wines," Virg added.

"That was almost funny, Virg." I then turned and leaned in close to one of the monks. "Actually, this guy over here is the one who needs Jesus. I think he set the hotel on fire."

Luckily Caiaphas failed to hear me.

The friar next to me said, "Great, they're shooting our holy water up into the building."

"It will be the most religious hotel around!"

At that we lost it. All the stress that had built up released in one belly-laughing outpour of misty breath. Even poor Caiaphas and Ruth smirked.

When Virg regained his composure, he turned around and told the glaring throng that we in no way were laughing at the situation across the street and that we would do anything in our power to assist.

"Up there," a lady of the crowd yelled, "on the ledge. Those men in the fancy robes. Look!"

The fog that grounded our flight had not lifted. As I peered up through it I noticed a few men walking on a narrow track outside the building as the hotel's stone gargoyles peered down on them from above. I had no idea how they got out there. Their white robes were stippled in that bright silver and gold, which glistened from the spotlights turned on them. I realized they were the ones who had been directing traffic on the thirteenth floor. They were the ones shouting at everyone to take the stairs and get out of the hotel. The hypocrites.

"Someone do something!"

The fully extended ladders on the fire trucks fell well short of the thirteenth floor. A fireman with a bullhorn warned them to stop moving. He said men were on their way up the stairs. Gasps rose up from the shivering crowd.

News anchors had arrived and were pushing-elbowing-tugging toward the front to record the event. A Latin cop named Jésus kept pushing them back from the cordoned off area. He was shouting many unintelligible words in Spanish that I cannot repeat here, especially since I don't remember what they were. A cop grabbed one of the news anchors and pinned him to the ground. He really did.

Beyond the crush of news anchors, more people were streaming out of the hotel lobby. I wondered how many it held when in full capacity, which Virg assured me that it was. I thought I saw Ruth and Caiaphas near the front of the people, but it was hard to tell. Light torched down from above, roiling back into itself.

Confusion reigned.

In the pervasive mist and smoke, a window was smashed by an ax. Then another. Glass sparkled down to the street and lay glittering and useless, which is the way I felt.

Yellow arms reached out one of the broken windows. Then another. Hands latched onto the gilded robes and slowly pulled each one inside from the ledge. When the last of them had disappeared, the crowd applauded.

This was the only good news of the evening. I was sure, however, that Bea could've made even more good news come out of it.

As we stood there watching the excitement from across the street, a loud explosion boomed from the hotel and fire shot from a window on our unlucky floor.

Drapes flapped and fire spewed out the sides of the new hole like a pernicious (that was Virg's word) reptile waking from its cave. Chunks of burning furniture scattered into the night. A few objects landed across the street and rolled to a burning halt at the feet of the berobed hotel guests who were quite good at hopping in their slippers. The crowd, which collectively ducked and weaved with the dexterity of a prizefighter.

"Fire in the hole," I kept repeating to all while bending down into the huddle. I actually liked the warmth from the closeness and hey, I wasn't about to get my head taken off by a flaming hotel Bible.

Virg was hunched down there with me.

Vanni Fucci

"I SHOULD ENCORPORATE fiery projectiles into my gigs."

"As long as they are soft."

Minutes passed without so much as a hunk of cushion shooting by us in our hunched positions. We hoped that it was now safe and took a chance by standing back up.

Wouldn't ya know it, another flaming piece of furniture spun toward me at such velocity I could not get out of the way. It skipped along the pavement twice, like a pitch in a cricket game the Indians play out behind my apartment, and bounced right up my robe without even asking me to dinner first.

I did a little dance and then an impromptu ballet move of sorts where I scissored my legs in the air. This was every bit as embarrassing as the move Virg let loose in the Bacheron Airport of Florence. And don't laugh because it's hard to move in bath slippers. Really hard.

Before I could go airborne again, I felt a tap on the shoulder. Actually it was more a hand pinning me down to Mother Earth than a tap. I flung around to behold the hotel clerk who checked us in. She was standing right behind me in her radiant glory.

I had forgotten her name. *Jesse? Julia?* Her big obnoxious nametag reminded me before she could set me straight. In all the uncertainty I was happy to see *Jennifer.*

"I know what you're thinking. I usually don't go out in my bathrobe."

She was pointing to the ground. Her eyes were saucers.

"I don't go out in bath slippers either and yes, yes, I will return them."

"Oh, I don't care about that. I just wanted to let you know your slipper is on fire."

I glanced down. "Jezebel!" I started pogo-sticking on my

other leg while flicking my other ankle. "Do something, Virg. Like now!"

"Hold still," he was saying as he tried to grab my ankle that I had up in the air.

The crowd of people around us stepped back and formed a circle eight with me in the center.

Jennifer got down on her knees and was fanning my slipper like it was her official job at the hotel or something. The moving air was only making it worse. Flames were up to my shin.

The slipper had the best idea of us all. It flopped off my foot after a karate chop that I did out of reflex more than anything else. Virg immediately grabbed the back end. He beat it against the sidewalk until the fire extinguished into a smoldering clump.

I was holding onto Jennifer's shoulder for balance. If my barefoot had touched the freezing sidewalk it would have been stuck there until summer. This was no mystery given the chill air rushing up my boxers and turning peculiar parts of me into ice cubes.

Virg handed the smoking, burnt footwear back to me. The pitchfork crest was charred. I didn't care with the wind whistling through my toes and turning them into ice pops. I slid it back on in a hurry. It felt warm and cozy. Believe me.

I turned to the circle eight crowd, which had taken an uncommon interest in me, and pointed at Virg. "Don't ever go on a trip with this guy. You might as well be traveling through Helicon. I said Helicon with a capital H."

Once I had calmed down I thanked Jennifer. She gave me a smile. I think the robe and slippers turned her on. She told us she had been working the graveyard shift when the fire alarms went off. Virg asked not to be charged for the room, which Jennifer said she would look into, but didn't think it a problem.

Those overhearing us in the crowd applauded. The applause, however, quickly turned to gasps as we noticed part of the reptile flying through the air with fiery wings. It caught a guy in the neck. Square on. He crumpled to the ground with a horrid purl of anguish that rose above any of the machinery or commotion going on outside the hotel. Emergency workers rushed over to him while Jésus, the Latin cop, pushed harder than ever on the wall of news anchors inching toward the hotel instead of away from it. The injured man quickly disappeared into the yellowy crescent the paramedics formed around him.

Standing there, freezing, I glanced down the street I noticed a few pickpocket kids having a banner night in all the confusion. They were targeting the valuables hotel guests had stashed in their robe pockets on the way out the door. I let Virg and Jennifer know there were thieves around. Jennifer indicated she would be back and then walked off. I assumed she was going to get one of the cops directing traffic at the lobby entrance.

Next to us a dark-haired man struck up a conversation. Right off we noticed he was not wearing the obligatory robe. This made me suspicious with the pickpockets stalking their prey. Yet, he was friendly enough in an Old World sort of way. I don't know how to describe him other than he could have been one of those guys you see on a pasta sauce label. I wanted to know his name. It struck me there was something familiar about this fellow. His clothes were fine and so were his looks. I could not place him.

"I'm Edward T. Nad. I know. It's my parents fault. Anyway, what's your name?"

He grimaced. "I would rather not for security reasons."

"Security is why I am asking. There are thieves out tonight."

"I understand. I'll show you my Id." The forthright man reached in his back pocket and pulled out his wallet. "I am not happy about this," he said before sliding his driver's license out with his thumb. Vannivauld Fucci is what I saw.

"Thank you. Your family makes nice handbags."

He struck me as odd. Oh he looked fine. There were no giant moles on his face or birthmarks. His hair was normal enough. It had a gentle curl to it. He certainly didn't have a swooping combover *a la* Virg. Still, I could not shake the overriding sensation that there was something weird about him.

Vanni Fucci asked us to step closer. He said he had a most amazing story to convey of his grandfather's time in the theatre.

"Let's hear it," I said, placing a hand on my wallet. "It will help us pass the time and hopefully take our mind off this cold."

"You see, fine sirs, my grandfather, Salvatore Fucci, used to be a renowned Shakespearian actor. I will never forget when he told me what happened to him after one of his performances in New York and the curse it branded on our family to this day. Lend me your ears and I will tell you."

Virg chuckled at that last part. I don't know why. I shrugged. There was nothing else to do. "We're all ears."

"Nonno, which is the Italian name we called Grandfather Fucci, had stepped off the platform, stage right, and into the dusty wings of Brant's Theatre after his curtain call. The audience was beside themselves. He had given one of the best performances of his magnificent career.

"Mary Brant, the stagehand and daughter of the owner, was waiting for him.

"Always the perfectionist, my grandfather chided her. 'You had the oil lamps behind the seashells too bright. I am still blinking them away.' Nonno was the first to admit that Shakespearean-trained actors can take themselves too seriously at times. 'My shadow was ten foot tall.'

"'Sorry. You know I'm a one gal outfit since the Depression started.'

"He collapsed onto a Shaker chair and began unlacing his boots. 'Standing room only. Just goes to show how people will pay for entertainment even in the darkest of economies.'

"Mary handed him a rag and he began wiping off the garish face paint (or what we today term 'makeup'), being careful not to get any on his ruffled Elizabethan shirt.

"'You knocked them out tonight. Mr. Fucci. Really. The audience may never stop clapping. Macbeth was swinging.'

"Mary always called characters by their proper names, my grandfather told me, as if they were real.

"'I'm sure Shakespeare just rolled over in his grave, but thanks.' He pinched her cheek. 'That made up for the oil lamps. Be sure to tell your father how good I was.'

"Once he had caught his breath (There were no smokier venues in the Thirties than theaters!) and changed into his street clothes in one of the carrels backstage, he left by the rear door.

"The Brant Theatre was rectangular and stretched toward Thirteenth Avenue where my grandfather hoped to catch a taxi after the patrons had cleared out. Adjacent the theatre was what used to be a real estate office or upper-crust restaurant or some other prosperous business in the Roaring Twenties that was now a Hoover Hotel where a multitude of homeless people were taking refuge. My grandfather saw one of them coming towards him in the alleyway. He was a short one at that.

"Slung over his shoulder was a large feed sack tied at the end with a chord, protruding and bulging at the sides. It appeared he had a squirmy animal inside trying to get free. He was struggling under the weight of it. At times the wriggling thing inside would knock him off balance, which required him to stop and readjust the sack.

"As he got closer in the sallow, quavering light of the alley, my grandfather was surprised to find this was not a man at all, but a boy. He couldn't have been over ten and was the most finely dressed child he had ever seen. That is saying a lot after being around the theatre and the finery of its patrons for so many years.

"During the Great Depression labor laws were routinely being violated. Kids worked night and day to help support their families, Mary Brant being one of them. Grandfather was used to seeing them in ragtag clothing, without coat or shoes, many begging for bread or even a little flour. But this kid! He was dressed to kill; hair slicked back, three-piece, pinstriped suit, silk hankie, tab collar, cufflinks, tie, buffed shoes that had a dark sheen.

"On his approach, my grandfather puffed out his chest. He figured he had slipped away from his wealthy parents after the show. 'Autograph, kiddo?'

"The boy looked puzzled. 'No, sir. What ever for?'

"Ego weakened, but curiosity remaining strong,

Grandfather asked, 'What do you have in there? In the burlap sack?'

"'Why shadows. I collect them.'

"Of all the responses Grandfather expected, that was not one of them. The kid said it in a way that made you think *everyone* collected shadows and carried them around in a burlap sack.

"Nonno laughed aloud over the bleating of horns on the avenue just outside the alley. 'Good one, kid.'

"'It's a lot of work, mister. To be honest, they fidget like the dickens.'

"Grandfather decided to play along. 'If you got shadows in there, let me see them.' The night was young and he had just given the performance of his life. At the far end of the alley he glimpsed theatergoers jostling for the few available taxis out on Thirteenth Avenue. He had time to kill.

"The kid slid the burlap sack off his shoulder and it landed on the brick pavement with a thud. He undid the leather chord tied around the neck of the sack. 'I'm serious, sir. Real, live shadows. Have a look. Don't open the end too much or they'll escape.'

"Nonno eased over the sack expecting a stray cat to spring out at any second and the joke would be on him. He flinched up every time a jab or bend stretched the material from inside. There was more than one animal in there all right. At last he was squarely over the mouth of the sack that was formed by the kid's two small hands. He slowly peered inside where he saw a cauldron of swirling nothingness the color of a moonless night. Dark shades of gray were churning, foglike. But there were no animals inside or Nonno would have at least seen their shimmering eyes. For a moment he regained his composure—composure that a man of the stage is never to lose—and reached his hand inside, expecting to pull out a tiny boy by the tuft of his hair, dressed in sable clothing and giggling.

"His arm plunged down to the elbow. Nonno's hand went on a search mission. Unbelievably he felt nothing but air inside. Swore to it even on his deathbed. He felt every inch of the sack only to come up empty handed. Yet somehow the sack had weight.

"'Nice trick, kid. Someday you will have to show me how you did it.' Shaking his head, Grandfather began to walk away. It had been a long night.

"'Oh it's no trick, sir. I can assure you. I'll sell the shadows to you. Hundred bucks apiece.'

"The sincerity in his voice caused Nonno to stop and turn back. 'Sure you will. Why not a thousand bucks each? Now it's getting late. You should be on your way home. If your parents are waiting for you out front of Brant's Theatre they will be getting worried.'

"'My rates are going up all the time. Imagine being at a beach on Long Island or a family picnic and having the shade of a giant tree with you at all times. I can sell you the shadow of the entire First National Bank Building to keep the sun away. That will be double the price.'

"'You have some imagination.' He ruffled the kid's parted hair and declined the offer. He once again began to walk away. The kid was not finished.

"'If you don't want yours, I'll take it, mister.'

"'My what? My shadow? You'll take my shadow from me?'

"'That's right.'

"The kid was persistent. He had to give him that. My grandfather knew he was going nowhere fast unless he abided him. Nonno took a deep breath and looked down. A distant streetlamp formed a crag of light along the kid's shiny hair and shoes. 'What's it going to cost me?' Nonno was fully ready to give kid a couple of bucks. The boy did not lack in the entrepreneurial department. Grandfather had witnessed many begging schemes on the streets of New York since the Market crashed, but never one like this.

"'Nothing, mister. My pleasure. I'll take your shadow for free.'

"'What's in it for me?'

"'What everybody is looking for these days, a way to stand apart from the millions of people in this city. Uniqueness.'

"Nonno played along. 'So having no shadow will make me unique.'

"'The most special cat around.'

"My grandfather nodded and smiled.

"'Remember to take off your shoes so I get the whole thing.'

"'Hope this won't hurt,' Nonno said with a smirk as he unlaced his brown and whites. 'Make it fast.'

"Grandfather watched him hold up the sack so that it was horizontal to the brick pavement. It was still jutting out in random places, what looked to be protrusions of elbows and legs and feet trapped inside. This was some trick the boy had mastered!

"He braced the large end of the sack against his bony chest and placed one skinny leg at an incline behind him to shore himself. Both hands were around the mouth of the sack and he slowly opened its pursed lip, then its throat.

"Nonno felt a great wind arise out of nowhere in the tight alleyway, but it was not a stirring wind. It had direction and purpose. A biting force. His lapels saluted and his derby began sliding off his head right toward the sack. His pant legs were flapping out in front of him and formfitting to his hamstrings. The tie encircling Grandfather's neck was pulling his head toward the kid as though attached to an invisible tugboat.

"Alleyway litter began collecting (and Nonno said 'collecting' because there was an order to its movement) like an air funnel was being used to force it toward the compelling suction generated at the mouth of the sack. He felt a tin can assail him in the back.

"He could not breathe—he swore to it—nor could my grandfather hold his footing any longer. His socks were slipping on the bricks. A crate hit the brick wall of the theatre and splintered into pieces. Just as he was about to go airborne, the sucking force died as quickly as it started. His derby fell to the ground and liter stopped pelting him.

"Once Nonno caught his breath, he said, 'Don't know how you pulled that off, kid, but it was real good. You should try Vaudeville sometime.'

"The following morning was Sunday and Grandfather slept until noon. His rousing performance of *Macbeth* the night before had sapped him of energy more than expected.

He was dehydrated—tongue a wad of cotton. He should have drunk a gallon of water when he got back to his apartment instead of collapsing.

"He peeled himself off the sofa and struggled into the tiny kitchen of his apartment where he threw down a glass of water and massaged a sore neck. The fridge was bare and he decided to hit a local diner for brunch.

"In the hallway of his apartment the elevator arrived after a short delay and the operator slid open the accordion gate. On his head was a monkey cap and he looked absurd as always. 'Heard you really knocked them out last night, Mr. Fucci.'

"'I try.'

"They must have had the express car because it went straight to the lobby without so much as a stop, which was fortunate because Nonno was in no mood for chitchat on an empty stomach. The floor indicator arm ticked off nine times without pause. On the way down he noticed out of the corner of his eye that the operator was shooting him a cockeyed look. A *strange* look.

"'There's something different about you, Mr. Fucci. I'm having trouble placing it. New haircut? Losing weight?'

"'No on both accounts. Just hungry if you can detect *that*.'

"The elevator came to a stop. The operator paused before unlatching the accordion gate. 'I'm not joking, Mr. Fucci. Broadway is eyeing you. Keep it up.'

"'You'll say anything for a tip.' The young man grinned as my grandfather pressed a quarter into his palm, but this time he actually *believed* the compliment. He *had* knocked them dead the night before.

"A few steps into the lobby and he realized he had forgotten his money clip back in the apartment. He turned to go back up the elevator. The operator was still there, holding the door open and considering him in the oddest way beneath the monkey cap. Patting his back pocket, Nonno felt a lump and waved him off, but he would not stop staring. *The morning reviews must be something!* Nonno thought.

"He made quick work of the lobby, saluted the doorman on the way past, and headed up Twenty-seventh Street. The day was bright and warm; so warm he peeled off his coat after the first block and by the third he was hugging the buildings to keep in the shade.

"Grandfather walked at a fast pace on his mission to get some food and drink. Flapjacks and coffee. The sudden blast of sunshine didn't strike him as odd until he was almost past it. A sense of unbelief made him pause. Right there in the middle of New York City was a pathway of sunshine, which is impossible to find in front of a building when the sun is behind it and the buildings on either side are casting huge shadows over the sidewalk.

"Was he the only one who noticed it? Those on the sidewalk were bustling past on their way back from Sunday morning services or racing toward the few department stores that had the gall to open on the Lord's Day. In their New York City minute none of them were noticing what, to Nonno, was plain as day . . . plain as daylight that is.

"Squinting up, he looked at that building from every angle to see if there was a missing overhang or glass-walled floor letting rays of sunlight past. What could it be about this one building? His false hope was dashed when he realized the façade was similar to the buildings casting shadows next to it. This left him counting the floors, but this was useless because the building was equal in height to the adjacent structures. Impossibly, the sun was making it *through* the building. At that moment he saw the chiseled stone faceplate: FIRST NATIONAL BANK. For the first time he remembered the kid from the alley and his words: *I could sell you the shadow of the entire First National Bank Building to keep the sun away.*

"The old First National Bank Building was not casting a shadow.

"And when Nonno looked at his feet, he wasn't either.

"A dozen people must have bumped into him while he spun in the middle of the sidewalk searching for it. One gentleman stopped to help him look for the money he had dropped or spectacles, but he told him it was hard to explain and he started walking. He was crestfallen on the way to the diner. No telling how many times people told him to watch where he was going on the busy New York streets or how many horns blared at him as he crossed the street against traffic in his daze. He tried desperately to deny it and pretend that it had not happened to him.

"When Nonno finally arrived at the diner he had forgotten why he was going there. Before opening its shiny glass doors he glanced up and noticed the sun waxing high overhead. That explained it. No one has a shadow when the sun's directly above them! It can get lost in the feet. That's what he blamed on his shadow's disappearance. He did a little two-step looking for it to no avail.

"Inside he blew right past the PLEASE WAIT TO BE SEATED sign and stole into a booth bathed in sunlight from high windows. He uselessly tried to make hand-shadows on the table, butterflies to match the ones in his gut. Something so simple had never been so frustrating. His greatest fears were realized when he made the napkin holder cast a dark gray shadow on the tabletop next to his nothingness.

"'. . . ask the manager if you can buy one.'

"Over the clink of plates and coffee mugs he began thinking of how important a shadow was. Like everyone else in the world he had never thought twice about it.

"'. . . couple bucks, tops.'

"The color of his skin was flushed more than ashen. He had no thirst for blood as best he could tell. He felt his canines and they were not growing into points. Vampirism was out of the question.

"'. . . your hearing?'

"A hand waving in front of his face caused him to notice the waitress. She had blue hair and pencils sticking behind each ear. She had been standing there for a while.

"'I said you can buy the napkin holder if it's so interesting. I can speak with the manager.'

"'No thanks,' he said sheepishly. She was speaking way too loud. The last thing he wanted was attention.

"'There's something different about you. Can't place it. You're not from around here, are ya? Midwest?'

"'Actually, I . . . never mind.' Nonno decided to dispense with any talk of the theatre.

"'Just going to sit there admiring your hands or do you want food? The breakfast special today is—'

"New York waitresses never cut you slack. He had yet to peruse the menu or even swipe a paper to read his review. 'Give me some coffee—black.' His hunger had disappeared and he just wanted to get out of there, to get back to his apartment. Everyone was staring or was it his imagination? 'Make that to go.'

"Fifteen minutes later Nonno arrived at his apartment and didn't leave for two days. Time was spent commiserating with himself. He shone lights on every part of his body to no shadowy avail. Over and over he was reminded of the things we take for granted in life: ten toes, lips, fingernails, eyelashes . . . the little things . . . little things like being able to cast a shadow!

"Tuesday night was the next performance of *Macbeth*. If Saturday night was the best performance of his life, then this was the worst. When he first took the stage he noticed the audience pointing and whispering . . . or thought he did. His performance as the lead in *Macbeth* was fine. In many ways he thought it was actually better than Sunday's. The reviews, however, were horrible. They had noticed his missing shadow. He just knew it. How could one not attract attention when on stage in front of a thousand people?

"Each succeeding night got progressively worse. He kept telling Mary to decrease the lamplight suffusing the stage from behind the seashells. Lower and lower. He found himself unscrewing light bulbs before the crowd arrived. Logic told him the darker he got the stage, the less people would notice his missing shadow. His plan failed miserably when Mary's father, the theatre's owner, got involved.

"'What happened, Sal? It's like you're not the same person out there.'

"'Nothing has happened. Believe me. It is the same performance I have always given. I am trying my best, I can assure you.'

"Harold Brant began sniffing around Nonno's clothing. He made a complete revolution. 'You have been great for this theatre and we have always been honest with each other.

Tell me straight out, have you been hitting the bottle?'

"'Not a drop. You know I am a teetotaler.'

"My grandfather knew Harold Brant didn't believe him, and his ensuing action confirmed that. His hand landed on Nonno's shoulder. 'I'm sorry, Sal. You know we go way back. Ticket sales have dropped thirty percent this week alone. The theatre will go under with those numbers. I have called up your understudy. When you are back to your old self, stop by. This summer we are going to run through the *Twelfth Night*. Come back for a reading.'

"Mary was crying off to the side. Over the last year they had become friends in almost a sibling sort of way. Nonno darted to his carrel and snatched up his belongings. The shelves had been ravaged in Harold's search for a liquor bottle while my grandfather was on stage.

"Jobless, Nonno had all the time in the world to look for the kid with the sack. He searched day and night for the dapper guttersnipe, down every alley and up every soup line, trash dumps and orphanages, shipyards. His quest took him to some of the worst of areas. One night he was nearly mugged along the docks of the Hudson. If the kid took his shadow, then it could be returned. He *had* offered Nonno the constant shade of the old First National Bank Building; so the mystic process was a two-way street.

"Grandfather was obsessive in his search. His livelihood and rent payments depended on it. Yet finding a nameless kid in New York City is near impossible. Street after street, building after building, he was relentless.

"Weeks passed. What little money he had stuffed under his mattress had run out and he was evicted. Landlords during the Great Depression had little tolerance for late payments from Italian immigrants. On that very day Nonno found himself not at the diner but in the back of a soup-line at a Hoover Hotel in lower Manhattan. He stood right next to bankers and lawyers. This made him feel no better. The fall from Broadway potential—theatrical darling of the rags—to homelessness, was a hard and brutal one.

"'What's the soup *du jour*?' he asked the guy in front of him in line.

"'Water flavored with salt-n-pepper.'

"'You really know how to cheer a guy up,' he was retorting when he glanced and saw him at the corner. The kid!

"Grandfather could have spotted him a mile away in his fancy little clothes. The guttersnipe was one of the most nicely dressed people in the entire city. The shadow trade had been good to him.

"Slung over his pinstriped suit was the squirming sack. Nonno had expected to find him on an ominous day in a dark alley. Alas, it was a beautiful, sunny day and he was standing right out in public, talking to some lady and pointing at the sack, trying to strike another deal.

"Nonno took off running in a dead sprint. The kid failed to see him coming from a quarter of a block away. Nonno latched onto his lapels, thinking he would try to escape, yet the boy made no movements to that effect.

"Instead he chided, 'Hey. Hey. Stop wrinkling my suit. A businessman has to look good in this town.'

"My grandfather did not let go. Instead he turned to the lady that was with the kid. 'What ever you do, Miss, do not let him take your shadow. It'll ruin your life.'

"Nonno was panting and unshaven. The lady gave him the strangest of looks before crossing the street in a hurry.

"'You just lost me a customer. What's the big idea?'

"'I should be asking you that! Give me my shadow back right now!'

"'Shhh! Keep your voice down. You're going to lose me more business.'

"You can only imagine the stares Nonno was getting from the others waiting on the corner, but he didn't care. He jerked the kid over to the side of a building where there was less pedestrian traffic and pushed him against the wall. 'Is that what this is to you, only a business? You're worried about money while I just lost my job and apartment. A career I built over a lifetime of acting. What are you going to do, charge me for my shadow?'

"'A thousand bucks.'

"Nonno had the kid by the collar now, right under his perfectly knotted necktie. He saw in his rage that he was lifting the kid off the ground, inch-by-inch. His polished shoes were dangling off the sidewalk. 'The shadow. That's mine. No different than my hand. It's a part of me and you took it.'

"'No, you gave it to me for free. Remember? Fair and square. Evens up. I offered you the shadow of the First National Bank and you didn't want it. I told you my prices were going up.'

"'That how you wear those fancy clothes? Conning people? Well I have news for you, I'm not paying a nickel for my shadow. And it had better be in there or else!' Nonno dropped him and tore the heavy sack away from the kid. He began untying the leather chord around its mouth.

"'Please, mister, don't that! You don't understand. It's very dangerous. *Please!*'

"Nonno had the mouth of the sack open. Back straining under the weight, he lifted it off the ground. Grandfather took the bottom of the sack and dumped its contents out on the sidewalk.

"The kid was pleading with him. '*NO!*'

"A blob of darkness spilled out of the sack like crude oil. It congealed for a moment on the sidewalk as if it had center cohesiveness, then began moving and spreading. The writhing mass quickly enveloped all who had gathered to watch the commotion. Nonno felt he was twisting through tattered, ashen sheets that the sunlight was useless in penetrating. The palpable gloom rose into the air, carrying with it the anguished screams of the horrified.

"An amorphous shape crept up one side of the building, staining the windows and brickwork, floor after floor. It hovered above the avenue. Men screamed and ladies fainted. Minutes later it began rising and expanding upward, a throng of shadowy angles, writhing arms and legs and chiseled stonework from which light neither escaped nor penetrated.

"And Nonno, defenseless, stood there mumbling lines from *Macbeth* to cover the screams:

> *What are these*

So withered and so wild in their attire,
That look not like the inhabitants of th' earth
And yet are on't?"

"That is a fantastic story!" Virg exclaimed.

"And your grandfather told you this on his deathbed?" I asked.

"We all knew the story. It is one told to the youngest of children in our family. It is one we must live with our entire lives. For you see, all of Nonno's descendants are under the curse."

"You mean—"

"None of us have shadows. The disease—and I am fully convinced it is a disease—is hereditary. No one is to know our family's name if they also know the damnation that has befallen us since the Great Depression." Vanni Fucci pointed and cursed me for making him tell his name.

"No offense, dude." Standing there, I realized why I thought there was something odd about him. I looked at the wall behind him and no shadow wavered in the tremulous firelight of the building across the street.

Infernally Yours

AFTER VANNI FUCCI concluded his story, Virg asked if I was going to faint again like I did in the jet bridge and I stomped his foot a good one. I forgot I was only wearing slippers. On impact it felt like every frigid bone in my foot shattered. I was beginning to really miss my combat boots. Might as well be missing my arms, but then I couldn't drum or anything.

Jumping around I noticed a glint of pink in one of Vanni's hands. It was not the shiny pink of a ring stone or bracelet, but rather a dull pink that did little to reflect the glow of the hotel fire. Immediately I recognized it.

"That's mine!" I shouted.

"What? What?" Vanni's thick eyebrows were cheap window blinds going up and down.

"In your hand. Open it. There. No, the *other* hand."

A folded piece of paper emerged as his fingers straightened. I stopped grabbing my foot and snatched it away.

"You're the biggest thief of them all. This was in my robe pocket. You should be ashamed." I immediately checked for my wallet and passport. Thankfully they were still there. "Let me tell you—"

I was not finished berating Vanni when he stole the slip of paper back from me in one quick snap of his wrist.

I immediately stretched for it and he moved away.

"This is a letter from a lady named Beatrice. Since Edward here made me divulge my family name and secret, I believe I should read it aloud for all to hear."

"Give me that." I was swatting at it, reaching, grabbing, robe flapping open.

Vanni cleared his throat.

"I'm not playing around. That is my property. Now give—"

Virg had to open his trap. "Besides your wallet and

passport that is the *only* item you grabbed out of the burning room. Isn't it, Edward? You thought more about this letter than anything else."

"That is not true. What do I care about any stupid letter from Bea? It's just that . . . it's just . . . it's mine, that's all . . . the letter must have fallen in my pocket in my hurry to leave the room."

"Hear ye, hear ye," Vanni Fucci said as he began reading.

> *Dear Eddie,*
> *Just wanted to let you know, for no particular reason, that I'm really into you. Sometimes I don't feel that I show it. From the start it has been a great ride (apart from the little fire in the oven, and hey, we got the manager to replace the fire alarms in the entire apartment complex so good came out of that, too). And speaking of rides, from our very first date (if you call getting coffee then eating snow cones in front of the Piggley Wiggley while riding mechanical cows and thinking of lyrics, a first date), to all the places we've been in the sputtering meter maid car with only a few breakdowns on Highway 51, the ride with you has been fabulous.*
> *I want to know—and you have probably already figured this out—I am down to earth and don't need fancy cars and bling-bling to be happy. I mostly like to write and play great music, and, of course, make the world a better place if I have half the chance. There is that whole obsession thing about my boot collection, but let's try to forget about that, k?*

A semi-circle of robed guests had formed around us. They were giving me a collective look that had, *Bea sounds like a great person,* written all over it. Can you believe it? Vanni played to the crowd, too. They appeared really into the letter as they stood there in the darkness listening.

> *Dad (AKA, random ghost) always taught me that when someone gives you a container of macadamia*

nut cookies you should return it full. In a strange way you are my cookie jar, Eddie. Not that you're hollow and round, or made out of ceramic or anything. Lol.

Did you know it's easier to smile when the sun is out? I have come to that conclusion ;o) It's my theory that people in the South get wrinkled faster not from the sun's rays but rather from all that sunshine that makes it easier for them to laugh and smile. Laugh lines get longer where it's sunny.

Alright, I feel like I'm rambling. Hope I'm not boring you. I truly believe our two-person band can work. It will be a good marketing tool if nothing else.

BTW, I am almost finished with the lyrics for our third song. Think you and me. Think we.

I am infernally yours.

"And get this, everybody," Vanni continued. "Instead of the letter closing with 'Best regards' or 'Take care,' it ends with 'Licks and nibbles,' and then it's signed 'Bea good.' Can you believe that, gentlepeople of the Trident Hotel? 'Licks and nibbles!'"

The crowd began laughing. A woman said she wanted to meet Bea. A businessman said I was lucky to have her. I heard a girl say she thought Bea's closing was cute. Cute!

"You finished?" I said to Vanni. "Feel vindicated now for having to tell us your family name and its dark secret?"

He paid me no mind and kept reading. "Listen to this everyone. There's more.

P.S. Hope you weren't attacked by clowns today!

I finally managed to snatch the pink letter out of his hands and tie back the sash on my robe.

"Come on, people, Bea, my *very* former girlfriend, has some real faults. Like San Andreas deep. You look at me like she's some great person. Bea thinks the only thing the ironing board is good for is stacking dirty clothes on. You know, colds on one end, hots on the other. One time it tipped over on me in the middle of the night, after a gig, and busted my shin all up. If I ask her about the dirty clothes, she goes into a whole story about how colors are never created or destroyed. They are merely transferred from one part of the world to the other. People, I totally understand the looks you're giving me right now. Believe me, she's unbelievable. She claims no rockers iron their jeans or T-shirts, and for once I agreed with her on that one. 'What about my dress T-shirts? Ones that I wear to church?' I asked her. Bea didn't have much to say 'bout that. She even handwrites thank you notes. She has major issues. So stop giving me those looks. Bea broke up the band not me!"

I thought about taking up a collection for the band right then and there. Virg was patting me on the back as if that would help calm me down (because that's the kinda guy he is). I was getting a major sympathy vibe from the crowd when the shadowless Vanni Fucci disappeared into it before I could call him a thief one more time.

In exchange for my opinion, the crowd spewed Jennifer from the semi-circular mouth it had formed. She strolled back to our little gathering place. She nodded over to where Jésus and a couple other cops had four urchins spread eagle against the wall. These thieves had very non-American names, which, of course, you would expect in Washington, D.C.

"Agnello, Cianfa, Buoso, and Francesco," Jésus called out as he scanned their Ids beneath a flashlight.

It must have been the stress of the evening or the late hour that was affecting my eyesight. As I peered down the street, the thieves appeared to change and morph in the quavering firelight. For a moment they were undulating and merging into one another, then separating again. One became translucent. They were no longer solid beings. Think of heat rising off hot pavement. I had clearly inhaled too much smoke inside the hotel.

Unsure of what I was seeing, I blinked it off and sucked in a chunk of chilly night air. I glanced down the street again. The bodies were shifting, vibrating into each other. The cops were conducting business as if none of it was happening.

"Virg, Virg, do you see—"

At that moment Jennifer, our desk clerk extraordinaire, stepped in front of our sightline. Her pulled back hair, her trim outfit with the lapels and nametag, gave her an aura of command in our chaotic environment. Jennifer, the minimum wage hotel clerk, had become Queen of the Frenzied.

"Obviously no one will be let back in the hotel tonight. You two are welcome to crash at my place."

Virg and I looked at each other. We were freezing and ready to agree to stay anywhere to get out of the cold.

I socked Virg in the arm. "See how people treat you when you're a rockstar?"

Virg launched into some big dissertation about how he would recommend the hotel at the Zany Zoo Travel Agency for all her kindness.

Jennifer smiled that million dollar smile. "You can fight over the sofa. I have a postage stamp apartment."

"There's no fight. Virg here will be happy to sleep on the floor. He really will. Don't look at me like that, Virg."

Pitchfork PJs

BEFORE THE THREE of us turned to leave, we took one last glance at the fire. Don't ask me how long we stood there. All fires have a magnetic way of attracting attention. All fires are hypnotic. That's why I had told Bea we needed fire in our show. The one that began on our floor (thanks to Caiaphas) was still firing occasionally in the fog. The fire was spreading. Windows were now lit on the entire thirteenth floor. As we stood there squinting, we noticed people moving behind the dancing flames. One of us said that we hoped it was the firemen putting the fire out.

We could take no more.

Thankfully the nearest subway entrance was close by. You would not believe the amount of cold wind that can find its way up a robe in Washington D.C. and right into a rockstar's innards.

We waited for the Greenline to Jennifer's apartment. It was to arrive at 3:08 AM. When it did, I saw zero eight on the side of it. I was seeing circles and eights everywhere in the subway station and blamed it on the fire.

When the doors retracted we hurried to get on and get warm. Virg hit my knee with his stupid suitcase on his rush to get inside despite us being the only people to get onto the Metrorail this time of night. Virg is the type'a guy who's scared the subway doors will close on him when no one is around and he will stuck there until morning.

I said something to him about it, too. Don't think I didn't.

Sitting down, looking in the back, it was just as I suspected. There were a few homeless people riding and riding the tube all night to stay warm. They were the smart ones indeed. Ever notice it's only the rich people who say wealth is overrated? I never met a homeless guy who tells me money is a big exaggeration.

The electromagnets soon were energized and the subway hummed off into a myriad of tunnels that snaked beneath the nation's capitol. It took me awhile to get used to sitting in a robe, especially with Jennifer positioned right across from me—legs crossed (too uncomfortable)—legs to the side (too awkward)—feet together, robe tucked between my legs (just right).

The events of the night had us all in a daze as lights flashed out the windows. Stops and colorful tunnels came and went. Announcements on the overhead speakers rang out in a tone of importance as if anyone was listening. Finally I said to Jennifer, "Aren't you scared? I mean inviting two strangers over to your apartment to crash?"

She flashed a grin. "What possible harm can a guy in a Hawaiian shirt and one in a stolen hotel robe with a burnt slipper cause me?"

I elbowed Virg. "She's got us there."

We stopped at a few more stations and shot through a few more tunnels with hellish artwork until Jennifer pointed out our stop.

We soon exited the Metrorail and climbed the stairs to street level, with Virg thumping his suitcase up every riser because the escalator was broken.

"Don't worry," I said to Jennifer, "he's always annoying. Just try to ignore him."

Her apartment was a block away. She lived on the second floor of a brownstone and shared her space with some broad named Cheryl who left a few days before to go home for Easter in Arizona. Jennifer clicked open the door and flicked on the lights. She had the classic layout of futons and a few velvet beanbag chairs scattered about. Dying plants sat along the window ledge that fronted the street. A square coffee table. A small TV. Folded tray tables. A cat (I hate cats). The usual minimalism.

This popped a name into my head. "The Extravagant Minimalists might work for our band, Virg, or the Wumpus Underground."

"Oh, so you two are in a band," Jennifer said with the usual excitement to her voice that I hear when a chic finds this out.

"Virg in a band? Ha! Does it look like he has a cool bone in his frumpy body? He's my bad-dressing manager and that's all."

"Don't forget tour guide."

"So you're on tour?" Jennifer asked while she removed her pumps and sat them next to the door in a rubber tray.

"I wouldn't exactly call it that."

"It's more like a miserable vacation that Virg suckered me into. More like a Hades hiatus. Especially after tonight."

"That explains why the rest of your band isn't around."

"Edward is pretty much it."

"Come on, Virg, you make the band sound so tiny. We need a perception of largess. What kind of promoter are you?"

"I'm sorry I asked. Have a seat, guys. It's been a long night for all of us."

Virg plopped into a beanbag chair and I leaned across the futon, making sure to tidy up the dark underworld of my robe. Next to me was a small bookcase with books by John Bunyan, Hiprah Hunt, William Cooper, Jeremy Taylor and Christopher Love. I had never heard of any of them.

A black cat came out of nowhere. It jumped on top of the bookcase, shot a glance to the strange men who had invaded her world, licked its paw and was done with us.

Jennifer turned on the TV on her way to the bedroom.

We just sat there watching some mindless infomercial with a whiny-voiced, hairy guy who was beside himself with joy as he explained the wondrous properties of an outdoor fire pit. "Look at the flames go higher and higher, all safely contained within the hand-painted ceramic basin and mesh cage. Taste the smores! Think of the fellowship! Clean burning, too!"

We were so used to watching fire that neither of us so much as reached for the remote to change the station.

Jennifer returned ten minutes later. Her hair was down. She had on flannel PJs printed with that awful pitchfork that served as the hotel's logo. Virg claimed she was going to extreme lengths to promote the hotel. I claimed she stole them. She called me the PJ police. I secretly hoped she would arrest me and put me in handcuffs.

Tucked under each arm was a blanket and pillows. She claimed Cheryl wouldn't mind and that Cheryl had a strict rule about not letting anyone sleep in her bed.

"It appears as though you are already situated, so I won't get in the middle of it. One of you can have the futon. I'm afraid a beanbag is all I have for the other."

"Funny you would say that," I responded, "because Virg loves to sleep on beanbags. Right, Virg? Doctor's orders. It helps his sleep apnea."

"I do not snore, Edward."

"Straight you do."

"Puh-lease."

"Jennifer will verify it. I want you to tell Virg in a few hours what a monster snorer he is. It will rattle your windows. You just wait, Virg. Just wait."

"Okay guys, I'll leave you to sort out the sleeping arrangements. I'm going to bed. If you're hungry the frig is over there and if you're thirsty, cups are in the cabinet above the sink. There's also bottled water in the frig and a pint of double chocolate ice cream in the freezer if you're so inclined."

"Virg'll be inclined all night in his beanbag chair."

Jennifer turned to go back to her bedroom.

"Our flight departs at noon," Virg blurted. "Can you set an alarm? I will also set one on my phone."

"How does eight sound? That will give us time to have breakfast and then I can get you boys to the airport."

"Very good," Virg responded in his mechanical way as Jennifer shut the door behind her. Despite what she said about not being threatened by us, I heard the metal on wood scraping of a bolt moving into its socket.

I watched Virg settle into his reclining position on the beanbag. The shape of it all was funny in the glow of the TV. Round lump of a head on big velvet lump, transitioning down to round belly and ending in stick legs. I thought of the urinals in the CAFC.

On stretching out I quickly realized the futon was not

long enough for me. My legs were two sizes too long. The pillow was too soft and the futon cushion too hard.

I rotated.

I stared into a plaster ceiling that looked as though a section could flake off and fall on me at any moment. I rotated again.

"Virg, you asleep yet? Did you know the kettledrum is the only drum in the whole world you can tune to a specific pitch?"

I flopped.

"Virg, did you know that a good violin contains seventy different pieces of wood? Think about it. Seventy."

I shifted.

"Virg, I can't sleep."

"Neither can I."

"It just struck me, this has been a really bad Good Friday."

"Yes it has, Edward, but it's actually the early hours of Saturday. Now if you would kindly stop talking and turn the TV off, it would greatly help both of our endeavors."

"The TV is a sedative. Why don't I change it from the infomercial and you turn away from the screen?"

I got up and searched for the remote in the anemic light. It was not easy in an unfamiliar apartment. I stepped on Virg twice and the cat once. Both made a similar noise.

"Hey Virg, did I ever tell you that oak drumsticks give a much richer sound than hickory or cherry wood?"

No response from the floor.

Finally I gave up on finding the remote. I knocked on Jennifer's door. "Uh, excuse me, Jen—Can I call you Jen?— but for the life of me I can't find the remote. I need to change the station. My ex-girlfriend used to always put it in some weird place, too. It's a girl thang."

I heard a slow stirring. "What?"

I repeated myself.

"Check the kitchen counter."

"Thanks."

Sure enough I found it where our host indicated. Only a chick would leave the TV remote out in the kitchen no matter how close it is to the living room. I scanned through the channels. The only thing good on was some old show about Ulysses and his journey through Greece or Rome or the underworld. I don't know.

By the time I settled on it, Virg was snoring away.

I gently tapped again on the bedroom door. "Jen, I hate to bother you one more time, but do you hear Virg snoring? Here, let me turn the sound down on the TV. There. Now do you hear it? That's not a freight train. It's Virg. Remember how awful it is for the morning and then tell him over breakfast. Okay?"

I thought I heard a grunt on the other side of the bedroom door. Vindicated, I took my place back on the futon. A fetal position was the most comfortable I was going to get.

Ulysses kept me company as Virg snored away. In my conscious-unconscious state I envisioned he was speaking to me. The TV droned on and on as I drifted off.

"...the poop rose and the bow went down till the sea closed over us..."

Guido

SATURDAY MORNING BROKE through the slats of Jennifer's blinds. The sun, strange as it was to see, slashed across my body. The TV was still on. Another infomercial. Where do they find the world's most annoying people to be on them?

Speaking of breakfast, I was famished. I lay on the futon with heavy eyelids. Virg rumbled from the bowels of Jennifer's living room floor. For a moment I closed my eyes to see if I could get back to sleep. That's when the cat went pogo stick on me. The little furball.

It jumped on my stomach out of nowhere. "Jezebel!" I exclaimed, not from my voice as much as from the air that shot out of me.

Fast as one could blink it bounded with poof and foop onto one of Virg's round bumps. All Virg could muster was the sound of a barnyard animal.

The cat darted under the dark recesses of the futon just as Jennifer appeared from her room. "Guido! Shame on you. He is so mischievous at times. I do apologize."

"Sooo, that's the cat's name?" I asked with suspicion.

Jennifer smiled. "You mean you don't meet cats named Guido every day? Let me tell you about him while I get breakfast on. Eggs and toast?"

"That sounds wonderful," Virg said.

"Coffee works, too," I informed.

Jennifer wandered a few steps into the tiny kitchen and began banging pans in search for the right one. "When I first saw Guido he was a stray who would play with two other strays outside our apartment building. They were always into some kind of roguish behavior. To make a long story short, an elderly couple lived in the apartment below Cheryl and me. The old man had named my cat the Sicilian Bull because of his big shoulders and brass-colored hair. I just called him Guido for short. The cat's Italian, what better name? It's like the Joe of America."

"Or the Francois of France," I added while Jennifer cracked eggs into a pan. I guess she assumed we both liked scrambled eggs.

"So the old man named one of the other strays Boniface since he looked like a pope from the rings of black and white fur around his neck."

"Yesterday I realized that The Dope Popes might be a good name for a hip-hop act," is what I whispered to Virg.

"What?" Jennifer asked.

"Oh nothing," Virg responded, "nothing at all. Edward has a way of mumbling."

While Jennifer popped two pieces of wheat bread into the toaster, she went on with her story. "Despite the other stray's religious name, he kept getting Guido to sin. They seemed to have an affinity for jumping on the old lady's bouffant hairdo whenever she wore a flower clip in it. I've never seen an old lady move so fast. So one day, coming back from the hotel, I saw the impish cats about to pounce on the old lady when I seized Guido by the scruff and took him in to live with us. He has been with us ever since. Either of you cat people?"

"I like cats," Virg offered.

"You would," I said.

In a couple minutes we made it over to the round table and began eating immediately. It surprised all three of us how hungry we were.

When I came up for air, I commented to Jennifer that room service was too expensive in her hotel.

"As if I have any say in the matter," she aptly said.

"I realize that."

"Not sure he does," Virg said. "Please don't encourage him."

I can't stand when Virg takes the side of other people. Where is manager loyalty when you need it? "All I'm saying, Jennifer, is that your minibar prices and room service are so expensive that you force hotel guests to go to the market around the block. The one with the U.S. flags in the windows run by Mexicans who serve Japanese food in Chinese takeout containers, which reminds all of your guests who are in a band of great names for their band."

"You really think that happens to any hotel guest but yourself, Edward?"

"Sure it does, Virg. Every day. And stop rolling your eyes while I'm telling a good story and eating breakfast. I'm tired of it and I'm tired of this sorry trip."

"You will be on your flight and out of D.C. soon," Jennifer reminded in an obvious effort to sidetrack me. "How about that coffee or some orange juice?"

"Both," Virg and I said at once.

"Jinx," I said.

As Jennifer got up, she commented that in a lot of ways she thought we were alike.

"Virg wishes," I said. "So your hotel guests are forced to eat at the Japanese restaurant run by Mexicans with unnatural cooking oil that may as well have a sign to replace the American flag that says: FREE CANCER TODAY! COME AND GET IT. HOW MUCH YOU WANT?"

"I'm sure this isn't your own story. I'm sure you didn't say that," Jennifer winked as the coffeepot gurgled to life.

"Naw. Just an example. Anyway, that's what's happening to your hotel guests simply because your minibar prices and room service are too expensive. I would have written it down on one of your 'How can we better serve you?' cards, and stuck it in that treasure chest box in the lobby if it wasn't so long of a complaint."

"I'll get right on that." I saw her look at Virg and smile when she said it. I'm unsure as to why. She poured our glasses of orange juice and brought them to the table. Next she brought over sugar and cream; not for the orange juice but for the joe. The coffeemaker soon dinged. She got three more cups out of the cabinet and slung coffee into each.

I drank to my heart's content. Virg kept staring at the clock with every gulp. Finally, he said, almost blurting, "We really had better get to the airport to make sure we get on our flight. It is an international flight, after all."

Jennifer backed quickly from the table. "Where to?"

"Barcelona," I confirmed.

"Color me jealous. You can take the tube so no worries about traffic, but I can understand."

"Well, we're flying out of Dulles instead of National."

"Oh, so you can't take the tube all the way. I like to get to the airport early, too, especially with the nasty weather we've been having."

"Uh, one problem," I said. "I don't have any clothes thanks to Virg here who made me leave our room before getting dressed." I was speaking to Jennifer but I glared at Virg for every word of it, then back to Jennifer. "Your shoeblacks have my combat boots. I go nowhere without my stompers. I have a rocker image to uphold."

"Okay, here's what we'll do. Finish your breakfast. We'll stop by the hotel on our way to the airport. I'll have some people check for your clothes."

"See, that's what a real tour guide does, Virg." I took my plate over to the sink while Virg talked about hotel rates and frequent stay clubs and asked why the Trident Hotel didn't have one since it increased customer loyalty by up to sixty-seven percent in the latest poll by the Hotel Association of America. Virg gloated that he was nearly up to gold status on two separate hotel chains.

"You're boring her. Jennifer, did he snore last night?"

She flashed her smile.

"See, Virg, see."

Section V

Let's (The La, La, Lee Song)

I TOOK A quick shower at Jennifer's before we left. When I got out, Guido was sitting on the sink, perched right on the faucet like a cleaning rag ready to whisk into action. I checked the bathroom door and it was still closed. I have no idea to this day how he got inside.

He would not move off the faucet no matter how much I shooed. If I touched him I would get cat hair on me right after getting clean. Cat hair! Besides, he might have clawed me. I don't trust cats. Not at all. Especially ones named Guido. He has a mafia name *and* he is a feline. Two major strikes.

So I let him sit there and watch me do things to my hair that are a trade secret in the industry. Just sitting there, pawing, licking, staring. When I turned on the faucet, low and behold the feline reached its head around and started drinking from the running water. This was one of the strangest things I had seen. "It's not like it's milk or anything," I told him. Later Jennifer confessed that Guido only drinks out of the tap. Put a bowl of water in front of him and he will turn his nose at it. The furball.

Virg knocked on the door and offered to let me wear one of his outfits in place of the robe. I laughed. He really busts me up sometimes. I said I would take my chances at finding my clothes at the hotel, especially my combat boots that any true rocker misses after being without them for any period of time.

Around nine in the morning the three of us left Jennifer's apartment for the Trident Hotel. Jennifer had gotten a phone call from her manager and learned that the firemen contained the fire mostly to the thirteenth floor.

On the way, back on the familiar subway, I asked her, "Hey, you never told us the name of the third stray cat.

There was Guido and Pope Boniface. Just curious."

"Sorry. It's Angiolello. I call him Angi for short. He doesn't like it because it has a girlish ring to it."

"Man," I said out of frustration with the whole feminine feline thing. "Does he drink from the tap, too?"

"Nope. That's unique to my Guido."

After the Metrorail passed through a tunnel with cologne advertisements plastered on the walls, Jennifer turned to me. "Let me ask you a question."

"Shoot."

"Last night, when Vanni read aloud that letter from your girlfriend—"

"*Former* girlfriend," I emphasized.

"Okay. It mentioned that she was about to finish the lyrics for a song. I would like to hear them."

I slouched and sighed. I was not about to recite Bea's lyrics for our third song. In a lot of ways it was the most personal of them all. "I would rather not, Jennifer."

"I'll tell you," Virg offered. "I really like what Bea came up with."

"Come on, Virg. Don't."

There was no stopping him. "It's from their Gush Sessions. 'Let's' is the name of it, but the end of each verse is so catchy, people call it the 'La, La, Lee Song.'" With that Virg saw the need to stand and recite to the entire subway car as he held onto the pole.

Let's (The La, La, Lee Song)

Let's wear fun hats, he and she;
Let's get cool tats, you and me;
Love's how it's supposed to be;
La, la, lee – Lee, lee, li – Li, li lo—love.

Let's have big hoots, he and she;
Let's wear big boots, you and me;
Love's how it's supposed to be;
La, la, lee – Lee, lee, li – Li, li lo—love.

Let's dance through flowers, he and she;
Let's prance through showers, you and me;
Love's how it's supposed to be;
La, la, lee – Lee, lee, li – Li, li lo—love.

Let's be free, he and she;
Let's be *we*, you and me;
Love's how it's supposed to be;
La, la, lee – Lee, lee, li – Li, li lo—love.

"Perfect," Jennifer announced. "Love it. Or should I say, lo-lo-love it?"

Virg was chuckling as he sat back down. I was put out.

"Now you see why Virg will never sing in the band. I keep him in the background; like way, way in the background. The next state if possible."

In a few stops the Metrorail dumped us off near the hotel. My slipper nearly got caught in the escalator on the way up to street level. I had to bend down, robe flapping open in places that it shouldn't, to get it. When I did the sash tied around my waist almost got sucked into the metal teeth of the beast.

Virg and Jennifer thought it was funny and so did some old woman behind me. The old shawl.

"It's dangerous in the subway, Grandma. Never saw a rocker in a robe before? Huh? Huh?"

When we got to the hotel it was still cordoned off by strips of yellow tape. The building looked malevolent (Virg told me that was a big word for evil) in daylight. It had taken on the form of a face. Angry glass, its broken teeth, lay strewn down the barricaded street. The lobby doors were a screaming mouth; the charred thirteenth floor a brooding unibrow curling at the edges.

We approached the tape with caution. There were at least half a dozen local and national news anchors pressing up against it in an effort to get a few inches closer than the competition. We heard some of the grumbles. They were all worked up about shoddy fire extinguishers and proper width of the stairwell for escape. Of course they had no proof and none of them had actually been inside the building since the fire to measure anything; yet they were fingerpointing nonetheless. It could not have been a simple accident by some guy named Caiaphas. It just couldn't have. It had to be the fault of a code violation. The city was to blame! The Code Enforcement Division had to be larger. Taxes needed to be raised. Action News 5 at 10.

The sowers of discord were everywhere.

They made me briefly think of Bea's failed attempt at getting the Bea Excellent Always cable program on the air. Once in awhile she is actually right, unlike me who am right all the time. Even when I'm wrong I'm basically right.

Out from one of the front doors that were encased in ornate wrought iron, I saw an Arabic man emerge. He looked official. Jennifer recognized him. His name was Mohamed and he was the manager of the entire joint.

They exchanged brief conversation, expressing how glad they were that the other was unscathed. Scathe would be a fine name for a rock band when you think about it or Scald.

So Mohamed the Manager starts going on about the police and how they would not give him access to the thirteenth floor and how that wasn't right and he had a fiduciary duty to the guests. He just kept going on and on, moving his arms in the air.

The Latin cop named Jésus we had seen the night before was back on the beat. Perhaps he had never left. He heard Mohamed cackling and walked over. He denied what Mohamed was telling us in so many words. The cop said Mohamed was given brief access to see the damage on the thirteenth floor. After the Cause and Origin guys had completed their investigation, he could have the run of the place. It would be a few days; maybe a week.

Mohamed said he was never given access to the thirteenth floor by the cop and that he was entitled to full and complete access as hotel manager.

"You don't have control over me. It is my right to be taken up. You're not God here," Mohamed said.

To this Jésus raised his eyebrows.

"He's creating a schism at the scene," Virg whispered.

"Watch your language in front of a young lady," I scolded, "or you might cause people's heads to fall right off."

After Mohamed told Jennifer that he was glad she was safe, Jennifer turned to the cop, "Can either Mohamed or I have access to Room—?"

"—Room 1313," Virg assisted.

"My stuff is in there," I said.

The cop hooked thumbs in his wide belt and swaggered a bit. "I can assure you all that everything on the thirteenth floor was destroyed in the fire. If anything survived, the hoses ruined it. We've got water damage six floors down."

At this Mohamed gave off a guttural wince.

"Okay, I'm trying to stay calm here," I said. "I'm trying to think. My clothes were up there, but my stompers were sent down for a polish."

"That's right," Virg confirmed.

"Mohamed," Jennifer said, "could you check the Buff Room for a pair of combat boots? It should be the only pair."

"I'll be right back," he said.

Arezzo

IT ONLY TOOK Mohamed a few moments to return from the Buff Room. Pinched between his fingers was the most beautiful sight I had seen: My polished stompers. I knew them anywhere.

"Sweet bipity bop," I said to Mohamed as he handed them over without pause. I clenched them in my arms and hugged them. If they had been left on the thirteenth floor they would have been char. A tear came to my eye as I thought about it. "I'll never leave you again."

Mohamed was giving me a funny look.

"I don't have a claim tag or anything."

"We'll take your word on it. They were the only pair of combat boots among the dress shoes."

"Go figure," Virg sighed.

I flipped off the slippers. They fluttered through the open lobby doors. I immediately began lacing the combat boots. They made me feel like a new man. Scratch that. Like a new rocker.

Jennifer was tittering. "Wearing combat boots with a white hotel robe looks funnier than slippers."

"Jezebel, I was just getting ready to like you."

"My name's not Jezebel. It's Jennifer."

I stood up and faced Mohamed. "That reminds me, now I need my clothes."

Mohamed shook his unibrow side-to-side. "Any clothes on the thirteenth floor were likely burned."

Jésus—who rarely agrees with Mohamed, mind you—nodded.

"Can I at least check?"

Jésus gave me a look of disbelief for even asking the question.

"Hey, never hurts to ask."

I pulled Virg and Jennifer off to the side where Jésus and Mohamed could no longer see us.

"I have got to get my clothes. Don't give me that 'here we go again' look, Virg. I'm serious! There is no way I'm wearing anything of yours on the trip to Barcelona."

"I could distract them," Jennifer offered, "so you can slip by. The stairway is to the right of the front desk."

"As if we didn't have to run down them last night," I reminded. "You go do your thing, Jennifer. Virg, leave your suitcase here. There is no way we take it up the stairs and there is no way anyone would want to steal it."

"Watch this. This should draw a little attention," Jennifer assured.

With that she spun away from us. We watched from the corner of the hotel as she strolled up and marched right through the yellow tape. It stretched to the breaking point across her flat stomach, then snapped, before slithering onto the sidewalk. In a few steps she was into the lobby via the open doors.

"Whoa, whoa, hold it right there," Jésus shouted as he finally realized the breach that had occurred. He raced toward Jennifer. Mohamed was right beside him.

Jennifer smartly turned around so she was facing the street and the mens' backs were toward us.

I yanked Virg by the sleeve. At the lobby doors we paused. When Jennifer went into pretend hysterics about customer service and how it is even more important during an emergency, we scuttled past them—me berobed in stompers, Virg beshirted in Hawaiian. Try to do that with two grown men and not attract attention.

Virg said nothing until two floors and four flights of stairs had gotten the better of him. He was sucking wind something awful. He exhaled his words on the way up in short bursts. "We—"

Third floor: "have—"

Fourth floor: "to—"

Fifth floor: "hurry,—"

Sixth floor: "Edward."

Seventh floor: "We—"

Eighth floor: "have—"
Ninth floor: "a—"
Tenth floor: "plane—"
Eleventh floor: "to—"
Twelfth floor: "catch!"

"Whatever," I responded as we reached the thirteenth floor. A dark starburst of stains around the metal doorjamb greeted us. While Virg was bent over wheezing, I yanked open the door with trepidation. The other side was burnt and appeared as though a blowtorch artist had taken a liking to it.

We gasped at the wasteland of char and smoldering artifacts that dotted the former hallway. It had the wet charcoal smell of an outdoor grill after a rain.

"Come on, Tub'o," I called to Virg.

He was leaning against the doorjamb, panting. "Don't know about this. We could get delayed . . . with questions from the . . . cause-and-origin . . . people."

"I don't hear any mulling around up here. Besides, if an inspector catches us, we'll just run back down the stairs."

Virg lifted his combover and wiped his forehead. He led me through a soupy mixture of ash that splashed beneath our feet. It made me cringe to think of my recently shiny stompers.

The doors to the rooms were all open. Emergency personnel had bashed a few of them off their hinges. Outside air sucked at the openings as we passed.

Virg was walking too carefully through the muck, so I took the lead. I hopped over a downed hallway table. Virg tripped going over it, which I expected since he doesn't have a coordinated bone in his frumpilicious body. I turned around and stopped and shushed him, but not in that order. He shushed me back right.

When I turned to continue to our room, I stuck my foot through one of those hunt club paintings that I was sure was bought at a starving artist sale. I imagine they are on the wall of every upscale hotel in America though I've stayed in none of them except the Trident Hotel and I'm unsure that I can even count it seeing how I didn't stay a full night.

Extracting my stomper I flashed back to when an angry Phil of my former band got his boot caught in the amp and I was about to smile when I heard, "Help me," from a tremulous voice.

"You hear that?" I asked.

"Please." The voice was quiet, yet desperate in its inflection.

We stopped dead in the hallway and listened.

"Virg, it sounds clos—"

"Shhh." Pointing, Virg motioned for me to enter Room 1308 (what is it with these circle eights everywhere?) first.

"That doesn't rev my monkey, Virg. You go. You're the travel guide."

"I am dying in here. Hurry!"

We swallowed hard as we stood abreast at the door. Dank air rushed to greet us as it tunneled through the smashed window of the open room. The flapping, black curtains still resembled giant reptile wings as they thumped against the walls. The drawstring had twisted into a hangman's noose.

"Help me. Somebody!"

Virg lurched across the threshold, looking otherworldly in his brightly colored shirt.

"Under . . . here," said the voice in a tone barely perceptible among the flapping sounds.

Virg glanced back at me and I nodded him toward the bed. I stood guard next to the door as Virg crept closer. I wasn't scared or anything.

Virg cleared an area of debris and went down on his knees. Slowly he peeled up the singed comforter.

In a blink he put it back down and looked back at me with ashen face. "There's a person under there."

"You expecting a fish? Do something."

"Help me, Edward. We need to drag them out."

"No *we* don't. You need to drag them out."

"Please," came the voice. "Hurry."

Virg gave me a pleading expression. I hate it when he does that.

Reluctantly I pitched in. I got next to him and threw the comforter off the bed so we could see better. A burned hand reached out for us. Instinctively we rocked back and landed on our backsides.

Sitting there in a panic I remembered the hand that grabbed me in the limo before returning to my senses. I tried to push away from the bed, but my back hit the wall.

The fingers were moving on the hand, trying to latch onto us. A blackened arm slowly emerged. It was a man's.

Virg turned on his cellphone to shed more light. I offered to hold it while Virg pulled the man out be grabbing him under the arms.

As we looked closer, we made out the man's face and neck. They were red and blistering.

"No. No. By my feet," the man said.

We got up and went around to the edge of the bed.

Virg took him by one ankle and I took the other. We began to carefully extract him from under the bed. He moaned and cringed as we pulled.

When he was fully out, we viewed a man of average weight and height. The left side of his body was burned and it was difficult for Virg and I to get him to a sitting position.

Although the electricity was out in the building, we were surprised to find that the water still worked in the bathroom sink. Virg found a ceramic mug by a melted plastic coffee machine and filled it with water.

The man downed it in large, sloppy gulps. The water spilled down the burnt side of his face as one corner of his lips struggled to close tight around the top of the cup.

Virg filled the mug twice more before the man was ready to speak.

He thanked us over and over. He told us the emergency workers missed him last night. They even checked under his bed at one point, but could not see him. He called out but no one heard him over the fire and streams of water being cannoned into the hotel.

Turns out, the man's name was Arezzo, a chemist born in Italy. They called him the alchemist early in his career for seemingly being able to change the form of common objects to precious metals. He was a devout Catholic now, but admitted he falsified results early in his career to make a name for himself. He felt that what happened last night was God's way of punishing him.

Virg told him that's not how God works. He said God was a loving God, but occasionally has to correct us as a father would. Arezzo didn't want to hear any of it, though.

To change the depressing subject I asked him where he lived now.

"Vegas. Where," as Arezzo put it, "there are a lot of evil impersonators, gamblers, counterfeiters and liars."

"Don't forget has-been singers," I added.

"And I guess alchemists, too," Virg said.

While Arezzo took a few last sips of water, I told Virg, "I would like to add one more job to my list of sorry jobs I will never work: Dressing up as a bunny for the miserable Zany Zoo Travel Agency, especially when everyone knows there are no bunnies in zoos. That's now front and center on my list. Another is being a Vegas lounge singer. Chalk that one up right under bar mitzvah belter and above cruise ship crooner. Got that? Don't give me that look, Virg."

"I'm not."

It was Arezzo who gave me a strange look then started going on about how he was traveling on business with some dude named Capocchio, a partner from Siena, when Virg reminded, "The time we have is short."

Virg got Arezzo to his feet as I trudged down to Room 1313 and searched for my duffel bag. All I found was a pile of ash that *used* to be my rock-n-roll clothes for the trip. I kicked the lump and watched it scatter.

A glimmer of metal skidded into the closet. My skull belt buckle rested on the floor. I saw it smile at me. The belt was burnt in places, but you could hardly tell against the black leather. I took my surviving remnant from the room. With stompers and skull I felt complete.

I walked back up the hallway where Virg was waiting outside Arezzo's room. Virg was promising to send help right away. "What's the matter?" he questioned, and I thought I saw him grinning ever so slightly.

"You know what's the matter. My clothes are toast."

Smackdown

WE WOULD HAVE made quick work of the stairs on the way back down to the lobby but Arezzo had an arm around each of us. When we finally got outside Jennifer—with shifting eyes that indicated she couldn't hold off Jésus and Mohamed any longer—noticed us step over the broken yellow tape.

We sat Arezzo against the wall. In the morning light there was a dull helplessness in his eyes as a medic ran over. Around the corner of the hotel we found Virg's suitcase just where we left it. He immediately began unzipping its perimeter and then began fishing for an item.

"What are you doing? We have to catch our flight."

"Wear this." Virg pulled from his suitcase one of his Hawaiian shirts and snapped it to attention as though it had the prestige of a military uniform. It had the appearance of being starched and ironed.

I threw up my hands and took a few steps back. "Not a chance. There is no way in Hades I am getting on a plane in that shirt."

"And you would rather wear a bathrobe?"

"Uh . . . yeah. Nuns and Tibetan monks don't have a problem with it."

"Honestly, Edward, a bathrobe?"

I thought about it. Shifted my weight. Tapped my stomper, knowing it has been scientifically proven by Bea that tapping a combat boot on the ground increases thinking capacity. When the answer came to me, I said nothing. Just stuck out my hand with head bowed in solemn disgrace. I felt the silky shirt land first. A pair of scratchy pants followed.

I took out my wallet and letter from Bea, then tossed the robe in the alleyway and got dressed. The stompers had to be peeled off to get the pants on, which were baggy and too short. The shirt was last. I wanted to delay wearing it as long as possible. Soon the final button had found its hole. The moment of truth had arrived. It was time to glance down at my outfit. Bright flowers, skull belt buckle, beige high-waters that revealed scuffed combat boots.

"This is very un-rock-n-roll, Virg. It's a sorry mix of cool and nerd. It's nool!"

"Dadgum, Edward, you do look nice."

"You would." I paused for a moment. "You know something? Never trust a guy who says dadgum. No. Wait. If people are ever standing around a guy that says dadgum they should just punch him right in the melon. There should be a law to that effect. If we had time I'd start a bill in congress before we fly out of D.C. The same goes for durn. Anyone who says dadgum or durn or darn or dagnabit or even dang, for that matter, must be—has to be—knocked in the head on the spot."

Just as I was rearing back to punch the cowering tour guide right in the snoz, Jennifer strolled around the corner.

"Ha! You guys look like twins!"

"Don't get me started," I warned.

"What kinda fashion statement are you trying to make, Edward, Hawaiian punk?"

Virg immediately started telling Jennifer about Arezzo in Room 1308 and how we had found him. She was horrified at the story and assured us she would get him further assistance immediately.

She gave us hugs, bid us a good trip to Barcelona, said she was excited about the band, and pointed us in the direction of the tube, which, of course, we were already very familiar with. She welcomed us back to the hotel any time.

"I'll look you up on my world tour," I told her.

"Well, when you do come back there will be crested slippers waiting for you that are not burnt."

"Gee, thanks. My slipper wearing days are over. Hey, now that I think about it, you know how to shred a guitar?"

"That would be a big negative."

Virg trundled down the street toward the Metrorail entrance and I followed. I got angry when I asked him to stop at a clothes store on the way to get some real duds before going to the airport. Virg said there was no time for that since we had to make an extra stop on the Metrorail and take the Metrobus for the final couple miles. He also enlightened me that clothing stores were hard to come by in Downtown D.C.

I said nothing to him on our way to the airport. Served him right.

We took the Orange Line and exited near some church because the Metrorail did not reach Dulles International Airport yet. Virg told me the Metroline connection to Dulles would be complete next year. I assured him he was a treasure trove of useless info as we climbed on the Washington Flyer bus to the airport. It was packed.

I had to suffer through the driver saying, "Nice shirts," when we stepped on and then all the looks from travelers on the bus. I think Virg took it as a compliment.

Out my window, street musicians were mulling about the churchyard, trying to get tips off their guitar playing, which only made me remember how good Bea was on stage. She is amazing on a six string, but when she gets out her twelve string, it will make you weep from the first note. Anything with a string attached she can play by ear. She was trying to acquire a sitar before she skipped town.

Virg stowed his suitcase and flopped into one of the remaining seats up front. I was sitting in the very back in a long bench seat that spanned the entire rear of the bus. It struck me as odd that there were no seatbelts. Silently I vowed to myself to never bring Bea on one of these shuttle buses. They don't have any seatbelts or airbags. Bea will cause a scene with the driver. Really, she would.

I sat next to a large man. Soon a latecomer sat on the other side of me who was even larger. There I was, squeezed into my seat right between two fat guys. And when I say "fat," I'm talkin' blimpo central (not a band name). Bellyrama (not a band name). Paunchlaunch (band name). Bellybrothers (not a band name). They were trading quotes with each other. I heard one in one ear and then the other in the other ear. Back and forth.

"O comfort-killing night, image of hell—" said the one on my left.

"Dim register and notary of shame—" responded the one on my right.

I began snickering and thought about telling them my ears were not speaking devices.

One of them said in a nasally voice, "There is nothing funny about this, good sir. We are highly trained Shakespearean actors on our way to—"

"Broadway," the other interjected.

I started to say that they didn't look like Shakespearean actors (not that I'm exactly sure what a Shakespearean actor should really look like in the first place) and instead just shrugged them off.

The diesel engine, which we were basically sitting on top of in the back, roared to life. The bus started moving toward Dulles International Airport. We rolled down the street for a couple minutes. My companions, wanting to show off, were glancing at me, hoping I asked the obvious question about their profession. It was the elephant in the bus and at that moment I realized I had one on either side of me.

"Black stage for tragedies and murders fell—" barked one.

"Vast sin-concealing chaos, nurse of blame!" blurted the other. "I quote from *Richard the III*," he professed.

"Thou mountain of mad flesh!" a guy said in the row in front of us.

He startled us all.

He had dark, wavy hair. "That's from *Comedy of Errors* and you both are a comedy of Shakespearean errors. You, my friends were quoting from *The Tragedy of Macbeth*."

"Take that," I said to my neighbors. "Snap!"

The guy on my right commanded, "Reveal yourself, oh soothsayer of Shakespeare."

A forty-ish man with a 1970s lounge singer mustache stood up in the front of us and held onto the back of his seat. I saw that he too had a round belly. Stretched across it was a shirt so tight that it revealed a sizeable dark circle of a bellybutton. For a moment I thought it was going to say something to me. Like rosebud or something.

Just as I was about to ask him what month of pregnancy he was in, he announced, "My name is Adam Crantz. I have a master's in Shakespearean literature from ______________ University. I am traveling to the Austin Shakespearean Festival."

The bus roared onto the main thoroughfare. The noise did little to mask the anger brewing around me.

"Well, Master Adam, *Macbeth* is a fine sixteenth century tragedy nonetheless," said one of the tubos.

"*Macbeth* was penned in the seventeenth century, my fellow," was the response.

One of the guys next to me, I'm unsure which, flicked Master Adam right in the earlobe.

"Oow! Hey!" He winched and grabbed at his ear.

"You must admit, Master Adam, that it is a lengthy tragedy of fine craftsmanship," the one on my left offered, as if trying to add something of value and a bit of credence to his very part-time job.

"It was Shakespeare's shortest," came the retort.

Again, I'm not sure which one did it, but I watched a flabby arm with fist attached punch Master Adam right in his distended belly.

It gave off the sound of a worn kick drum.

Master Adam responded with an elbow to the face of the guy on my left. In slow motion I saw jowls fluttering and a belly button screaming. Mayhem ensued in the back of the bus. Straight up. Rounded knuckles and fat rolls flew under the colorful background of my bright shirt. I thought I saw two (I'm not sure which two) bellies hit each other with sumo wrestler force.

"Smackdown in D.C.!" I yelled.

The rest of the passengers began panicking, especially Virg.

It took me awhile to pinch down from my seat and climb out of the fat foray. I thought of my time spent on the floor of the plane going to D.C. and was just hoping I didn't latch onto any woman's panties this time. You never know what you'll find on the floor of a plane. You really don't.

Once I had crawled a few rows toward the front, the bus

had stopped at a tollbooth. I found Virg's leg and stood up next to him.

"You look disheveled, Edward."

"Your hairdo isn't looking too hot, either."

From the time it took the driver to scan his toll pass and for the bus to slowly move back on the toll road, things had pretty much settled back to normal. Luggage that had fallen (a few pieces right on the back of my legs as I crawled, thank you very much) got put back on the rack.

Minutes later the bus pulled into the airport. It angled toward the International Departures lane and the driver began calling out the various airlines. The first grouping was skipped. We stopped at the next one.

That's where Master Adam piled off. Not a one of my Shakespearean friends would look at him as he exited. Outside the bus he made a hand gesture to them and a beeline for the terminal.

My seat buddies also started getting off the bus. I was still put off by their brouhaha. There was no classical training about either of them if you ask me. Once they were a ways down the aisle I told them to, "Have a nice trip you bards of lard!"

They must've forgot to wave to me as they got off. At the next grouping of airlines, Virg and I wandered out.

They Might be Giants

DULLES INTERNATIONAL AIRPORT appeared different in daylight. The pervasive gloom of yesterday had lifted with a spring and a bounce. Gone was the foggy air that cloistered (if that's a word-I think Bea used it once) about the massive windows that welcomed passengers. Today we could see buildings in the surrounding Virginia area and its many trees. Heck, we could see across the street.

Once inside, Virg and I walked past a bank of flower vendors on our way to check in for our flight. I remarked how our shirts made us invisible in front of the flowers.

Virg got a kick outta that.

"You know, Bea's the type of girl who runs her fingers across flowers petals as she walks by."

"Those girls are hard to find, Edward."

"Like you would know."

"You miss her something terrible. Admit it."

"I mean, I miss a few things like trying on leather pants together and picking out new tats. Little things that truly matter in a relationship. But hey, she's the one who walked out on the band. It hurt your pocketbook, too. Don't forget that. I really hope I never see her again and if I do—" I broke off.

"What? What are you going to do if you see Beatrice again?"

"Don't know. It won't be pleasant I tell you. I might just slamdance her right into the ground. That's what I'll do. And stop shaking your melon head like you disagree with me all the time. You're embarrassing me."

Twenty minutes later we had made it through ticketing and security. This time I did not get patted down or even wanded. I felt like the girl who no one asks to dance at the high school prom. And if you must know, I *did* go to my miserable high school prom but I didn't dance or anything. There was a terrible band playing. I jumped on stage and pushed some loser drummer off right in the middle of a sappy love song. I took his sticks and began pounding the skins. I barely had a good rhythm going when I got tossed out on my ear. The school administrators said my music was deemed "inappropriate given its pulsating rock inclusions." Whatever that means.

My beats got the kids excited. That much is for sure. I saw plenty of grinding out there. I was almost expelled the following Monday, but the dudes and dudettes liked it and petitioned for me. The three Italian chefs we met in D.C. were some of my biggest fans.

Once through security, I told Virg that I thought the security checkpoint lady had a thing for me. What lady doesn't?

Virg joked that it was because of my stylish shirt and high water pants.

I didn't laugh. Virg is the worst person in the world at telling jokes.

We glanced at our tickets and learned that today we were at Gate Nine. It had a big circle around it on the Departures screen. Virg said that meant our plane was on time.

Even with the running around we did in the torched Trident Hotel that morning, we had gotten to the airport an hour before takeoff. Virg informed me that that was cutting it close for an international flight.

"Did you realize it's the day before Easter, Edward?"

"Easter Eve. Want me to hide plastic eggs around the airport for you to find?"

Soon we found the seating area and flopped into the fake leather chairs—two bright American peacocks on their way to Barcelona.

The chairs were comfortable. Having nothing better to do I stretched out and leaned back. I must have dozed off. When I awoke, I blinked my vision into clear view and noticed a city of towers standing in front of the floor-to-ceiling windows that I had failed to see when we sat down. For a moment they appeared a tad fake, as though formed by some airport artist on a grant from the city.

But when I took a closer look I noticed the objects were not buildings at all. They were giants; or at least what I imagined to be giants. As I got closer I heard the calling of names. Ephialtes. Briareus. Tityos. Typhon. Antaeus. Only in the breadbasket of America would one hear names like that. They were being spoken in soft, high pitches and excited tones.

The voices of children calling out at play.

The children were in a vast pit of plastic balls that had been laid out like a tiny city. From a distance they were giants I tell you. *Giants.* This made me think of a band Bea used to enjoy.

I watched them jump and throw balls. The tikes were fun to watch. Their parents were calling them by name. Briareus took one off the noggin. Antaeus did a face planter. Clearly Typhon the Terror was getting the best of the others in the germ factory of brightly colored spheres.

Just as one of my stompers was about to step into the pit to right the injustices therein, an announcement came over the loudspeaker. Our plane, though at the gate, had a "minor mechanical issue" that had to be checked out by airport personnel. I had been asleep for longer than I thought.

I got away from the giants and hustled over to Virg. "What does that mean?"

Virg's forehead was crinkled. "It's not good. We could be delayed fifteen minutes to a couple of hours."

The last bit was all I heard. "A couple hours?"

"Afraid so."

"Well do something."

Virg slumped up to the counter and got in line behind ten other concerned people. When Virg reached the beleaguered attendants, he started gesticulating and acting like he was all bad and tour guide tough. Then I saw him pushing paperwork across the counter and pointing at it.

The attendants punched numbers into a computer and soon pushed different papers across the counter. Virg shuffled back with his combover all mussed.

"Well?"

"It's a landing gear issue. It will be a while. Grab your luggage and follow me. Oh, I forgot, you do not have luggage."

"You think that's funny don't you. Well I'm getting tired of this rotten shirt of yours and everybody staring at me like I'm not a rockstar. Where are we going?"

Virg was already trundling his suitcase into the open expanse of the concourse and I noticed I was talking to the back of his combover, which almost looked as ridiculous from the back as it did from the front.

"I booked us on another flight. We are going to have a connection or two until we get to Barcelona."

"And you call yourself a tour guide," I said from behind. "I would be embarrassed if I were you. Think about it."

For the next hour we sat at yet another gate waiting for our flight out of Dulles Airport. I made Virg spring for lunch. I got an individual pizza and he got a panini, as if you care.

Finally I heard, "This is a call to begin boarding Flight 909 to Amsterdam. Now seating those who need assistance and our first class passengers. Please have your passports and tickets ready to ensure quick boarding. We have a full plane today."

Virg was mulling around near the counter annoying the clerks to no end. When I saw him he was standing and waving frantically. He was doing it for no other reason than to express his feelings that if we didn't get on, right that very second, the plane would leave us. I began sauntering over to him at a slow enough pace to get him really nervous.

When I reached him the line was thirty deep waiting to board. Virg huffed his displeasure at my laidback ways.

"What?" I threw an arm around his shoulders. "We're fine, Virg. I take my time in a Hawaiian shirt."

He shook that melon head of his. "We are in first class. Follow me."

The first class line began moving quickly and in a few shakes we were only five back from the ticket scanner.

"See? Plenty of time."

"You don't want to mess around with international flights,

Edward.”

“Yeah, yeah, yeah. Hey, look at the scanner guy. He's a giant. Must be near seven foot. I'm seeing giants everywhere in here.”

“Bet he played basketball or volleyball.”

As we got up to him I noticed his nametag said Nimrod. I snickered as he glared down at me. He scanned my passport and ticket. Virg was next. He also made it through under the glare of Nimrod. When we got onto the jet bridge, I said, “That guy's name is even funnier than yours.”

“Mine is a classic one, Edward, with hints of romance and religious undertones tied to the Catholic Church of antiquity.”

“It's not a wine.”

“If you must know, my parents named me after Virgil in Dante's *The Divine Comedy*.”

“Like anyone's ever read that. Didn't Dante write some book about hell or something?”

“That's one of the three books that make up *The Divine Comedy*.”

“Eww, Mr. Literature.”

We stopped at the usual line that forms near the end of the jet bridge. There was a long pause. The line was not moving.

Virg asked, “So you really don't want to see Beatrice again? Or to put in your vernacular, you don't 'like ever' want to see her again.”

“Can I make it any clearer by saying that does not rev my monkey?”

We stood there. We looked around. Virg began fidgeting.

“What are you doing?”

“I have many of Beatrice's lyrics stored on my phone. Remember 'Collecting Angel Eyelashes?'”

“Not every word, but yeah, I remember it. We only played it once in concert. Gave it away for free on the Internet. Not the concert version, but the Moxie Mix that Bea edited. It got us some attention.”

“Giving it away for free was my idea,” Virg reminded. “This is one of my favorites.” With that Virg started reading back the lyrics.

Collecting Angel Eyelashes

President's a taker not a giver.
Let's hold hands by the languid river.

They rant, "The queen's heart's impure."
While we escape to autumnal fields of azure.

Everyone wants rebellion.
Ours is a life of absolution.

"Anarchy, anarchy, anarchy," the cry.
Kiss me, love me, thrill me 'til I die.

The economy is a big ouch.
Let's you and I curl up on the couch.

The president's got a bug.
We'll write songs and shrug.

Is global warming manmade?
I'm your sylph in a forest glade.

Bombs are dropping from the sky.
While Seraphim 'round you fly.

They dress in sackcloth and ashes.
While I walk behind collecting angel eyelashes.

"You have to admit that it's topically good, Edward."
"Big deal. We needed a ballad. Every band needs a ballad
on their debut album. I can write lyrics. You wait and see."

Moxie Mix

WE FINALLY MADE it to our first class seats, which Virg said were actually "business class." I reminded him we were not traveling on business so how could we be traveling in business class. He had no answer for that humdinger.

I had the middle seat in a row of three. As this was an international flight, the seats were wider than normal and reclined almost to a sleeping position. I verified that immediately and a guy behind me got a bit perturbed.

Virg had the window. He immediately began adjusting the overhead vents and lights to get them just the way he wanted. Hadn't been seated for half a minute when he asked to excuse himself. He had to use the john (my term, not his).

"What is this, Virg? I'm flying with you for umpteen hours and you already keep getting up and disturbing me?"

"We haven't even taken off, Edward."

"That's exactly my point," I said as he lumbered-knocked past me. I watched him disappear in the front of the plane and the lighting of a red stripe across a lad and dame sign.

———

"Ciao!"

"Beatrice?"

"In the hot flesh. Where in the world are you two?"

"We're about ready to take off for Barcelona via Amsterdam from D.C. Don't ask."

"I can't wait to see you guys. Sounds like you're talking in a closet."

"I am in the bathroom of the plane."

"Eww! Please tell me your pants are pulled up and securely fastened."

"No worries there, Beatrice."

"Be sure to use hand sanitizer. I have a theory that germs, just like colors, are neither created nor destroyed.

They are just passed from person to person."

"Chaos theory for germs."

"Oh no. Germs are highly organized. They would put any army to shame. They are especially organized on planes. Either of you sick?"

"No, but our hotel caught fire last night. The very floor we were staying on."

"Treble clef! Eddie didn't start smoking again?"

"No. No. We are both fine. The fire started a few rooms down the hall. Edward's duffel bag with his clothes inside got burned. He is wearing one of my Hawaiian shirts."

"That's hilarious! I've never seen him wear anything but black T-shirts. I can't wait to see him. Is our big secret safe?"

"In answer to your question, no, Edward doesn't suspect a thing, especially since you're in Venice and we are going to Barcelona. He is always bringing you up, though. I think he misses you. In the airport I just quoted your sterling lyrics for 'Collecting Angel Eyelashes.'"

"The Moxie Mix! That's sweet."

"You know how Edward can be . . . well, a bit cantankerous at times."

"Say no more, Virg. And who says cantankerous besides you?"

"I'll be out in a minute. Sorry, Beatrice, someone is trying to get in the bathroom. Our flight is on schedule. I'll—or rather, we'll—see you soon."

"Thanks for bringing Eddie back to me, Virg. I owe you."

"The pleasure is all mine."

When Virg returned to his seat he was rubbing his hands with sanitizer, or at least I hoped that's what it was. "You may find this hard to believe, but I am actually glad you're back." I dialed my voice down to a whisper as Virg climbed into his seat. "See that guy on the other side of me? He must've sneezed fifty times while you were gone. So he pulls out a long wad of paper from his pants pocket. It kept unraveling like some kind of magician's trick."

Virg's eyes followed my hand up and down.

"When I took a good look at it, I saw it was a stream of

toilet paper. *Toilet paper*, Virg. That's the kind of guy he is, a guy who would roll up a stream of TP instead of bringing tissue onto the plane. When he was finished blowing his sizeable honker, which generated so much embarrassment for me from the infernal noise of it that I almost knocked on the captains' door and asked them to let me off. Next the guy took the snotty wad and stuffed it into the magazine bin on the seat in front of him. He is someone who leaves his snotrags deep in the magazine bin for the stewardess (oh sorry: "flight attendant") to dig out later at the same time she is catching his germs. You're staying with me on this one, right? I'm almost finished. By the way the guy hacked, I figure the entire plane will be sick when we land. Bea says germs are neither created nor destroyed. Just like colors. God created them all at the beginning of time and there will be no more. Bea says it's a positive thing in relation to germs."

"I think I've heard Beatrice say that somewhere," Virg smirked, which was totally random and useless. "A gentlemen gets better in Bangalore and a little girl comes down with a cold in Calcutta. The whole concept of germs just dancing and hopping around the world on a—"

"Mucus merry-go-round," I interjected.

"—is very intriguing."

"Leave it to Bea to find something positive about germs. Anywho, this guy next to me—" I stopped abruptly and adjusted my tone down a few notches. My voice has a tendency to get louder the more I talk. "—has about half the world's germs right in his snoz and he's trying to transfer them to the magazine bin and to me!"

A flight attendant came by and questioned if we would like a beverage before takeoff.

"Orange juice," we said in unison and glared at my neighbor. The mucus monger. The sultan of snot.

Soon we were in the air. It is amazing how such huge planes can get enough lift under them to get off the ground. Virg said he will never get over this feat of human engineering no matter how many trips he takes with the Zany Zoo Travel Agency.

As the plane rose I heard the gruff talk of a bunch of women bowlers. They were off to some tournament in Amsterdam. I didn't know there was bowling there, maybe lawn bowling, but not real bowling. The ladies, if I may be so bold, kept hacking when they talked, and cursing worse than me when I was in the bunny costume.

The flight attendant got on the blower and informed us that electronic devices could now be used. I unwrapped my earphones and plugged them into the entertainment center mounted on my armrest. A rocker gots to have his music.

Virg punched a few keys on the touch screen in front of him. I wouldn't have believed it if I had not seen it myself. He actually brought up a videogame and started playing it.

Amazed, I tried to watch. Virg, in all his whizz-bang excitement, did not notice that the sun was in his face. I motioned to him that he had left the window shade up. He took a break from the action to close it. When he did I clearly saw a type of videogame where the landscape was ice. There were four concentric rings that Virg had to get through. I could see that if you landed in the center you would die.

In the first ring, referred to as Caïna, he fought some guy named Cain as he danced around these gross people frozen in ice with only their heads showing above the surface. Virg was uncoordinated at working the controller. I suspected as much.

What may have been hours later (or just felt like it), he finally defeated Cain and reached the second ring, called Antenora, where a vicious Trojan warrior lay in wait. The warrior had shiny armor on his arms and legs, a breastplate of bronze. He wielded a sword and beat his chest. So far, his fury was unmatched in the game. Virg went at him. A blow to the leg. A blow to the head and neck. All blocked. Virg next tried a move that can best be described as a robot dance on ice.

"Come on. Give me that." I snatched the controller out of his hand. "You're embarrassing me at thirty thousand feet. Let me show you how a rocker plays videogames."

My thumbs went at it. "Take that and that," I said. "Want some more of that? Huh? There's a lot more where that came from!" It is impossible for me to play videogames and not talk aloud. It really is. "See how it's done, Virg?" After I finished making ninja on Trojan warrior boy, I started kicking the frozen heads in the ice and yanking out their hair just for the fun of it. When I was through with the devastation I gave the controller back to Virg and blew on my fingertips.

"Whoa, Edward, you have pent-up anger."

"That's the rocker in me. Straight up."

Choose Strife

NO SOONER HAD Virg taken the controller back when I heard a slurping sound coming from the disgusting guy next to me in Business Class. From the corner of my eye I saw he was sucking his fingers like they were summer sausages. He had brought a greasy chicken biscuit sandwich onto the plane. The slob crumpled up the wrapper and stuffed it into the bin on the chair in front of him where he had stowed his snot rags. Guess he thought it was his own special trash bin.

Then he started touching everything, putting those greasy slimy fingers everywhere. Suddenly he grabbed the sleeve of my Hawaiian shirt. I almost freaked. Fortunately the videogame still had my reflexes on edge and I jerked away.

"Sup?"

"Do you happen to have a napkin or perhaps a tissue?" he asked.

"Why don't you give the bathroom a try? There's a thing in there called the sink with soap and water and everything."

The guy issued me a perturbed look and headed down the aisle. The sucking of fingers is one of my pet peeves.

Human spit has tons more germs than dog spit. That is not a good feeling. It really grosses me out when someone around me is licking and sucking their digits. When Bea saw me turning green at some fast food restaurant she would try to help me out by saying, "Not only is dog saliva cleaner, but it is also friendlier. If you look at all the squiggly dog germs under a microscope you would see them wagging their tales at you."

"Still, I'm not going to go around kissing canines," I told her. She had nothing for that one.

"What are you smiling at, Edward? I am having great difficulty on level three," Virg informed.

I saw that ice ring three was named Ptolomea. Obviously

the videogame programmers didn't know how to spell.

Virg was at a horrific part. Count Ugolino, who was stuck in the ice up to his neck, was gnawing the head of an archbishop next to him.

And I thought the slob sucking on his fingers was gross, I said to myself.

Virg told me I missed the storyline in the game where the archbishop caused the count to die of starvation. The gnawing was his payback. It's beyond me where these videogame designers come up with this stuff. The archbishop reminded me of something.

"Virg, you know how people shout it from the mountain tops what they gave up for Lent? 'I'm giving up donuts.' 'Well I'm giving up barbeque.' 'I'm going vegetarian.' Don't you think it should be a personal thing between them and God? Evangelicals don't shout it from the mountaintops because they have Lent 24/7/365. No smoking. No drinking. No visiting the movie theatre. No swearing. No revealing clothes on women. Here's something for you: What if someone gave up bellybutton lint for Lent? Stopped wearing sweaters so lint wouldn't build up. Maybe started wearing T-shirts under their sweaters to block bellybutton lint. Huh? *Huh*? Wouldn't that be something?"

Virg kept playing away. "It doesn't seem like a sacrifice to me."

"Sure it does. They can't wear the clothes they want anymore. And speaking of bellybuttons, you should've seen this guy on the bus. Huge! Cavernous! Hey Virg, you listening? I may give up stompers for Lent."

"Really?"

"Naw!"

My neighbor returned from the john as Virg was shaking his head. The flight attendant followed behind him with a basket of pretzels and nuts. Virg asked for both and so did I as I said a prayer about the fingersucker. But God didn't hear it. Know why? Because the guy next to me promptly ordered the *salty* nuts and went to town on his digits shortly thereafter.

"Those aren't spareribs," I informed him.

He kept going at it.

Finally I said to him, "Would you mind not sucking your fingers? That really sucks."

"It's quicker than going to wash my hands all the time."

Virg nudged me. Guess he didn't want any issues on the plane. I noticed he was really into the videogame. I told him to move here, kick there, and do that.

"You and your infamous hypotheticals, Edward. I have been around you too long. The Infamous Hypotheticals would be an excellent name for the band."

"Like right, Virg. That's a stupid name for the band. Why do you come up with such bogus names that have no potential for greatness, unlike my names? Now, The Infamous Theoreticals would be a fine name for the band. The stupid factor is very low on that one. What about Apocalips for an all girl punk band? Or Chose Strife. Now that would rock for a punk band; Fidget Midget would work, too. There are other names. I'm not in a punk funk for names. How about Men-o-Pause for a girl band of aging hippies? Never mind. That sounds like a name you'd come up with, Virg."

Virg just nodded.

"What about Probe or Dead by Sunrise or, or Hurricane Over Havana? Now those, my colorful shirted friend, are pure, unadulterated rock-n-roll names. Maw is another one, too."

The flight attendant came by to pick up our trash when I threw out Better Carousing by Chemistry as an exemplary name for a chick band. Virg laughed and the flight attendant gave me a sourpuss look.

Once she was gone, I spun back to Virg. "Foraging Westward or perhaps Turendotcom for an operatic band? You with me? Ghetto Stilettos has a nice ring to it and so does Mr. Ladybug. Butcher's Floor for a thrash metal band is spectacular and so is Keystone Corpse for a Goth band."

"So you're all tapped out of punk names?" Virg questioned.

"No, because there's Unsocial Security. That would be a great name for a punk band. Cow Tipping would be awesome for a grunge band."

"What about Metal in the Microwave?"

"Get serious. I only want cool names. Just pipe down will you? This is my brain dump session. Where were we? Oh yeah, Grain of Sand and the Clams! That would be a stupendous name for a band."

"No arguments there," the guy next to me blurted. He had taken his fingers out of his mouth long enough to offer an intelligent comment.

"Epistles for Missiles strikes me as an upstanding name for a Christian band but Evangelicalifornians does not. The Bludgeoned Curmudgeons. DieNasty instead of Dynasty. Still with me, Virg? Got plenty more inspiration here. Plenty." I pointed to my head. "I'm all about inspiration, like Tattoo Blue or Lather for a girl band, which reminds me, Bea had better not try to strike out on her own. She will have to find a drummer better than me, which is utterly impossible. She will have to entirely write new songs because I own all the rights, and that would take mundo time."

"Beatrice has no trouble in that department, Edward. She wrote 'Riven by Chance' while I was sitting in front of her having tea."

Virg started to add on to what he was saying when the flight attendant brought the guy next to me a scoop of vanilla ice cream with caramel drizzled over the top.

While I waited for the slurping to begin, I said, "Charnel Sunday has a nice rock ring to it and so does Punkyard Dogs. Socialdarks instead of Socialites is a rippin' name. So is Mayhemp."

"How do you do it?"

"There's more to it than just my frantically active imagination," I said. "Take for instance the term falsetto. Let's say you want to play off it and turn it into a name for a band so you take the false part of the name and flip it to Truesetto. You have more than one person in your band so you add the plural to Truesettos. There, you have a pretty good name if you have a barbershop quartet, yet it doesn't quite have the bite one is looking for in a rock name—the tang, if you will—so you change true back to false and modify settos to setthoes. And there you have it. The

Falsesetthoes, which is great for any girl band on the planet."

"I see. I see."

"I'm not sure you do. Listen and learn. You can even apply the Edward T. Nad Band Naming System to phrases. Take for instance, 'Pew, who's got gas?' Modify the last word and you have a fine album name: *Pew, Who's Got Vegas?* You can even modify chemical compositions to come up with great band names. Take $Ache_2O$ for instance as opposed to H_2O."

"Very good, Edward."

"What if the band name was They Have No Name so when some big music exec asks the name of the band, Virg, you can say, They Have No Name. And the fat suit will reply, 'What do you mean they don't have a name?' To which you'll snap back with joy, 'They do have a name.' And the suit will say, 'Excuse me, but you just told me they have no name.' So Virg, you just stand up straight, look 'em in the eyes and say, 'That, my good fellow, *is* the name of the band.'"

"It's like who's on first."

"Stop using sports metaphors, will ya?"

"There would be some good marketing in that name.

"It's aces, Virg."

"Sort of like proving a negative as buzz marketing for the band."

"Can you tell I'm struggling with the perfect name for the band?"

"Just a little bit."

"I want it to be the right one. Names mean so much. I don't want to be some band that is a one hit wonder and spends the rest of its musical life playing at rich guys' barbeques and county fairs while toothless fat kids gorge on funnel cakes and scream, 'Rock on'—"

Judecca

"—OR PLAYING REDNECK weddings with car racing themes on the walls or bar mitzvahs where boys throw sparkly kippah skullcaps at Bea—I mean whatever hot chick I've got on the mike. It obviously won't be Bea. Perhaps Jennifer or that law clerk we met at the CAFC. What was her name? And I'm not going to rock out in some dingy fish restaurant by the shore where they pay us in all-you-can-eat-peel-and-eat shrimp. And then when we get back to Florence we have to lay down tracks for on-hold phone recordings so we can get a little bread to pay rent. I really don't, Virg."

I took a deep breath and reclined my seat. It's a lot of work educating Virg about the music business and I realized it for the hundredth time as the plane barreled through the sky toward Amsterdam.

I must have dozed for about an hour with my seat in full recline mode. When I awoke, I saw that Virg had a bunch of crumpled wrappers on this tray and a can of soda.

"What gives?"

"They served lunch while you were out. I didn't want to wake you, Edward. I'm sure you can ask the flight attendant for more."

On the other side of me I heard the sucking of fingers. They'll bury my neighbor with fingers in his mouth. They should do a sculpture of him with fingers in his mouth or a garish painting that hangs in a hallway of the Trident Hotel. I turned and questioned, "Where are you from, sir?"

"Canada."

He said it as if it was a big city. I had no clue who the president of Canada is and I bet neither did the rest of the Americans on the plane. I read somewhere that only 8% of U.S. residents can name the Canadian president at any one time. And if you dug in the data further, most of them say 'eh' at the end of the question because they are Canadian transplants.

"I've never been."

"Fantastic lakes and forests. We like to keep the beauty of our country a secret from Americans."

"Name's Edward T. Nad. I would shake your hand, but . . . you know, eh? I'm in the music business. Have my own band."

"What's its name?"

"I'm working on that as you may have heard previously. You?"

"Natas is what everybody calls me. I travel a lot. Guess you could say I roam the earth and look for things that interest me."

My eyes got wide. "You one of those journalists who makes a living interviewing bands? I'll be happy to do an interview right here on the plane."

"I am sorry, but that is not my line of work."

"S'ppose it's for the best. Those guys crack me up. They really do. Someone trying to describe how a song sounds in words is one of the funniest things you'll ever read." I lowered my voice. "'The pitch rises and falls throughout the song as the snare drum snarls and a host of guitars whine to a whimper in over three minutes of audio assault.'" I raised it again. "After reading a review like that do you have any idea what the song sounds like? Didn't think so. I just read another one that described a new tune by a British band as, 'A blend of synth-laden pop and rock-infused anthems that relentlessly assault listeners' sensibilities.' Whatever that means."

"I have to agree with you. The only way I tell if I like a song is to listen to thirty seconds of it online before purchasing. As for my line of employment, I guess you could say I'm an insurance agent."

"I'm pretty sure the mortality rate is one hundred percent," I said. "Everyone has their time to go. I just don't want to be on a plane when it's a pilot's time to go. Know what I'm saying?"

The flight attendant closed the curtain that separated

Business Class from the rest of the plane and walked past our row. I tried to get her attention so I could get some lunch, but she didn't see me.

"So Natas, forget insurance agents. What about real estate agents? Why do they always have to put their ugly mugs in those home magazines? I mean, what other business does that? You don't see accountants rushing to plaster their faces in magazines. By the squirrely way most of them look that makes perfect sense. You don't see morticians plaster their faces anywhere. If there's anyone you should base a decision on because of the way they look, it's the guy who's going to be cutting open Granny. Think about it. I could care less what my real estate agent looks like, unless she's a fine hoochy mama."

"You just say, hoochy mama?"

I slapped my knee. "Man I get a kick out of those real estate agent grids with all of their pictures side-by-side. They strike such goofy posses. It's like, 'I got the googly eyes so I can sell your house.' 'No, no, take a gander at me, I just got my roots streaked, I must be able to complete a half a million dollar transaction better than the lady next to me.' 'My hair's bigger than hers and I just got my nails done so I will be able to sell your place faster.'"

Natas smiled. He told me I was on the right track as far as he was concerned, which made absolutely no sense.

Over near the window Virg had made it to ring four; called Judecca in the videogame. He was still fighting away. I didn't know he had it in him. At the center of the ice was a giant Lucifer in pixilated form. From his mouth spewed an icy steam that froze upon meeting the air and shattered when it hit the ice. He had the classic horns and fiery eyes, long fingernails and amber skin.

I tapped Virg on the shoulder. "That's not right. Bible says the devil was God's most beautiful angel and I have to believe the horrific images of him handed down from Renaissance painters to modern videogame designers have gotten it all wrong. That's why sin is so enticing. It comes from the devil who is so beautiful. He would melt the flowers on our shirts he is so good looking. He would make Bea seem like a trash heap in his presence.”

On the other side of me Natas was nodding. His eyes were wide in agreement.

“I’m unsure what this has to do with me getting past ring four. You do not appear well, Edward.”

“This isn’t about ring four of any stupid videogame. This is about my miserable love life and getting the band off the ground. I just feel like I am fighting the flames of Hades with a plastic squirt gun. Just squeezing and squeezing and squeezing and getting nowhere. That’s how I feel. My life is getting so hot and wretched I run to the spigot that is just floating there in the middle of the room, not attached to anything, and keep filling my little squirt gun over and over. I dash back to the flames and empty the squirt gun into them, but they keep getting higher and hotter. That’s when I book it back to the spigot, crank it open, and fill up the squirt gun with the coldest water I can find. I mean freezing water in the hopes that it will help with those flames. In my madness I try to stuff more water into the squirt gun than it can possibly hold. I finally realize that won’t work because the reservoir for the water is too small.

“I put the cap back on while cursing the Chinese maker of the gun for not making it larger. I dash back to the flames of Hades and give them hell. Muscles rippling, stompers firmly planted on ash, I pop off as many rounds as my plastic weapon can handle. Just when I think it’s doing some good, the flames torch up even higher and melt the end of the squirt gun.

“At this point I’m so frustrated that I just throw the plastic gun into the flames, as far and as hard as I can as if that might help extinguish them. Then I just stand there, watching it melt into a blob of useless plastic, which forms into the rounded shape of the heart soap I envisioned I dropped in the cheap Poconos motel shower that represents my shrinking, dwindling love life. Across the way I notice you, Virg, and you are doing the same with a different colored squirt gun and it’s not having any affect on the flames either. In fact, for all I know your squirt gun is filled with lighter fluid because the flames get higher and higher every time you squirt them. That's what my whole life feels like right now in so many ways. It really does. Squirt guns in Hades."

I noticed Natas had disappeared. I would never see him again for the rest of the flight. I guessed he went to the back of the plane to suck his finger in some corner.

Whether it was my lack of lunch or sapped energy from my tirade on life, I nestled back into my seat and nodded off.

I slept hard—rockstar hard.

The night of sleeplessness in Jennifer's apartment had caught up to me. I had even fallen asleep in the airport before I awoke to giants. A rocker needs at least ten hours of sleep so I needed about six more just to break even. As the plane jetted through the sky I wrestled with more band names, tossing in my seat and moaning (I would later find out from Virg). I strangely thought I heard a voice whispering, almost hissing, a subtle name for the band. It wasn't until the flight attendant came on the loudspeaker and announced that we had begun our descent into Amsterdam International Airport that I awoke with an odd clarity.

"Why'd you let me sleep so long, Virg? Get me some water or something. I'm parched."

"You've been out of it."

"Why're you eating prunes? Did you bring those?"

"Yes. I have constipation issues when I travel. These keep me regular."

"Is there no end to the lengths you'll go to to embarrass me?" I collected myself before continuing. Took a calming breath. "What really matters though is that I've come up with a spectacular name for the band while I slept. I tell you it's the best name I've ever thought of for a band."

Virg handed me an unopened can of carbonated water from his lap tray. I popped the tab and chugged.

"Okay, let's hear it, Edward."

I wiped my lips with the back of my hand and blurted, "The Divine Dantes!"

The Divine Dantes
Paella in Purgatory

Chapter 1

"Beatrice? It's Virgil."

"Hoppy Easter, Virg!"

"You sound far away."

"I'm in another country and you woke me up. You know how I am without my coffee—tetchy with a swirl of sketchy."

"Forgot we're in the same time zone. Sorry. Just wanted to let you know that we finally touched down in Barcelona."

"Cool. Speaking of sketchy, how's Eddie?"

"Fine."

"Big booted rocker touring Barcelona with his manager, fine? Or just jetlagged bloke, fine?"

"The later. Edward is wearing one of my Hawaiian shirts."

"Shut the floral pattern up!"

"He looks quite handsome in it, I must say."

"You would, Virg. Take some pictures for me. Oh, and this is the funniest thing. I had a dream about Eddie in the bunny costume. Hope you have video."

"I do, but don't tell him."

"Yes!"

For those joining us while Virg is across the way blathering on his cellphone like he is important or something, let me summarize the miserable situation for you: young rocker—great American band—dumped in New York by his girlfriend—forced to parade around in a bunny costume in front of the Zany Zoo Travel Agency—on way to Barcelona—not going to Venice because that's where said former girlfriend is—scared of clowns—hotel caught fire— wearing embarrassing Hawaiian shirt—secret neck tattoo— still not going to Venice to get girl and band back together.

Did I mention our never-ending flights? DC to Amsterdam: rubbery chicken, even rubberyier green beans. Amsterdam to Paris: Zip. Paris to Barcelona: squib of brie (that's a fancy French cheese) and champagne, stewardess (Bianca) who was so friendly I told her she couldn't be French.

Beyond tired, we arrived on the dawn of Easter morning.

————————

"You're a day late, Virg, or maybe I had my time zones off."

"It was quite the trip."

"And Eddie still doesn't suspect anything?"

"No. All Edward knows is that he's here on a two week vacation."

"Great. The quickest I can get there from Venice is tomorrow afternoon. I doubt the trains even run today. We can arrange a meeting place."

"Fine, Beatrice."

"What if I showed up in a bunny costume?"

"That would be humorous. He will be glad to see you no matter how you're dressed. He misses you. I'm sure of it."

"I don't think Eddie really meant to hurt me. I could be someone's daughter after all. Ciao, Virg."

————————

When Virg returned from his call he started snapping pictures of me with his phone. No joke.

"Would you stop? You're creeping me out."

"Just wanted to get a photo or two of our arrival in Barcelona."

"Don't put me on one of the Zany Zoo travel brochures or I swear I will kill you dead."

We continued trundling across the Barcelona concourse, which pretty much looked like every other airport concourse we had visited. I could no longer tell them apart.

"So let me get this straight, Virg. To get to Barcelona we took a plane from Florence, New York to DC—where we got fogged in for a day and all manner of disturbing weirdness happened to us, not to mention the hotel fire and me having to wear a robe around the city in the freezing cold—then we missed—correction: *you* rerouted us to Amsterdam where we hung out with those cute waitresses in their official-looking, navy-blue flight outfits with the red collars, and then we were routed to Charles de Gaulle—whoever that guy is—at two in the morning Paris time to make our connection to Barcelona where we got served *fromage* on the plane and champagne in those fluted airline glasses—for breakfast, mind you—after flying all night?"

Virg crinkled up his forehead. "Afraid so, Edward. That must have been some experience for you having never flown before our journey started."

"Hades. That's what it was." I looked at a rising sun out the concourse window and turned back to Virg. "Know something? You're the worst tour guide on the face of the planet. Straight up. I would've gotten here a lot faster without you. I really would have. If I swam the Atlantic Ocean in my combat boots I would have gotten here faster."

We skirted a bunch of college exchange students from Mexico and got in one of a thousand lines backing up for Customs. For what seemed hours, we stood with the rank and file shuffling forward at the next shout of a Customs Agent.

"Hate to say it, Edward, but you look pretty haggard."

I peeled open my eyes. "Who says haggard anymore?"

"I call it as I see it. You do look worn out."

"Like you don't, Mr. Pasted Down Hair, Travel Agent Slash Tour Guide, Haggard Word Using, Whatever Da Da Da. At this point I don't care how I look. Besides, what fans will recognize me in Barcelona, especially in a Hawaiian shirt?"

"The skull belt buckle may give you away."

It took us another forty minutes to make it up to the first available counter. The entire time I said nothing to Virg. I watched a scrolling display tick off the minutes until it was 5:47 A.M. on the tenth of April. Neither of us said a word to the other. You may find this a surprise, but I get tired of Virg sometimes. I really do. Finally, an ancient dude waved us over to a finger-smudged glass booth. A gray beard clung to his dark skin like filings on a magnet. Furrows ran down his cheeks and his ears had a gelatinous sag to them that reminded me of the bacon grease the guy in the alley dumped on my head when Bea and I broke up.

His nametag told us he was Cato from Utica and I told him, "We're from New York, too."

"That's obvious," he snarled in perfect English.

"Florence, New York. I've never been over to Utica."

"I have," Virg piped up. "It has a very nice park system interwoven in behind the National Distance Running Hall of Fame. And your pierogis. Oh, your pierogis are excellent fresh out of the oven. I prefer the traditional potato pierogis."

"Excuse him, Cato. He's a compendium of worthless travel information and a giant nerd to boot." I fished my passport out and slid it under the glass. "Virg?"

My supposed tour guide did the same.

Cato took the passports and opened them. His fingers were knotted twigs; his teeth the spent colors of November trees. He took long, hard looks at the photos in the passports. He squinted, extended his arms and squinted some more. Then he extracted reading glasses from his shirt pocket. His face pinched together in a look of concern.

Virg and I glanced at each other.

The Customs Agent set the passports down and consulted what appeared to be a loose-leaf binder with more photos in it. I caught a glimpse of the cover when he held the binder up. It said *Fugitiu.*

Cato did a double take at the photos in the binder and then looked back at each of us. What he did next shocked us both. He called over a much younger agent and began whispering in his ear. I couldn't make out any of it, which I expected given that it was in Spanish. Virg said it wasn't actually Spanish. He called it Catalan.

"Who's ever heard of that? Quit making up languages," I told him.

"Catalonia is made up of four regions, or provinces. Barcelona is one of them and is its capitol city. About thirty-seven percent of Spaniards speak Catalan and forty-seven percent Spanish."

"And you speak tour guide gibberish."

Virg claimed to know a little Catalan and I searched his

face for guidance. He was visibly concerned.

The young agent nodded and stepped to the side. He put a hand on his sidearm, which caused Virg to step back on my ankle. I tried not to hop from the pain shooting up my leg.

Suddenly Cato's finger unfurled. He pointed in a way that clearly indicated the both of us. "You are fugitives from America!"

"Fugitives?" I said. "That would be a smashing name for a punk band, but we are not—"

Virg pushed me back with his arm and stepped on my ankle again while he angled to the forefront. "I can assure the both of you that we are merely tourists here in Barcelona and not wanted by any authorities in any jurisdiction."

Cato opened the binder and pressed against the smudged glass a photo of a chubby man with a comb over. I had to admit that if you slapped a cheap Hawaiian shirt on the guy, he would bear a striking resemblance to Ole Virg. As best I could tell from the printed description he was wanted for drug smuggling.

"But that is not me," Virg exclaimed in a rather high tone. "My name is not even close to that guy's."

"It may be a fake passport," Cato informed with the agent behind him nodding, hand still on pistol.

"But look at the hair. Mine is different." At this Virg stretched his hair up in the air. It had to be nearly a foot of comb over goodness. I was so embarrassed I turned away. Behind us I noticed a bunch of perturbed travelers, arms crossed, feet tapping, watching from the line behind us.

"Chill," I told them. "Get in another line or something."

When I had turned around Cato was thumbing to the back of the binder. He stuck another photo up to the glass. A version of me (albeit not as handsome) with spiked blonde hair and a silk polka dot shirt came smiling back.

"Whoa. What do you think I am, a popstar? Give me some credit here people. If that was me in the photo I would have jumped off a building by now. Think about it."

Virg angled in front of me once more. I was quick to get my ankles out of the way. "What he is trying to say is that he does not resemble the photo and neither do I. Our passports clearly show that we are not these individuals. Please. Please let us go through. You are making a mistake."

Cato thought about it for an intolerably long time.

"There has to be some way we can prove we are not the fugitives in your binder."

"You tell'em, Virg," I whispered from behind. "Give 'em Hades."

"We're beyond that now," he whispered back and I had no idea what he meant.

Cato's twiglike fingers massaged his beard. "There is one way. The last fugitive I showed you had a particular marking on his neck. A tattoo. Without disclosing what it is, have the guy behind you show me his neck."

"Wait a minute, Virg. I'm not ready to reveal to *anyone* the tattoo on my neck."

"See, he does have a tattoo on his neck. Show it and hope that it is not the same as the one on my cut sheet."

Virg looked back over his shoulder. "Do it, Edward. It's our only hope that he will let us pass."

I gave out a big sigh and eased over to the glass window. I undid a couple of buttons on my shirt and pulled the collar down.

I was a good bit taller than Cato, who I imagined had shrunk over the years, and he was having difficulty making out my tat. Cato unlatched a half door and exited his station. He got close up and was still having problems.

"Get low," Virg implored.

I stooped.

"No. Lower. Kneel."

"You kidding me?"

I felt Virg's hand on my shoulder, pushing me to the floor. The people in line were snickering. I soon found myself kneeling on the hard tiles and smelled the horrid breath of one Cato of Utica, Customs Agent of Barcelona Extraordinaire while he searched all around my gizzard. Close up his eyeballs were a root system of red.

"Ah, it's an insect," he announced to the other agent.

"It's a bee to be exact. My old girlfriend is named Beatrice.

I called her Bea for short. Late one night after a gig I got it for her. Get it—a bee?"

"Yes. Yes," Virg said. "Beatrice is a fine young woman. They are very much in love and we are going to meet her. Kindly let us pass in the name of love."

"Yes. In the name of love," I repeated.

"They want to pass in the name of love," Cato announced to the other agents and then chuckled for an embarrassing long time. "That's the first laugh I've had and my graveyard shift is almost over."

The people in line behind us were laughing, too. "What? What, people?" I said.

After a delayed silence, he continued, "You may pass. Clean this young man up and go along."

"Oh, thank you," Virg exclaimed as he latched onto his suitcase to move on as soon as possible. "Thank you so much."

I unfolded myself and got up on my stompers. I made two steps behind him and stopped in my tracks. "Mr. Cato, sir. What was the tat you were looking for on the fugitive? Just curious."

"A large race car. There is no way a tattoo artist could have turned it into a small bumblebee so I let you go."

"Luckily Bea's name isn't Carlotta."

That's when Cato pointed me toward a hallway called Reed and said, "*Vamoose!*"

Virg was waiting. We got away from the agents as fast as we could. As we moved along Virg kept dabbing his forehead with the sleeve of his shirt. He was visibly shaken by Cato. It didn't take long for me to ask that we slow to a walk. My ankle was throbbing. We kept walking and walking in a straight line. It felt as though we were trundling down the hallway for a mile or more. Just when I thought we had reached the end—a play of light from a bank of mirrors—the corridor kept going, stretching.

"It's like the hallway is getting longer, Virg."

"I know. Strange."

After a football field or four, we reached an escalator jammed with jetlagged tourists. The escalator disappeared into a wall that had colorful artwork hanging on it. It appeared we were going underground.

"Sometimes you have to go down to go up," Virg explained.

We stepped onto one of the moving stairs. Virg's suitcase was between us, which didn't leave much room. Halfway down I had to get something off my chest. "Can't believe you lied to Cato. Bea and I are in love? We are going to see her? You kill me."

Virg brought his shoulders to his ears.

"Didn't think you had it in you. I really didn't. Lying to a Customs Agent. Next you're going to tell me you drive without a seatbelt."

"Only on Tuesdays, Edward."

"Or you're going to smuggle Cuban cigars back to the US in your white tube socks."

"I've done it before."

I shot Virg a disbelieving glance. "Really?"

"Naw!"

"Hey, that's my word. And by the way, that was embarrassing how you made me get down on my knees back there in front of everyone. I didn't appreciate it. You stepped on my ankle a hundred times. You really did."

I thought I saw Virg smirk.

About Andrew

Andrew Barger is the award winning author of *Coffee with Poe: A Novel of Edgar Allan Poe's Life*, a short story collection: *Mailboxes – Mansions – Memphistopheles,* and *The Divine Dantes Trilogy.* He is also the editor of a number of other books, including *Edgar Allan Poe Annotated and Illustrated Entire Stories and Poems, Phantasmal: The Best Ghost Stories 1800-1849,* and *Mesmaerion: The Best Science Fiction Stories 1800-1849.* He hopes to start a band someday if he can settle on a name for it.

Connect with Andrew Online

AndrewBarger.com

Blog:
AndrewBarger.blogspot.com

Amazon:
Amazon.com/author/andrewbarger

Facebook:
facebook.com/AuthorAndrewBarger

Goodreads:
Author Andrew Barger

Twitter:
@andrewbarger

Edward T. Nad Facebook Page
facebook.com/edward.nad.9

Reading Group Guide

The Divine Dantes
Squirt Guns in Hades

1. What was unique about the travels of Edward and Virgil and how did it enhance or take away from the story?

2. Can you relate to their travel predicaments? To what extent do they remind you of yourself or someone you know?

3. What specific themes did Andrew Barger emphasize throughout the novel? What do you think he is trying to get across to the reader?

4. Edward claims that he never wants to see Beatrice again since she broke up the band. Does his view change throughout the novel? If so, what event was the catalyst to change his mind?

5. Did Andrew Barger capture the speech and idiosyncrasies of a young rocker in Edward T. Nad? What about the way he dresses?

6. How is Edward treated by his parents, especially his mother? Does this help to explain why he acts a certain way?

7. In reading the book did you get a sense that Andrew Barger incorporated underlying meaning that is linked to "The Divine Comedy"? If so, when?

8. In what ways are Beatrice, Edward and Virgil like their characters in "The Divine Comedy"?

9. Did parts of the book make you uncomfortable? If so, why? Did this lead to a new understanding or awareness of some aspect of your life you might not have thought about before?

10. Do Beatrice, Edward or Virgil remind you of anyone you know now or have known in the past?

11. Did the lyrics of Beatrice's songs provide a window into the relationship between her and Edward?

12. Were you aware Edward T. Nad has a Facebook page where he enlightens the world on all things rock-n-roll? **Facebook.com/edward.nad.9**

www.ingramcontent.com/pod-product-compliance
Lightning Source LLC
Chambersburg PA
CBHW051302210726
48287CB00002B/623